ROBERT B. PARKER'S
BUCKSKIN

This Large Print Book carries the
Seal of Approval of N.A.V.H.

ROBERT B. PARKER'S BUCKSKIN

ROBERT KNOTT

WHEELER PUBLISHING
A part of Gale, a Cengage Company

GALE
A Cengage Company

Farmington Hills, Mich • San Francisco • New York • Waterville, Maine
Meriden, Conn • Mason, Ohio • Chicago

Copyright © 2019 by The Estate of Robert B. Parker.
Wheeler Publishing, a part of Gale, a Cengage Company.

ALL RIGHTS RESERVED
Wheeler Publishing Large Print Hardcover.
The text of this Large Print edition is unabridged.
Other aspects of the book may vary from the original edition.
Set in 16 pt. Plantin.

LIBRARY OF CONGRESS CIP DATA ON FILE.
CATALOGUING IN PUBLICATION FOR THIS BOOK
IS AVAILABLE FROM THE LIBRARY OF CONGRESS

ISBN-13: 978-1-4328-4700-5 (hardcover alk. paper)

Published in 2019 by arrangement with G. P. Putnam's Sons, an imprint of Penguin Publishing Group, a division of Penguin Random House LLC

Printed in the United States of America
1 2 3 4 5 6 7 23 22 21 20 19

I told you that. Didn't I? I have someplace to be, ya see?"

More fireworks lit up the sky, one after another after another. A large pinwheel was lit, spewing sparks that cast a bright glow on the kid's boyish face. He beamed like a child, watching in awe.

"You oughta see this. Boy, oh, boy."

He watched, wishing he was part of the fireworks and festivities taking place on the town's plaza. The band ended the slow waltz and started up with a lively tune that brought hoots and hollers from the crowd.

"I should be out there among 'em. Not in here, out there. How about letting me out? I should be out there."

"I told you to shut your mouth."

"I should."

He watched for a minute, then said, "Lands alive, food smells good out there. Don't it? I'm hungry as a bear. If you won't let me out, why don't you go out? You should go out, dance and have some fun. Get something to eat and bring me back something, too. No reason to sit in here with lil' ol' me. Hell, what am I gonna do? Nothing. That is damn sure plain to see. Nothing."

The jailer was fuming but didn't glance up from the newspaper he was reading as the kid continued.

"You know as well as me that it doesn't make good sense, me being in here and all. Hell, I was doing nothing. I was minding my own business yesterday. I was passing through. I'm heading up north. I got business up north. Important business."

The jailer continued to ignore the kid, who'd been talking nonstop since he got locked up.

"I could have danced right off, ya know. I should have, but I didn't. Know why?"

The jailer spoke without looking up from the newspaper.

" 'Cause you was riding the dead man's horse?"

"I won that horse fair and square. Wasn't my fault that drunk put his pony on the table 'cause he had no money."

The jailer lowered his newspaper. Then tipped back in his chair so he could see the kid eye to eye, but said nothing as he stared at him.

"I won that pony, even got a bill of sale."

He pulled a piece of paper from his pocket, jumped down from the bunk, and moved to the bars. He held out the paper, waving it at the jailer.

"Take a look-see, why don't you? I tried to show you and that other brass-buttoned bastard this, but you wouldn't look at it. I didn't do nothing wrong. Nothing at all. Here, take a look. I didn't have nothing to do with shooting that fella. Got this telegram, too." He removed a telegram from his pocket. "Requesting I come as soon as possible."

"Shut up, kid."

"I didn't. I was nowhere near that cantina where he got shot. I mean, yeah, I had been there earlier, like I said, when I won the pony, but was nowhere near there when it happened."

"Save that crap for the judge."

"You don't know nothing . . . You're a dumb shit is all."

"What'd you say, boy?"

"You heard me."

"Don't you push me, boy. I've had enough of your yapping."

"Or what? What you gonna do?"

The jailer stared at the kid. And the kid could tell he was getting to him.

The kid smiled.

"You're just one of those dumb-shit soldier boys. One of those that follow orders 'cause you can't think for yourself. I should have just danced, just danced right off."

"Keep it up and I will come in there and dance your ass around till you quit breathing, save the court money."

"Fuck you, dumb shit."

The jailer slammed down his newspaper.

11

He lifted out of his chair, snatched the keys from the desk, and marched to the cell.

The kid moved away from the bars as the jailer fumbled with the keys, trying to unlock the cell.

"No need to get all worked up," the kid said.

The kid was small, not tall at all and one hundred thirty pounds soaking wet. He backed away as the cell door opened and the burly jailer charged him. He slapped the kid so hard blood flew from the kid's mouth and splattered on the wall. He hit him a second time, sending another stream of blood flying in the opposite direction. The next strike came from the kid. It was swift and to the jailer's throat, and it was the sharp spoon handle that burrowed into the man's neck. The jailer felt his neck where blood was flowing. He reached for the kid, but the kid was swift and moved out of his grasp. Then the kid kicked the jailer hard in the groin and stabbed him again, another blow to the jailer's neck. The jailer stumbled, hurt and bleeding. He dropped on the bunk and the kid stabbed him again and again. Then the kid held up the stabbing tool. He showed the spoon knife to the jailer. The jailer was now weak, and blood flowed from the many wounds to his neck.

"This here spoon was from that lousy plum pudding your asshole buddy gave me yesterday. That was all I had to eat. You realize that?"

The jailer stared at the kid and blood poured out of his neck and bloomed out across the front of his shirt.

"You dumb fuck," the kid said. "You and him didn't have smarts enough to make sure you got the pudding spoon back, did you? I was up all night working on this. While you and that Yankee friend of yours were playing checkers with each other like little children. Telling each other lie after lie. About how you did this or how he did that, I was working on this. I told you I had business to attend to, didn't I? Didn't I? Now look at you. All you had to do was go out like I said and have some fun, bring me something to eat, and this might not have happened. But it's happened now, ain't it? Ain't it?"

2

Two coyotes stood on the road, staring at us as we approached. They were bleached white by long days of harsh sun. It'd been hot and bone-dry all summer. And like most critters enduring the continuing drought, the coyotes were suffering. They were skinny, parched, and hungry-looking. When we got closer, they moved off the road and into the short brush. The smaller of the two stopped and stared at us as we passed.

Virgil and I were riding out of Appaloosa to pay one of two competing mining camps a visit. There'd been ongoing friction between the two outfits. Ever since the first day they found gold in the jagged hills north of town, there'd been nothing but trouble.

Half of the gold discovery was on land owned by a consortium: a group of Appaloosa businessmen known as the Baptiste Group. The other half belonged to two Irishmen, ranchers, the McCormick brothers.

The McCormicks purchased the land from the Baptiste Group a year prior to the discovery. The transaction turned out to be a misstep that prompted Henri Baptiste to regret the sale. So much so, he hired gun hands to intimidate the Irishmen. But the move only made the McCormicks hire their own gunmen in case tough talk turned to triggers pulled.

The two groups had camps on opposite sides of the discovery, but they had to share the same road coming or going. Virgil and I had not encountered any of these men. We'd heard about them and about reports of skirmishes on the road, but that was it, only reports. We figured it'd be a matter of time before we had the pleasure of making their acquaintance.

And sure enough, now, on this sweltering day in mid-August, Virgil and I were riding out to get our introduction.

Two days previously we moved some convicted felons down to Yuma. When we returned and stepped off the train in Appaloosa, Deputy Book was waiting there to meet us. He let us know one of McCormick's men had been missing for three days. Book informed us that the missing man was not one of the hired gunmen but rather one of the miners.

The McCormicks, of course, suspected the Baptiste outfit and threatened retaliation.

Virgil and I had paid a visit earlier to Baptiste's office and the hotel where he resided in Appaloosa, but we did not locate him. Nor did we find any of his business partners, so we took the short ride out to the mines to see what we could find out.

When we arrived at the Baptiste location, the foreman, Frank Maxie, walked out of the office to greet us as we neared. He was a grizzled old-timer Virgil and I had known for years. Frank was a retired man of means who knew the gold-mining trade likely better than anyone in Appaloosa.

Before taking a position with the Baptiste Group, he'd made a considerable amount of money. He'd worked for decades operating his own strike in Laverne that played out a few years ago.

He stepped off the porch and shook his head as we came to a stop.

"Well, well, well, if it's not Virgil Cole and Everett Hitch. I'd ask you what I did to deserve the pleasure of being visited by you marshals of this here territory, but I won't, because I know why you are here."

"You do?" Virgil said.

"Not dumb," Frank said, squinting up at Virgil.

"No?" Virgil said.

Frank smiled.

"Henri Baptiste here?" I said.

"No, too dusty out here for Henri . . . Now and again he comes, but not much."

"Know where he is?" Virgil said.

He shook his head.

"No. I'd offer you some coffee if it weren't hotter than a well digger's ass."

"So, what can you tell us?" I said.

"Come down, let's go inside."

When we entered the office Frank moved around a small table covered with maps and papers. He poured Virgil and me a glass of water. We sat across from him as he dropped his big frame into a swivel chair.

"I come up here to show these nincompoops how the cow ate the cabbage," he said. "I know my veins."

"And?" Virgil said.

"And that's it. That is the extent of my business here. I don't know a damn thing about what happened."

"What did happen?" Virgil said.

Frank took off his hat and dropped it on the table. He leaned toward the rear wall in his chair then put his big hands on top of his bald head. He grinned as he looked back

17

and forth between Virgil and me.

"Look, I told him, the Frenchman, not to hire no gun hands. I told him. I'm not saying they had anything to do with the McCormicks missing a hand. But I warned Baptiste and them other dumbasses working with him to not go and get greedy."

"Meaning?" I said.

"Meaning, let the McCormicks work their side and we work ours. I don't have to tell you boys gold makes people crazy. It just does. Like giving an Apache corn liquor, they can't handle it, can't handle the rush. Don't forget I started on the big one, in California back in the day, and I know what gold does to a man's soul. It eats it up."

"How did you know about the McCormick hand that was missing?"

"I heard about it from one of my miners. He said he was drinking beer at the Rabbit Inn and he heard about it from some of the other fellas. Shit happens, people talk."

"What do you know about these men Baptiste hired?" I said.

"Very damn little."

"What little do you know?"

"They don't come around here, really."

"But they've been here," Virgil said. "You've met them?"

"Met? No. Been here? Yes. They come and go."

"More than once," I said.

"Yes, more than once. They make themselves known, then go."

"How many are there?"

"For sure there are seven of them. As far as I know . . . Just talk to Henri Baptiste. He'll tell you . . . Well, maybe."

"Oh, we will," Virgil said.

"Like I said. I told Baptiste and the others to leave well enough alone. But that's gold for ya."

"Know where these seven gun hires live?" Virgil said.

"No," he said. "Appaloosa, I imagine."

"Lot of good they are doing there," I said.

"Fine with me," Frank said. "We have guards here to guard. So do the McCormicks. The gun hands are just chest puffers, ya know?"

Virgil nodded.

"Know the gun hands' names?"

"No. Well, know one. Heard one's name and 'spect he's the leader, too. Bart, he was called. Looks to be the oldest. He's a tall, skinny fellow, meaner than a windblown grass fire, too. He put one of the others in his place with a fucking bullwhip to the back of his head. No shit. Just like that. Whap!"

Virgil glanced at me.

"Victor Bartholomew?" I said.

Frank shook his head.

"Bart was all I know. That's what they called him. Why? Know him?"

"Skinny fucker with a bullwhip?" I said.

"Victor Bartholomew," Virgil said.

"That's not good," I said.

Virgil moved his head from side to side real slow.

"No," he said. "It ain't."

"Was there another? Looked similar to him, but bigger, taller, older?" I said.

"No," Frank said.

I glanced to Virgil.

"That's good," I said.

"That is," Virgil said.

3

The McCormick brothers and Baptiste had offices on opposite ends of the prestigious Appaloosa Avenue. The avenue was the central thoroughfare of the city. It was the only road in town made of cobblestone and it was lined with fancy brick buildings that stretched out across three city blocks. Known before as Vandervoort Avenue. But the Vandervoort name was history. Removed from all the previous places bearing the Dutch namesake — the brick factory, the town hall, the theater, and the avenue.

After the death of Vernon Vandervoort, all vestiges of his name were no longer visible. Vandervoort, it turned out, was a criminal and murderer. Less than six months ago, an altercation in the town hall unfolded before a huge crowd. Vandervoort shot and killed his own son and wife before Vandervoort was also shot and killed.

Before we paid Baptiste a visit, Virgil

wanted to stop in to see Allie at her dress shop on the avenue. We'd been away a few days, and without my encouraging Virgil, he thought it a good idea to let her know that we had returned.

Allie's shop — Mrs. French's Fine Dresses — flourished into a profitable business ever since it had opened its doors. And it was situated in a prime location: the center of Appaloosa Avenue, directly across from the town hall and the theater.

As we walked down the boardwalk we could see Allie through the window, setting up a large poster on an easel. It was a colorful poster with big block letters announcing APPALOOSA DAYS. An upcoming street fair with food, shop sales, street dancing, and music.

Virgil shook his head.

"Appaloosa Days," he said. "Always something."

"Allie and her ladies' social pretty much put the whole thing together," I said.

"Pretty much all her doing."

"She's quite the entrepreneur."

"Among other things."

We watched her for a bit. Once she got the poster secured, she retrieved one of the dresses out of the window display.

"Successful," I said.

Virgil nodded.

"That she is."

"One of these days you can quit marshaling altogether, Virgil, and let Allie support you."

I was watching Allie but I could feel Virgil's eyes on me.

"Could," I said. "Or I suppose you could work alongside her."

"Alongside her?"

I nodded.

"Sure."

"Doing what exactly, Everett?"

"Oh, hell, I don't know. Who knows? You might make a good salesperson or, hell, even a seamstress."

We waited on a buckboard followed by a buggy and when the buggy was past, Virgil moved on across the street without saying anything. I smiled and followed.

Allie opened the door as we neared.

"There you are," she said.

Virgil moved ahead of me, and when he got up the few steps to the shop's entrance, Allie met him and they kissed.

"Welcome back," she said. "Are you just getting here?"

"Got here a bit earlier, but we had to do a few things."

"Before you visited me, you had to do a

23

few things?"

"I'm here visiting you now. Everett, too."

"Well, I missed you."

"We was only gone two days."

"Well. So? Still, I missed you."

"Missed you, too, Allie."

"You did not."

"I did."

"Phooey."

"Everett missed you, too, didn't you, Everett?"

"I did."

Allie smiled.

"You two. Y'all come in, I'm just helping someone." Allie leaned in to me. "Some someone you might want to meet, Everett."

"We got some business," Virgil said.

"After you already had some business? Now you already have more business?"

"It can wait," I said.

She smiled.

"Come, I have some lemonade, too."

When we entered, a tall, slender woman was standing in front of the mirror. She was holding up the gray gingham dress Allie had retrieved from the window. She held the dress in front of her, looking at her reflection. When we walked closer, she turned toward us and smiled.

"Martha Kathryn," Allie said. "I'd like you

to meet, Marshal Virgil Cole. He's my . . . my companion."

Virgil removed his hat.

"How do you do?"

"Fine, Marshal Cole," she said. "A pleasure to meet you."

"And this is his partner, Marshal Everett Hitch."

I, too, removed my hat.

"Nice to meet you," I said.

"A pleasure," she said with a sweet smile.

"I take it you are new to Appaloosa?" I said.

"Well, not exactly."

"She would be hard to miss," Allie said. "I know."

"I arrived here about six months ago."

"Six months?" I said.

She nodded and I smiled at Virgil.

"Appaloosa has gotten way too big," I said.

"It has," he said.

She blushed.

"I have been sequestered, I have to say, though. Pretty much the whole time."

"Locked up?" Virgil said.

She laughed.

"No, I've been working in the Appaloosa Theater just across the way."

Virgil smiled and nodded some.

"We are in and out of the jail all the time,"

25

he said. "I'm sure we would have caught wind of you being locked up."

"Martha Kathryn is an actress and a singer," Allie said. "She has been practicing there for the new play."

She nodded.

"Rehearsing."

"Yes," Allie said. "Rehearsing. And I took the opportunity to ask Martha Kathryn if she would perform something for our upcoming Appaloosa Days, and I'm grateful to say, she has accepted."

"That's good," I said. "You're with the traveling theatrical company?"

"Yes, that's right. Our manager heard the theater was not in use, so he rented it out to develop shows for our season on the road."

"Yes, I remember reading something about that," I said.

"I saw her a few times on the street," Allie said. "She caught my eye, let me tell you, but she never came in until last week."

She nodded.

"We have been doing nothing but working and sleeping and working and sleeping."

"But all that is about to end," Allie said.

"There's a show opening," I said. "Right?"

"Tonight," she said.

"I remember reading about that, too," I said.

I could feel Virgil looking at me, but I didn't look at him.

"It's her opening night here in Appaloosa," Allie said. "Isn't it just divine."

"Sure is," Virgil said.

"And we," Allie said. "We will be there."

"We will?" Virgil said.

"We will," Allie said. "We will be dressed for the theater."

"Allie, you don't need to speak for Everett," Virgil said. "And there are a few things that need some tending to."

"You have something else you need to do, Virgil?" I said.

"He does not," Allie said.

"I don't?" Virgil said.

"You do not," she said. "And neither does Everett."

I smiled to Martha Kathryn.

"We look forward to it," I said.

Allie looked back and forth between Martha Kathryn and me then cut her eyes to Virgil.

"Lemonade," Allie said. "Let me get us some lemonade."

Allie started off toward the rear of the shop. She said over her shoulder as she walked, "And Virgil, you will assist me?"

"Anything you say, Allie."

He smiled at Martha Kathryn then followed Allie.

Martha Kathryn turned to the mirror and held the dress up in front of her again.

"What do you think?" she said.

I moved behind her to look in the mirror.

"Don't think that is your color."

She smiled.

"Really?"

"Really."

"And what would be my color, pray tell?"

"White, black, yellow. No, not yellow. But not that, not gray, gray is not right for you."

She met my eyes in the mirror and said nothing.

I said nothing back as I returned her look.

She smiled.

I smiled.

4

Virgil and I left Allie's shop and walked toward Henri Baptiste's office at the opposite end of the avenue.

"Pretty woman," I said.

"Is," Virgil said.

"Refined."

"You figure?"

"I do."

"Last time you was dallying with a refined performer, she up and took off on you."

"She was a fortune teller."

"Point?"

"Don't think I would have called her *refined.*"

"What would you have called her?"

"Mysterious."

"Hell, Everett, they're all mysterious."

As we approached, Henri Baptiste stepped out of the office door. Following him was one of his associates, a man Virgil and I had dealt with before. Eugene Pritchard, a big overgrown blowhard attorney who had more money than sense.

They moved off in the opposite direction without seeing us. We followed them until they got to the corner. They waited for a mule team pulling a load of lumber to pass. Before crossing the street, Eugene turned, seeing us.

"Marshals," he said.

Henri turned toward us, then pulled his shoulders back and tucked his thumbs into the pockets of his vest.

"Need a word," I said.

"I'm afraid you'll have to wait," Eugene said. "We are off to an investor meeting we are already a little late for."

"Investors can wait," I said.

"Well . . ." Eugene said with a jackass smile. "Another time would be better."

"You'll just be a bit later than you already are," Virgil said.

"What is it?" Henri said. "What can we help you with, gentlemen, Marshals?"

Henri was a Frenchman, no doubt, but he spoke with pretty clear diction, void of sounding altogether foreign. He was a small man in stature, but his presence loomed large.

"There is a man that has been reported missing," I said. "A McCormick hand."

"Yes, I heard," Henri said.

"How?" Virgil said.

"Well, hell," Eugene said. "The news has been all over Appaloosa."

"Who did you hear the news from?" Virgil said to Henri.

"He heard it from me," Eugene said.

"And where did you hear it?" I said.

"Good Lord."

"I asked you a question."

Eugene pulled an *Appaloosa Star* newspaper from the inside of his coat pocket and pointed to a small article on the back page.

"Made the news, for God's sake."

"We know nothing about it," Henri said.

"You hired some gunmen?" Virgil said.

"I have," Henri said.

"Why?" Virgil said.

"Protection."

"No law against protection," Eugene said.

"Where are they?" I said.

"At this moment in time I don't know," Henri said.

"And they are your protection?" I said.

"It's not that I feel I'm in current or constant danger."

"Then what is it?" I said.

"Their presence is all that is needed," he said. "Please understand this. I want people to know that I have a lot at stake and that

I'm not to be fucked with, as it were."

"Who would want to do that?" I said. "What people would want to fuck with you, as it were?"

"I will not be intimidated or pushed around by McCormick or anyone else."

"Since the gold was found, you realize we have to be extra careful with our business," Eugene said.

"McCormick has hired his own men, too, Marshal Cole, I'm sure you know this, and I have my men. I am not certain about the men McCormick has hired, but my men are not breaking any laws. They're only there if there is trouble, and they're not wearing firearms in town."

"That's the law," I said.

"Yes, as well as my strict instruction. It's no secret that I do not care for the McCormick brothers and they do not care for me, but I don't want to take any chances."

"You hired Victor Bartholomew?" Virgil said.

"Is that a problem? Have I broken a law?"

"Don't know. Have you?"

"Listen, Marshal Cole. I'm just trying to protect my interest. This is one of the most colossal finds in decades. And as we have said but will reiterate, there is a hell of a lot of money at stake here."

"You don't need to reiterate nothing," Virgil said. "But what you do need to do is take care of your business without causing others trouble. You do that and everything will be *muy bueno.*"

"Look, we need to be extra cautious. That is all. I have instructed my men to watch his men. I don't want to be confronted with some kind of Irish Mob takeover. But that is it, and they know nothing of the missing man. Now, if you will excuse us, we will be on our way."

"His brother with him?" I said.

"I'm sorry, what? Who?"

"Victor's brother?" Virgil said. "You hire him, too?"

"No. I have no idea who you are referring to."

"Where did you find Victor?"

"I have a business associate in San Cristobal who recommended him," Henri said. "Said he was reliable."

"Reliable?" I said.

"Yes," Henri said.

Virgil nodded.

"Appreciate your time," Virgil said.

The two men turned and faced the street. They waited for a rider then crossed. We watched after them a second or two, then Virgil glanced at me and smiled.

"Not the most likable," I said.

"No," Virgil said. "They're not."

5

The McCormick brothers were new to Appaloosa. They were not the rough-and-tough, and often crude, Irishmen we normally encountered. They were very different. Educated and civilized. They were older, industrious men who moved to town with money in their pockets. And from what we knew of them, they were not crooks. They started up a number of businesses within their first year of residency, and they employed a good number of people. They were ranchers with a decent-size cow/calf operation, but they also owned a dry-goods business, a furniture store, and now a gold-mining outfit.

But Appaloosa was growing so fast it was getting harder and harder to keep up with all that was happening. Who was moving in and who was doing what. And like so many of the newcomers in Appaloosa these days, Virgil and I had never met the McCormick brothers. We'd seen them, and knew of them, mainly through Allie, who was friends with the wife of one of the brothers.

There were three young men in the front office. They were all dressed in nice clean suits and wore lace-up shoes, and each was busy sorting and unsorting papers when we entered. One of them, a thin young man sitting behind the center desk that separated the large entry from the main offices, finished some writing and smiled up at us.

"May I help you?" he said.

He leaned back in his chair as we walked to his desk. A huge map of the McCormicks' gold mines loomed large behind him.

"Here to see the McCormicks," I said.

"James is out, but Mr. McCormick, Daniel, is in," he said. "May I tell him who is calling?"

"You may. Marshal Virgil Cole," I said. "And Deputy Marshal Hitch, Everett Hitch."

"One moment," he said.

He got to his feet.

"I'm Lawrence Newcomb, by the way, I'm the office manager here at McCormick Enterprises."

Lawrence was tall and very thin and moved like a graceful dancer. He walked off down a short hall and turned the corner.

The other men stayed busy as we waited, and after a minute Lawrence returned.

"Right this way," he said.

We followed Lawrence into Daniel McCormick's office. Daniel, the older of the two brothers, stood to greet us as we entered.

"I figured it was only just a matter of time before we met," he said with a very slight Irish brogue. "I've heard a great deal about the both of you."

Lawrence left, closing the door behind him. Daniel got up from behind his desk to shake our hands. He held out his hand first to Virgil, but I reached out to him.

"Virgil doesn't shake hands," I said.

His eyes rendered a glint of curiosity but then he smiled and nodded.

"Oh. Well, fine."

He shook my hand, then motioned to the chairs facing his desk.

"Please, have a seat."

We did just that, then he moved around and sat behind the large oak desk.

"Why'd you figure it'd be a matter of time?" Virgil said.

"Oh, just a figure of speech."

He opened a cigar box and held it out to us.

"Cigar?"

I held up my hand, declining, but Virgil nodded and retrieved one from the box.

Daniel offered a tip cutter and lighter. Virgil clipped the tip and lit the cigar. Then Daniel did the same. Once Daniel got his going good, he blew a roll of smoke, set both of his hands on the desk, and narrowed his eyes.

"Not really a figure of speech, is it? It's of course more than that. It's serious business to have an employee go missing. And know that it is the work of a sonofabitch little Frenchman and his band of no-goods."

"What all do you know about this?" I said. "Your missing employee?"

He shook his head.

"His name was Randal Fisher. By all accounts a good, hardworking young man. Honest and showed up to work on time. That is, until he didn't show up."

"And up to the time of Randal Fisher not showing up, was there any sign of trouble between him and anyone else?"

"None that I know of."

"Where was Fisher living?" I said.

"Boardinghouse here in town."

"And you have checked with them," I said. "When they saw him last and so forth?"

"Yes. Well, my brother did, and they had not seen him. What few things Fisher had to his name were left under his bunk. But one night he did not come back, and that was it. We shared this with the Appaloosa deputy. Deputy Book, I believe."

"And you think the Frenchman's men are to blame?"

"Of course."

"What makes you say that?" I said.

"Who else?"

"We know you have hired gunmen," I said.

He puffed on his cigar and stared at us before turning his gaze to the window. He rolled his fingers on the desk as he thought, then he leveled a harsh look at us.

"I have managed many businesses in my time. And I have worked hard at all of them, and never have I been involved in criminal activity. I hired the gunmen, yes, I had to."

"Had to?" I said.

"Yes. When the Frenchman and his group hired men to intimidate my men. Well, I did the same, and since then I have felt better about my entity."

"How did you find these men?" Virgil said.

"I placed an ad in *The Territorial Gazette.*"

"How many men do you have?" Virgil said.

"Six."

"Who are they?" I said.

"Do you mean what are their names?" he said.

I nodded.

"Yes," I said.

He opened his desk drawer and retrieved a piece of paper and slid it across the desk. I picked up the list and read the names out loud.

I shook my head.

"Never heard of them."

"Where are they?" Virgil said.

"They spend a good deal of time at the mine."

"How is it you came about owning this mine?" Virgil said.

"I bought it."

"Why?" Virgil said.

"Originally to run cattle."

"Not the best land for cattle," I said.

"We have always been in the cattle business, and when we arrived here in Appaloosa, it was our intention to continue with the cattle business. So we searched for some land to buy."

"But how was it you bought it," Virgil said. "How did you come about it? Was it for sale and you just came across land where gold would soon be discovered?"

"I paid a good price for it. More than it was worth."

"Did you know there was gold on the land before you bought it?" Virgil said.

"No."

"But you wanted that land. Why?" Virgil said.

"It's not bad cattle land, that is why."

"Not great," I said.

"No, but not bad. My brother approached the Baptiste Group and worked out a deal with them."

"What kind of deal?"

"We knew he owned the land. And my brother, James, simply asked him if he'd be willing to sell a portion of the property. And that is what happened. They were not using the land. We struck a deal. Paid the Baptiste Group the money, and the land became ours."

"How many head do you have out there?"

"Now, not many. Once the gold was discovered, we naturally shifted our focus."

Virgil nodded, puffing on the cigar.

"Who discovered the gold? The Baptiste Group, or was it you?"

Daniel rolled his fingers in a drumming rhythm again.

"We did."

"And you had no idea about the gold prior?" I said.

"No," he said. "Like I said."

"You said you found it?" Virgil said. " 'We'? We who exactly?"

"My brother, James, discovered it."

"He just stumbled across it?" I said.

"No. Well, kind of. No cattle had been on that land to speak of, and, as you know, water is scarce in these parts, and James was looking to see what possible water source there might be. There was little water, so we figured maybe it was a good idea to dynamite, to open a water source underground. Sure enough we got water, but we also got gold."

"So how did Baptiste find out about what you found?" I said.

"James had hired a few men who helped with the dynamiting and, well, they said they'd keep quiet about it, but . . ."

"They didn't?" I said.

"No. Gold excites people, makes people do strange things. Things they might not normally do."

"Like making people disappear," Virgil said.

6

The kid walked out of the jail with the jailer's Winchester, his Colt revolver, and what money the jailer had in his pocket. He skirted around the plaza and stayed in the dark under the awnings. But once he was to the other side, where the festivities were still going on, he stashed the guns and moved out into the crowd.

He figured it would be morning before someone found the dead-and-gone jailer. So he settled in and enjoyed himself. He ate a big plate of food until he could eat no more. Then he got up and danced to the music. He even asked a young *señorita* to dance. He told her not to be concerned with his busted lip and bruised face, that he'd just had a horse fall but was a good dancer. And he was a good dancer, had grace and a rhythm that the *señoritas* admired. He danced and danced, first with one *señorita,* then another. He danced so much his feet got tired. He drank some beer and got some more food.

After he got his belly full again and danced with his favorite *señorita,* he excused himself. He gathered up his weapons and poked around the Army corrals behind the jail.

He was thrilled and not too surprised to find the pony he'd won. The kid really liked the horse. He was a small, friendly tricolored geld that was easy to ride. The kid was an expert rider. He had a way with horses, even the rank ones, but this one he felt comfortable with.

In the tack room he found an even better saddle than the one that was originally on the pony. And even though the party was still going on, he figured he best not push his luck. So he mounted up and rode off into the dark night.

He cleared a good amount of distance away from the town the first night. He found a cool place to sleep in the morning for a few hours. Then, after another half-day in the saddle, he came to a depot, where he rested and got more food. He played some cards and drank a little whiskey with some section-line fellas. Then lit out again, staying on the move.

The following day he came to a farm, where a friendly couple offered him a place to bed for the night. That is, if he helped with the chores.

They told him there was a village a few hours' ride up the road, but since they had been without their regular help they'd be appreciative if he'd pitch in. And he did that; he pitched in and did some feeding, hauling, paint scraping, and cleaning. The kid was no stranger to hard work. He'd spent his youth bouncing from one family to another and they always put him to work.

After the work, he washed up and sat at the table with the couple. The husband was quiet and hardly said a word all day, but the wife was friendly and chatty. She was also pretty, for an older woman who'd spent hard years on the farm. Her skin was dark and her face was thin, with high cheekbones. She had deep-set blue eyes, kind of like his, and the kid thought she likely resembled his mother. Her hair was up and freshly washed. She wore a white cotton dress with a wide red scarf that draped over her shoulders. The kid thought about what she might look like under her dress. She said they had not had children, so he thought her breasts most likely were in good condition and not worn out from nursing. He thought she smelled good, too.

"So, young man," she said with a warm smile, "just where will you be heading to tomorrow?"

"Well, I'm not sure, ma'am, just how far I will

get. I'm sort of taking it easy."

"That's nice."

"Yep, I've waited this long, I mean, it's been a long time, so there is no need to hurry."

"Waited?"

"Yes, ma'am."

"For?"

"Let the boy eat his supper."

"No, that's okay. I'm going home."

"Well, that's nice," she said.

"I'm hoping so."

"Where is home?"

"Trinidad."

She smiled and looked to her husband, who remained focused on cutting up his pork chop.

"Well, I think I have heard of it," she said, "yes, but I've never been there."

"Me neither."

She frowned.

"But you said it was home."

He smiled.

"Home is where the heart is."

She smiled and reached out and touched his hand.

"That's nice. I'm very happy for you."

"Thank you."

She squeezed his hand, then took a sip of water.

"That's a beautiful scarf," he said.

"Why, thank you. It was my mother's."

46

"That's nice."

"I hope you, you don't mind me asking, but what happened to your face?"

He touched his lip.

"Why, I almost forgot about it," he said with a mouthful of whipped potatoes.

He laughed, which made her smile and chuckle, too.

"Well, I was arrested by these two no-good soldiers and they beat the tar outta me."

She glanced at her husband then turned her attention back to the kid with a concerned expression.

"Arrested?"

"Yep, yes, ma'am, arrested and locked up. Behind bars in an Army jail down on the border."

The kid kept on eating as she stared to her husband, who was no longer focused on his pork chop.

"What were you arrested for?" the husband said.

The kid took a few bites before he answered.

"Murder."

The woman's concerned face changed to fear. Then she lowered her fork slowly and rested it very gently on her plate, careful not to make any noise.

"And they let you go?" the husband said.

"No."

"How did you get out of jail, then?"

The kid held up a spoon.

"Well, I whittled down a spoon handle like this one here, carved it into a sharp point, and jabbed it into the soldier jailer's neck a few times, and that did the trick."

The wife started shaking. She moved her chair away from the table.

Her husband stared at the kid.

Then, with a sudden burst of energy, the husband went for a rifle near the door.

But he was way too slow.

7

There was an Appaloosa Days poster set up outside the main entrance of the Boston House Hotel when I entered. I thought about the upcoming event and all that Allie had put into it thus far. And it made me think with all the advertising and with all the people now living in Appaloosa, it was no doubt bound to be one hell of a crowded event.

I made my way through the busy lobby, walked into the saloon, and was happy to find a vacant stool at the end of the bar, where I waited for Virgil and Allie to arrive. The place was jam-packed and noisy. Wallis was having a hard time behind the bar keeping the service coming, and I sat for a bit before I even got his attention.

The saloon was always busy these days, from the time the doors opened until they closed. People were changing, too. Folks were becoming more refined. They seemed happier, too, in general. No doubt because there were plenty of jobs to be had and there was more money. People were living better lives. The population of Appaloosa was now nearing four thousand, and it seemed that everywhere you went you would most likely have to wait on one thing or the other. When Wallis finally did make it over to me, he had sweat dripping off his nose, but he smiled wide.

"Well, take a look at you."

"What?"

"What? What do you mean 'what'? Don't think I have ever seen you looking so fine and dandy, Everett. I mean, you have always been a sharp dresser, but you have outdone yourself. Damn dandy. What's the special occasion?"

"I'm going to the theater."

"The theater?"

"Yep."

Wallis shook his head as he collected a mug.

"As I live and breathe."

He chuckled as he poured me a beer.

"Seriously?"

"Seriously."

"If I didn't know better, I'd think there might be a woman that is seriously involved with this theater business."

"I'll take a shot of whiskey with that."

Wallis set the foaming beer in front of me, then placed a glass next to it and poured.

"I'm dying of thirst over here," somebody called out from the opposite end of the bar.

"Hold your horses," Wallis said over his shoulder, then leaned in toward me. "What's her name?"

"None of your business," I said.

"Well, hell, Everett," he said. "How can I ever be of consoling service if I don't know her name?"

"Martha Kathryn," I said. "And I just met her."

"Ohh. I like the sound of that."

"Me, too."

"Everett," Virgil said.

Wallis eyed Virgil behind me. Allie was in front of him as they moved past a few customers standing near the bar. I got out of my seat and reached for Allie's hand.

"Here, Allie. Sit."

"Why, thank you, Everett," she said as she stepped up onto the stool, eyeing my attire.

"Brandy, Allie?" Wallis said.

"Why, yes, Wallis, thank you."

Virgil nodded to my beer and whiskey.

"Same as Everett there."

Allie leaned her head left, then right, looking me up and down.

"My, oh, my."

"You told me to dress up."

"And you look so handsome, Everett. Don't you think, Virgil?"

"Well, hell, Allie. He did what you asked him to do."

"I did."

"I've tried to get Virgil to step out of the black and he just won't do it."

"I'm clean, my suit is clean, and my hat is clean," Virgil said as Wallis handed him a mug of beer.

"Look here," I said.

Virgil followed my look to see a tall and skinny man with long hair and a beard. He was looking in our direction.

The bearded man held up his beer to us and nodded.

"That'd be none other than Victor Bartholomew," I said.

"None other," Virgil said.

He stood with two other men. He stared at us over the top of a beer mug as he took a swig.

"Know those other two?" I said.

"They was with him before, weren't they?" Virgil said.

"Yep, the Mexican I remember. He's Johnny Rodriguez," I said. "The other, the big one, not sure, but I think he's Ward . . .

Ward something?"

"Sounds right," Virgil said.

Victor lowered the mug and smiled wide, like we were all old friends.

"Here they come," I said.

"Allie, do me a favor."

"Yes, Virgil."

"Just take a little fresh air out the side door there so Everett and me can talk to these fellas."

Allie regarded the men we were talking about, then turned to Virgil.

"Be a good idea," Virgil said to Allie.

She raised her hand and I helped her off the stool. She moved off through the folks crowded around the bar and walked toward the door. Victor came striding over and the two men with him followed.

"Virgil," he said with a nod.

Then his eyes drifted to where Allie walked. She turned back, and Victor tipped his hat. Then he smiled at me like he was my friend.

"Everett," he said.

He tipped his head toward his men.

"You boys remember Johnny and Wayne, don't you?"

"Not much to remember," I said.

Virgil did not acknowledge them.

"We meet again," Johnny said with a smile

and showing the missing tooth under his bushy mustache.

Wayne, not Ward, said nothing. He just glared.

"We heard you fellas was here," Victor said.

"What do you need, Victor?" I said.

"Just saying howdy," he said.

"Why do we know that is not the case?" I said.

"Don't know what you mean, Everett," he said. "Good to see you, too."

Then he opened his jacket with the handle of his bullwhip to show us he was without a gun.

"Not heeled," he said.

Virgil didn't say anything.

Victor grinned an arrogant grin.

"Just following your law."

"Keep it that way, Victor," Virgil said.

"That's a fine how-do-you-do."

"Fine as it will get," Virgil said.

"You, too, Everett," Victor said. "You feel the same way?"

"What do you want to tell us about the McCormick miner?" Virgil said.

"Got no idea what you are talking about," Victor said.

"Not a good idea to lie to me," Virgil said.

"Just being friendly."

"No, you're not," Virgil said.

"What makes you say that?"

"We're not friends," Virgil said.

"Sorry you feel that way."

"Your brother with you?"

He turned and turned again as if he was searching.

"Nope," he said. "Not that I can see."

"He here in Appaloosa?" Virgil said.

"No."

A silence swelled and filled up a strange uneasiness as Victor stared at Virgil.

"You're the one who locked me up, Cole."

Virgil nodded.

"I did."

"Not the other way around, Virgil."

"Nope."

"I'm the one that should have the grudge."

Virgil didn't say anything.

"I'm the one with the debt to settle, Virgil."

"Bad idea to threaten me."

"Just stating the facts."

"The fact is, you only got a portion of what you deserved," Virgil said. "That is the fact."

Victor stared at him, unblinking.

"I'm here on business and —"

"I know goddamn good and well why you are here."

"Good, then you know I mean business."

"Get on before I get pissed off and drag you outta here and down the road to jail with that whip wrapped around your neck."

"No reason for that kind of talk," Wayne said.

"Do like I tell ya," Virgil said.

Wayne moved forward.

"You don't scare me none," Wayne said.

Victor pulled Wayne back.

"No reason for any misunderstanding," Victor said.

He smiled, staring at Virgil. Then he made a point to look off toward Allie. He smiled at her and tipped his hat. He turned and walked away.

8

The kid left the farm after the sunset. It was a beautiful end to an eventful day, with purple and gold and orange spread out before him as he rode. His pony was well fed and rested and even had a little extra spirit to his step. When it turned evening, the moon was near full and the road was easy to follow. And it wasn't too long before he came to the town that the husband and wife had told him about.

It was a small place but bigger than a village, and it had a good peaceful feeling to it. He passed a few houses before he came into the light of the town. It was early enough that folks were still awake. He could see a few people behind their windows doing one thing or another. He was glad to see people were still out and about. A blacksmith was even working the evening hours; the sound he'd heard from almost a mile away. The kid figured it was better than working the hot iron in the heat of the summer day.

He could hear music, too, a piano and fiddle, and that lifted his spirits. Not that his spirits were not already high. But he enjoyed people having fun more than almost anything else. He followed the sound and arrived at a saloon on the far end of town. It was a two-story building, and his first thought was women. Maybe there were workingwomen here.

He tied up his pony and entered, and to his delight it was the type of place that suited him. It was full of life. In the corner under the stairs there was an old fella playing the piano. Next to him was an even older man sawing on a fiddle. And there were women. One was up dancing; another two were sitting with some fellas about his age. And before he could get to the bar another woman, one he'd not seen, mainly because she was so small, tugged on his sleeve.

"Hey there, handsome," she said.

"Hello, cutie pie."

"You think I'm cute?"

"I don't think, I know."

She laughed.

"Well, I like you!" she said.

And she did have something. Beautiful, he thought, might be an exaggeration. But she was fetching and there was something about her that made him excited. Made him feel randy.

She was little and skinny, and her body barely touched the insides of her dress. Her hair was blond and stringy and thin. She had freckles across her cheeks and nose, but her brown eyes were as big and round as half-dollars.

"Those are some eyes you got there."

She blinked them.

"Buy me a drink?"

"Damn straight."

She hooked her arm in his and they sauntered to the bar like they were old friends. After he got a bottle and two glasses, he wasted no time in letting her know he had some money. He told her he would be more than happy to spend it on her upstairs.

"Doing what?" she said with a coy laugh.

"Oh, I don't know. Bet we can think of something."

She gazed into his eyes and smiled.

"I think I like you," she said, leaning in close to him.

Then she reached down between his legs and smiled.

"No, I don't think, I know I like you."

She grabbed his hand. Then turned to one of the other women, an older, heavyset gal with large breasts and a painted face.

"Georgina, I'm going up."

Georgina gave the kid a once-over, then

nodded her approval and he followed the little blonde up the stairs.

"What's your name?"

"What's yours?"

"Becky."

"Pretty name."

"Thank you. And you? What yours."

"I don't have one."

She opened the door to the room.

"Silly, everybody has a name."

"Everybody but me."

They entered the room and she closed the door behind them.

"So what am I supposed to call you?"

"You don't have to call me anything."

"But what if I want to get your attention?"

"You already got my attention."

He leaned on her and moved her back to the closed door and kissed her. She returned his kiss then batted her big brown eyes. She touched his cut lip and cheek.

"Does it hurt?"

"Not really."

She kissed him gently.

"What happened?"

"That's funny," he said.

She kissed him again, gently, on different parts of his lips.

"What's funny?"

"My mother asked me the same thing."

She kissed him again and again.
"What did you tell her?"

9

Allie had been in the Appaloosa Theater in the past, but Virgil and I had not stepped foot into the place before this evening's production. The play was *Evangeline.* A life-size illustrated image of Martha Kathryn in the center of the lobby placard made it obvious. She was portraying the central character, Evangeline.

"Oh, my, will you look at that," Allie said. "Isn't she something? So beautiful."

I nodded.

"She is at that."

Atop the placard, it exclaimed *The World's Popular, Fascinating, Musical Extravaganza,* based on the poem *Evangeline* by Henry Wadsworth Longfellow.

"Longfellow," Virgil said.

"Yep," I said.

"This is so exciting," Allie said.

"Not sure how a poem gets swiveled into a musical extravaganza," Virgil said.

"Looks like we're fixing to find out," I said.

The theater was like every other place in Appaloosa, crowded. But it was an impressive place, no doubt: grand as some of the theaters I'd seen in my early days in New York City. Ornate carvings outlined the wide proscenium stage painted in gold and silver. A fat cherub blowing wind into the sail of a ship marked the centerpiece above the stage. The theater had red-velvet seats in wide rows for at least five hundred people. A balcony covered half the seats, and private boxes lined each side. And there was an orchestra pit, where a band was tuning their instruments. Vandervoort had built the theater and had a few successful shows. But after his demise, the playhouse had no real ownership or guidance, until the Appaloosa City Council took over management.

When we settled in and the orchestra music started, Allie squeezed Virgil's hand and mine as if she was holding on for dear life. And when Martha Kathryn stepped out on stage Allie clapped so hard I thought she might hurt herself.

Martha Kathryn was stunning as well as captivating in every way. She was elegant and commanding, and it was hard to take your eyes off her. She danced and sang and laughed and made everyone in the audience laugh.

The show was entertaining and comical. And actually turned out to be one hell of an extravaganza for certain, with lots of ladies dancing and singing and a plot that somehow traveled from Arizona to Africa.

After the show we waited in the lobby along with a crowd of admirers wanting to get cast members' autographs. Martha Kathryn emerged with some of the other actors, and it was clear to see that it was Martha Kathryn who the crowd was waiting for. She got swarmed. We stood back and waited for her to thank each one. Finally she had to let them know that she had plans and bid them good night. When she came to us, Allie hugged her tight.

"That was one of the most incredible experiences, I have to say," Allie said.

"Well, good, I'm so glad you enjoyed it," she said. "Now, I could use a sip of some wine or a shot of bourbon."

Virgil glanced at me.

"Sounds right," I said.

"Does," Virgil said.

"To the hotel?" she said.

"Indeed," Allie said.

Martha Kathryn took my arm and we walked, following Virgil and Allie toward the Hotel Windsor.

"What'd you think, Mr. Hitch?"

"Think you're damn good."

"About the show."

"I enjoyed it, didn't completely understand the plot, but I enjoyed it."

She laughed.

"Yes, it is a rather nonsensical show."

"But I enjoyed it, enjoyed you."

"I have my moments."

"You have much more than moments."

"It's all part of the act."

"That's not what I'm talking about."

I figured I had no reason not to get right into the middle of what I really felt about this woman, and there was a web being spun between us.

She smiled.

"Why, Mr. Hitch."

"I could go through the list, but then I would be meandering through the obvious."

"That right?"

"Best not try to explain the unexplainable."

"No reason to define it."

"No reason I can think of."

"What you see is not always what you get."

"Even better."

She smiled. I felt like leaning in and kissing her right there. I was pretty sure she felt the same, but I figured I'd let us both think about it.

Martha Kathryn and the main members of the cast were staying at the Hotel Windsor. When we arrived, we settled on the back porch for a drink.

A few people stopped by the table to let her know they had seen the show and how much they liked it. After they cleared, Allie held up her glass.

"To Martha Kathryn."

"Why, thank you," Martha Kathryn said, "but this toast is to you, to my new friends in Appaloosa, and thank you for coming."

"Well, my gosh, like I said, that was the most exciting thing I think I have ever seen, just incredible. And I am so over the blessed moon to say just how pleased I am that you will be helping out by performing for us at Appaloosa Days. Do you think you will do something from the show? That would be marvelous if you did, but of course whatever you decide, I'm certain it will be amazing."

"Rest assured, I'll do something fun and entertaining for your Appaloosa Days, Allie."

"Thank you, thank you, thank you!"

Martha Kathryn turned to Virgil.

"Did you enjoy the show, Mr. Cole?"

"Virgil thought it was fantastic," Allie said.

"Didn't you, Virgil?"

"I did."

"Do you like the theater, Marshal Cole?"

"Sure," Virgil said.

"He told me walking over here how much he liked the dancing cow," Allie said.

Martha Kathryn laughed.

"And the spewing whale," Virgil said.

"Yes, those two are crowd pleasers," she said. "Well, again, thank you for coming."

I felt her rub her foot on my leg under the table. Then she smiled. It was a seductive smile and her eyes were speaking way more than the words she was putting together.

"Thank you," she said, "and please, come again."

10

Later that night, after he'd had his way with Becky, the kid got on his pony and resumed his journey north. He rode most of the night and into the early-morning hours, putting as much distance as he could between him and everything in his wake. He camped off the road in a thicket near a brook and slept for the better part of the morning before he saddled up and continued.

He topped a hill to see a wagon coming his way, and behind them he could see a large town in the far distance.

When the wagon neared, he could see it was a family: a mother, a father, and a boy sitting between them. The boy was a dark-haired kid with golden-colored skin just like him. As they got closer, he could see the boy also had blue eyes, just like his.

"Howdy, folks," the kid said as he slowed up.

The wagon also slowed in a cloud of dust

as the father pulled the mules to a stop.

"Hello," he said with a nod and a smile.

The mother and the shaggy-haired son were smiling, too. The kid thought they sure looked like a happy family.

"Mind telling what town that is back there?"

The father turned looking behind them.

"That's Saqui."

"Saqui? That sounds Indian."

" 'Spose maybe it is."

The kid nudged his pony closer.

"Not that many Indians around these days."

The father nodded.

"No, not like it used to be."

"Don't know that's not a bad thing," the kid said with a grin.

"No, I suppose not."

"Looks like you're pulling up stakes?"

"We are."

"What's the matter with Saqui?"

"Nothing wrong with it," he said.

"Just moving on?" the kid said.

"We are."

"I know the feeling, I feel the same way, staying in one place too long ain't good, things just start closing in on you."

"We have family south, be better for the boy and the one on the way."

"Well, good for you. How old are you, boy?"

The boy turned his face up to his dad.

"Go on, tell him."

"I'm nine."

"You are a fine-looking young boy for nine years old."

"What do you say?" the father said to his son.

"Thank you, sir."

"Heck, I'm not a lot older myself."

"How old are you?"

"Well, it's hard to say."

"You don't know how old you are?" the boy said.

"No, you see, I'm not real sure when my birthday is, to tell you the truth."

"You don't know your birthday?"

"No, but I reckon I'm about nineteen or twenty."

"I can't wait to be that old."

The kid laughed.

"Know what I was doing when I was nine?"

"What?" the boy said.

"I was already working."

"You were?"

"Yep."

"Doing what?"

"I was skinning animals."

"Really?"

"Really."

"What kind of animals?"

"All kinds. I skinned mostly beaver and deer,

70

but I also skinned elk and some bear, too."

The father smiled to his wife, then nodded to the kid.

"Well, we best be moving on," he said.

"Hold on one minute," the kid said.

He moved his pony a bit closer.

"You sure are a nice-looking family."

The husband glanced at his wife, then mustered a smile.

"Thank you."

"I got something for you."

The kid smiled real wide.

"Well, for your wife."

The kid turned in his saddle to retrieve something from his saddlebags.

"Here you go."

"Oh, no, I couldn't," the mother said.

"No, here, please, it's yours."

He leaned out and handed her the red scarf.

She hesitated.

"Please, it's yours. A good-luck keepsake for your travels, your new beginnings."

She glanced to her husband.

He nodded and she took the scarf.

"It belonged to my grandmother."

Then he tipped his sombrero.

"Have a nice journey."

11

The long night of sweating and tossing and turning exhausted me. The whole night I thought about Martha Kathryn. I don't think that I had slept more than an hour at a time, and I was appreciative when the sun finally showed up. It gave me an excuse to get up, get my ass out of bed, and get the day started.

I dressed and went to the barn to work with a pair of horses I'd recently bought, a dam and her filly.

They were both anxious to get out. I let the filly out first. She ran around the corral, kicking up dirt and tossing her head. She waited for her mother's release. They were both light in color and tall, with dark manes and tails. They settled with feed. And after I worked with each of them for a good half-hour, I put them up and walked to the sheriff's office.

After last year's murder of Sheriff

Chastain, Appaloosa's lawlessness had been at a low for a long stretch. And as a result, the city aldermen were yet to fill Chastain's position. The main reason for the delay was the simple fact that there was a seasoned interim lawman, Lloyd Somerset, who had offered his help until a sheriff got elected.

Lloyd was a retired Texas Ranger who moved to Appaloosa to be close to his daughter and grandkids. Word was, in his day Lloyd was a feared and revered lawman. Even in his older age, Lloyd gave off the impression he was somebody you might not want to cross. Nowadays, though, he was more of a jailer than a peacekeeper. But he was available, and all the deputies seemed to like and respect him. They enjoyed his stories about his Texas Ranger days and dealing with the Comanche.

It was only in the last few weeks that the city officials had even begun making efforts to elect a new sheriff. For the time being, the main man who was dealing with the actual policing duties was Deputy Book. Book was the senior deputy, but he'd yet to see his twenty-fifth birthday. So finding a man with some authority and experience was high on the Aldermen's agenda.

When I entered, Lloyd was drinking coffee with Book.

"Morning, Everett," they said in tandem.

"Fellas."

"I was telling young Book here about the time I brought in the Chiricahua prophet warrior princess Lozen."

"Victorio's sister?" I said.

"Yep. Pretty as a cactus flower. Stronger than most of the men warriors and could ride like a goddamn Comanche. She escaped the first night. Turned out one of them greenhorns who was supposed to be in charge of watching her thought he might get a little piece off her. But it turned out she got a little piece off him. The whole top-half piece of his red hair is what the fuck she took, along with the skin that his red hair was attached to."

I poured myself a cup, and before I could sit, James McCormick, the younger of the two McCormick brothers, entered. He was taller than his older brother, with thick, dark hair and a chiseled face. We could tell before he opened his mouth that he was angry.

"Something has to be done," he said.

"About?" I said.

"Another one of our hands has turned up missing."

"How do you know?"

"If you don't do something we will have to retaliate," he said. "We can't just sit back and let those bastards pick our men off one by one. Won't stand for it."

"Just hold on," I said. "How do you know he's missing? What happened?"

"Just like the other hand we lost, he just did not show up."

"When?"

"He was supposed to show to work yesterday."

"Maybe he's off on a bender," Lloyd said. "Or shacked up with one of the gals on the north end?"

"No, I don't think so."

Lloyd leaned back in his chair.

"Maybe he was throwed," he said.

James shook his head.

"Not this fella."

"What's his name?" I said.

"Hastings, Mel Hastings."

"Melvin Hastings?" Book said.

James nodded.

"Know him?" I said.

"I do," Book said. "Known him for a good while. He's a cowhand by trade. Last fella I could think of to get thrown off his horse and end up in a ditch."

"Know where he lives?"

Book shook his head.

"No."

James shook his head, too.

"I don't, either," he said. "He'd not worked with us too long. Don't know much about him other than he was a capable and hardworking young man."

"Let us look into this."

He nodded.

"My brother was the one who hired the men to protect us from this sort of thing, and I don't think he was wrong in doing so. Not now, anyway, but we are respectable businessmen and I want the law to be aware of this and take care of it."

"Like I said, let us look into this."

He stood there for a second, wondering if there was anything left for him to say. He shook his head, then nodded and left.

12

Virgil and I set out to see what we could figure out about the disappearance of Mel Hastings. After some investigation we found one of the other miners who knew Mel. He told us that Mel lived with a young woman in a small boardinghouse near the stock corrals by the railway tracks.

Following up, we later learned from the caretaker of the place that the name of the woman Mel was living with was Belle. She was a rush weaver, working in a small chair factory on the river. And we rode out to visit with her.

Her boss, a big bald fellow with muttonchops, led us through the factory to where a line of workers stood weaving chair seats. He pointed to a pleasant-looking young woman, with a round figure and face.

"That is Belle," he said. "The one on the end."

"Much appreciate," I said. "We won't be long."

The big man nodded then left us to talk to Belle.

She was focused on her weaving work but smiled when we stepped up.

"Hi," she said as she continued to work.

"Belle?" Virgil said.

She stopped her weaving and nodded.

"Yes."

Virgil opened his coat a bit, revealing his badge.

"I'm Marshal Cole. This is Deputy Marshal Hitch."

"Yes."

"We are looking for Mel Hastings," Virgil said.

"What did he do?"

"Have you seen him?"

She shook her head.

"What makes you think he did something?" Virgil said.

She shrugged.

" 'Cause you're here."

"When did you last see him?" I said.

Her bottom lip started to quiver.

"Day before yesterday."

"Where was that?"

"At our room. Where we live. At our boardinghouse."

"And you have no idea where he is now?"

"Might be with her."

"Who?"

"His whore."

"And what makes you say that?"

"Would not be the first time," she said.
"Why, what happened?"

"He didn't show up for his job," I said.

She blinked and blinked, and then her eyes started to water.

"Oh, no."

"What?" I said.

"You don't think . . . You don't think . . . He told me that one of the other fellas he worked with did not show up at work, was missing or something, and that there was bad blood with the other mining company, and, well . . . do you think, is that what you are thinking, too? Has something happened to Melvin?"

"We don't know," I said. "That is why we are here, we wanted to know what you knew."

"All I know is he did not come home from work. I had his supper ready and I never saw him."

"I'm sorry to ask," I said, "but who is this other woman you are talking about? The . . ."

"The whore?" she said.

"Yes."

She told us the name of a woman who also lived in the boardinghouse. The woman that Belle referred to as the whore and suspected Mel had been sleeping with on the side.

Belle was not wrong. We found the woman and had a talk with her. She told us she had been seeing Mel some but she had not seen him in a while, nor was she intending to ever see him again.

When Virgil and I got back to the sheriff's office, Lloyd was sitting, cleaning a shotgun. It was disassembled, with the pieces spread out in front of him on the desk.

"There ya'll are."

I leaned my eight-gauge on the desk and nodded to it, indicating that it, too, could use a cleaning.

"Next?" I said.

"Do I look like a damn gunsmith?" he said.

"Matter of fact," I said.

"Well, hell," Lloyd said. "Line 'em up. I got nothing but unlimited time. Or in my old-ass case, I reckon I got nothing but limited time."

Virgil grinned as he poured a cup of coffee then turned to face Lloyd.

"So?" Lloyd said. "Anything?"

"Enough to know the missing fella is damn sure not to be found," I said. "Not yet, anyway."

"Hard to figure with so many fucking people crawling in and out of the woodwork around this place," Lloyd said. "Surely some poor sonofabitch would have some idea about him and that other fella's whereabouts, whether they're dead or alive?"

"You would think," I said.

13

Lloyd finished putting the shotgun together, then got up and lumbered around the desk. He was stretching his back as he moved.

"Getting too damn old to sit," he said. "And too old to move."

Lloyd turned where he was standing by the edge of the desk when a big, red-bearded man with a naturally surly disposition strutted in the door, followed by two other men.

"What can I do for you?" Lloyd said.

Virgil turned from the stove to face the three men standing just inside the door.

"Who's in charge around here?"

"Charge of what?" Lloyd said.

"Who's the sheriff?"

"For the time being, that'd be me."

"I'm Edward Hodge. I work for the Mc-Cormick Brothers Mining Company."

"Good for you," Lloyd said. "Good for you."

Hodge turned slightly and nodded to the two men standing behind him.

"This is R. W. Gibbs and this is Hugh Kane. They, too, work for the McCormick Brothers Mining outfit."

"Well, good for you, too," Lloyd said. "What can I do for you employed fellas?"

Hodge leveled his eyes at me, and then Virgil.

"This is Marshal Virgil Cole," Lloyd said. "And this is Deputy Marshal Everett Hitch, of the United States law enforcement variety. It appears we are all employed here."

Virgil took a sip of coffee, then said, "You fellas need something?"

"We are here to help."

"Help with what?"

"Arrest or kill them hands who work for the Baptiste Mining outfit," he said.

"Why would you want to do that?" Virgil said.

"For what they've done."

"What have they done?"

"Took two miners," he said. "Of course."

"How do you know that?"

Hodge sneered.

"Who else would have done it?"

"Do you have proof?"

"It's obvious," he said. "What they are doing. Taking out the workers."

"You know that for a fact?" Virgil said.

Hodge squinted. It was clear he didn't appreciate Virgil's question.

"Can't say I know it as a fact."

"Well, there you have it," Virgil said.

"Have what?"

"Nothing to be done," Virgil said. "Can't go after people that you don't know for a fact have committed a crime that you *think* they have committed."

"Well," Hodge said. "All right, then. Let it be known that we come to you to offer help. You don't want it, fine. We'll take care of matters as we see fit."

Virgil glanced to me, then shook his head.

"Not a good idea," Virgil said.

"Baptiste hands are responsible for the missing workers," Hodge said. "And we aim to reckon this situation, it is what we were hired to do."

"You can best help us by not getting in the way."

He shook his head.

"No, that's not gonna happen," he said.

"It is," Virgil said.

Virgil set down his coffee and moved toward the men a few steps. The big man stared at Virgil longer than he should have.

"We will do what we were hired to do," Hodge said, showing his teeth, "and we'll go from there."

"Go to jail from there," Virgil said.

"We were hired to protect the McCor-micks and their assets, and the men that are missing and presumed dead are part of the assets that we were hired to protect."

"Might be a good idea for you to take care of your assets first," Virgil said.

"Or what?" Hodge said.

"Find your assets locked up."

Hodge glared at Virgil, then me, then Lloyd, then Virgil again.

"Tell me your name again?" he said.

"I didn't," Virgil said, then nodded to Lloyd. "He did."

Hodge's eyes narrowed.

"Virgil Cole," Lloyd said. "Marshal Virgil Cole."

Hodge nodded slowly as he stared at Virgil. He tipped his hat.

"Be seeing you, Virgil Cole."

Virgil dropped his chin.

Hodge turned and walked out, followed by his partners.

"He don't care for you," Lloyd said.

"What gave you that idea?" Virgil said.

"Just a feeling," Lloyd said.

14

The night was warm and bugs were swirling under the streetlamps along Appaloosa Avenue. There weren't too many folks moving about where I stood under the awning across the street from the theater.

Everything seemed to be calm for a Friday night, until the sudden sound of applause erupted through the doors of the theater. The clapping echoed out into the street.

Soon the theatergoers came streaming out. Groups and couples walked out, going this way and that. They were animated, talking and laughing and recapping their evening's experience. Most of what I overheard was about how wonderful a performer Martha Kathryn was. How talented and beautiful and funny and what a great dancer she was. I agreed.

In a short time most all had moved on and only the autograph seekers remained. Then after a while through the window I saw her come into the lobby with the other cast members. She was smiling and talking and signing programs, one after another after another.

After most all the folks began to thin out, I started to walk across the street, all set to greet her. Then the door opened and Henri Baptiste stepped out with Martha Kathryn.

I stayed where I was in the shadow of the awning as they turned and moved off up the sidewalk. After they walked a ways, Henri offered his arm and she took it. She was almost a full foot taller than Henri. *I'll be goddamned,* I thought.

I remained in the shadow, watching them. Then, as I was about to move off in the opposite direction, I saw the two men. They were the men who came into the sheriff's office earlier with Edward Hodge, R. W. Gibbs and Hugh Kane, and right away I knew they were following Baptiste and Martha Kathryn.

I stayed on the opposite side of the street, remaining in the shadows, and tailed them. They stayed back, making sure they were not seen as they followed their quarry. The couple turned up Main Street and walked some blocks, headed presumably toward the Hotel Windsor.

When they got to the hotel, Gibbs and

Kane did not follow Baptiste and Martha Kathryn inside. They held their position, watching through the windows.

And I stayed a few buildings away, watching them. After a bit they turned and looked around. I stood still across the street in the shadow of an alley, observing them.

Then they moved off the porch and walked across the street, closer to where I stood. I moved farther into the shadows, making certain I was not seen. I stood where I could keep an eye on them. They lit cigarettes, settled in, and sat on the boardwalk.

They must have rolled and smoked a dozen cigarettes as they sat there across from the hotel. I was curious as to what the hell they were up to, what they were going to do. Were they going to wait on Baptiste, were they out to scare him, harm him, or, worse, were they poised to ambush him, kill him? And at the same time, I wondered, too, what Martha Kathryn was doing with Baptiste.

Were they out on the back patio having an after-theater drink, like we had with her? Or had she taken him up to her room for a good time? I wondered if she knew he was a wealthy man who had become wealthier by striking gold. *Gold. Makes people do things,*

things they might not otherwise do, I thought.

My mind was racing thinking about Martha Kathryn fucking someone else. Then I thought, *But, hell, I don't even know her, she can fuck whoever she wants to, gold or no gold.*

Then, after another cigarette, Gibbs and Kane got up and crossed the street and walked to the hotel. They stood on the porch, glanced around some, then entered.

I moved out and crossed to the hotel and eased up on the porch to have a peek through the window.

They stood in the lobby, where a few people were sitting. A desk clerk said something to them and they shook their heads, then the clerk smiled and moved away.

I could see through into the double doors leading to the busy patio. Martha Kathryn was sitting with her back to me. And I could see Baptiste, too, sitting in front of her, facing toward the front, laughing and talking with her.

Then Kane turned as if he was going to exit and I saw he had a pistol tucked into his belt. Gibbs grabbed his arm and said something. Then Kane nodded and the two of them started for the patio. I thought they'd be fools to ambush Baptiste here, in front of other people.

Regardless, they had guns, or at least one of them did, and that was enough. There was no reason to be too little too late, so I pulled my Colt and entered the hotel.

As they reached the door leading to the patio, I called out to them.

"That's far enough," I said.

A few people gasped when they saw I held my Colt out at arm's length, pointed at Kane and Gibbs.

"Do not take another step."

The men turned to me as I moved to them.

"Get your hands up," I said. "Right goddamn now."

Now everyone in the place was staring at me, Kane, and Gibbs and what was happening.

"Not sure why," Gibbs said. "We ain't done nothing."

"Up."

They raised their hands up and I moved to Kane.

"Do not make a move or I will drop you."

I eased up to Kane, keeping my Colt to his head, and reached in and pulled his pistol from his belt. Then looked to Gibbs.

"You, you carrying, too?"

Gibbs did not answer.

"Are you?"

"What if I was?"

"Lie to me and you'll be sorry. Likely dead."

Gibbs nodded and I moved to him. With my Colt to his head, I removed his pistol.

"You are both under arrest."

"Thank God, Marshal," Baptiste said, as he started to get out of his chair.

"Sit down and shut up," I said.

"But," Baptiste said.

"Do like I tell you."

He wanted to say something else but he did what I said and lowered into his seat.

"Now, you two, we are going to take a little walk," I said. "And I will follow you, you know the way."

I could sense everyone in the crowd was focused on me, including Martha Kathryn. I could feel her eyes on me, but I did not glance at her. I remained focused on the men and we walked out the front door of the hotel.

15

"I got money," the big fellow said. "I got paid today and I got plenty of money."

"I don't care," the bartender said.

The bartender was big. Way bigger than the big fellow he was standing in front of as he pointed to the door.

"Not gonna tell you again," the bartender said. "Get outta here before I throw your ass out in the street by the seat of your damn breeches."

"Okay, okay, I'm going, no need to get all mad, I was just having a little fun with her."

"Not going to tell you again."

"Okay, damn, come on, kid, let's get the hell outta here, too damn stuffy in here anyway."

The big fellow staggered from the saloon, followed by the kid.

"What an asshole that sumbitch is," the big fellow said. "I should have just let him have it."

"You want to go back?" the kid said with a

grin. "It's early yet. I can watch you let him have it."

"Naw, fuck him. Fuck it. I got some whiskey," the big fellow said. "Let's drink some whiskey."

The big fellow pulled a bottle from his coat pocket as he walked unsteadily into the narrow passageway between the saloon and the building next to it. The kid glanced around, then followed the big fellow. The big fellow took a swig, passed the bottle to the kid, then stopped and fumbled with the buttons of his trousers.

"She wasn't much to look at no ways," he said as he relieved himself. "She liked you, though, kid."

He watched himself pee. Then he chuckled and raised his face to the sky.

"Yep, she was batting her eyes at you. But you get that all the time, don't you?"

He grinned at the kid.

"Pretty like you are. You are. You are pretty . . . Let you touch my dick for a nickel."

"That all it's worth?"

The big one laughed as he continued peeing. The kid walked past him toward the rear of the building.

"Where you going?"

"Sit and drink some whiskey," the kid said.

When the big fella finished, he stumbled out and met the kid behind the buildings of the town square. The kid walked on, and the big fellow followed.

They sat on empty crates behind a livery stable and the kid passed the bottle to the big fellow. The big one's eyes were watery and his mouth stayed wet from habitually licking his lips.

"We should have both gave it to her," the big fellow said.

The kid laughed.

"What's so goddamn funny?"

"Just that," the kid said.

The big fellow grinned at him and leaned back.

"Ain't you ever done it like that, with a buddy?"

The kid laughed again.

"Don't laugh. Nothing wrong with it," the big fellow said.

"I didn't say there was."

The big fellow's tongue did a loop about his lips, then he took a pull from the bottle and passed it to the kid.

"You'd'a liked it, wouldn't you?"

The kid shrugged.

"You would. She'd'a liked it. Us filling her up."

"Maybe she would."

"We can find us another one. Maybe one that ain't so fucking ugly. I got money."

The kid shook his head.

"No need."

"There is always a need. Hell. I know a gal that would be up for it. She'll be in town tomorrow. She comes on Saturdays. She works at the Saturday market, selling her family goods. What her family don't likely know is she also sticks around and sells her own goods on Saturday evening before she returns to the farm like fucking nothing happened. As long as she can make a little, she'll give a lot, and thing is, she fucking likes it and she's a hell of a lot prettier than that dumb bitch in there that got me in trouble."

"Won't be here tomorrow."

"Where will you be?"

"I'm just passing through."

"Ain't everybody?" the big fellow said.

"Well, I don't know about everybody, but that's what I'm doing."

"We are all just passing through. That is what the Good Lord said. We are just here temporary."

"You believe that shit?" the kid said.

"Not shit, it's the written Word, God's Word. Ain't you Christian? Don't you believe in God?"

"There is no God."

"Fuck yes there is too a God," the big fellow said with an almost belligerent tone to his voice. "My daddy is a preacher. I know all about God and Jesus and all and the different books."

"I did not get none of that growing up, so consider yourself lucky that you got spoon-fed that malarkey before you had sense enough to think for yourself."

"Bullshit. Mark and Matthew and Luke and John and Jesus and Mother Mary is God's Word. And the Old Testament, too, Genesis, Ezekiel, Adam and Eve and Cain and Abel. Shit, you should read it."

"Why?"

"Don't you want to go to Heaven?"

"That what you want?" the kid said. "You want to go to Heaven?"

"Hell yes, it beats the other damn direction."

The kid took a swig and passed the bottle.

"Whatever. But I'm currently expected else-where."

"Who's expecting you?"

"Well, the thing is, they don't know I'm com-ing."

The big fellow frowned.

"Fuck, kid."

"What?"

"How the hell can you be expected if they don't know you're coming?"

"Well, it's just that it's been a long time com-ing."

The big one shook his head.

"That don't make no sense."

"No?"

"No."

"How much money do you have?" the kid said.

"Least twenty-five dollars."

"That's good," the kid said.

"Yeah?"

"Yeah."

"What makes you say that?"

" 'Cause I'm gonna need to get me a few things 'fore I take off."

16

The following morning, Virgil and I were drinking coffee in the sheriff's office. Lloyd, Book, and a few of the young deputies were also present as Hodge and James McCormick walked in. Hodge moved toward Virgil, with furious red eyes.

"You arrested my men?"

Virgil shook his head.

"I did not."

Hodge squinted, then glanced at James.

"What do you mean?" James said.

"We heard," Hodge said, "that you arrested them and they are locked up."

"Where did you hear that?"

"From the Frenchman himself," Hodge said.

"I saw Baptiste on Appaloosa Avenue," James said. "And he told me and he threatened me."

"How did he threaten you?"

"He told me that if any of my men came

near him again I could expect more trouble than them just being arrested."

"So," Virgil said, "your men got near Baptiste and it pissed him off?"

"I'm not sure what exactly happened."

"Not sure?" Virgil said.

Hodge eyed the closed door that led into the hall of cells.

"So they are not here?" he said.

"I didn't say that," Virgil said.

Hodge squinted at Virgil with meaner eyes than he'd entered with.

"You said you didn't arrest them."

"I didn't. Everett did, didn't you, Everett?"

"I did."

"Goddamn it. Why?"

"For one thing, carrying firearms," I said. "That's against the laws here within the Appaloosa limits."

"Well goddamn it," Hodge said. "Why didn't you say that?"

"You know the law," I said.

"You said 'one thing,' " James said. "What is the other thing? Is there something else?"

"You tell me," I said.

"Not sure what you mean," James said.

"What was the purpose of having those two follow Baptiste?" I said.

"Look," James said. "It is *my men* who are missing. *My men.* Good working people of this community. And you are sticking up for that no-good sonofabitch, Baptiste?"

"Answer the question," Virgil said.

"Are you listening to me?" James said. "It is my men who are missing, damn it."

"Answer the question," Virgil said.

James shook his head.

"Just to watch him," James said. "That is all."

Virgil glanced at me.

"Why?" he said.

"To keep an eye on him is all."

"They approached Baptiste with fire-arms," I said. "Why?"

James bit the inside of his cheek as he pondered the question.

"Just to let him know we are watching him," James said.

James removed his wallet.

"How much to get them out?" he said.

"Not gonna be that easy," Virgil said.

"What, then?" James said.

"We will have to keep them locked up for a while," Virgil said. "Until the judge has time to see them."

"When will that be?" Hodge said.

"You'd have to ask the judge," Virgil said.

"You can't do this," Hodge said.

Virgil smiled.

"We can and will."

Hodge shook his head.

"And how long is 'a while'?" James said.

"Long as we like."

"You'll fucking regret this," Hodge said. "Fucking regret it, I will guarantee."

"You are on the wrong side of this," James said. "Have you no conscience?"

"We are here to uphold the law," I said. "We are doing what we can to find out what has happened to the missing men. But above all, we uphold the law. And with the exception of the two of you, that is what every one of us in the room is paid and assigned to do. So don't ever question our conscience. Not ever."

"I have had enough of this bullshit," Hodge said as he walked out.

James stood there trying to think of something else to say but then he, too, walked out.

"Damn," Lloyd said. "That was a good fucking scalding, Everett. If I live long enough and ever get the chance to use that speech, I will do my best to dole it out with that same sea-parting, Moses-like authority like you just done."

17

Bells from the Catholic church on Main Street were ringing, echoing through the streets of Appaloosa. Churchgoers dressed in their Sunday best were hurrying to get into their seats. I thought about the church people as I walked. I often wondered what life would be like to be one of them, to be one of the followers. The believers.

When I entered the Hotel Windsor I saw Martha Kathryn right away, sitting on the patio and facing the lobby. As I walked toward her she smiled, seeing me, and immediately got up and moved toward me. She reached out, took both of my arms, and kissed me on the cheek.

"You got my note?" she said.

"I did."

"Thank you for coming."

"You wanted to see me?"

"Yes, indeed."

"Well, here I am."

She held me at arm's length, studying me.

"Yes, you are," she said with a warm smile. "Yes, you are."

She took my hand, turned, and led me to her table.

"I'm just having a late breakfast. Please, sit."

I took a seat next to her and she sat.

"Are you hungry?"

"No. I'm good."

"Well, how about a beverage?"

She held up her glass.

"This is a lovely wine," she said.

"Kind of early, isn't it?"

"Never, especially on my day off. Won't you please join me. I insist."

"If you insist."

She held up her glass to the waiter.

"Please, would you be so kind, another for me and one for my handsome friend."

Then she turned to me and squeezed my hand.

"It's so nice to see you," she said.

"Likewise."

"I so needed to see you."

"Why?" I said.

"Well, my God. I have never in my life experienced anything like what happened the other night."

The waiter brought us two glasses of wine.

"Thank you," she said.

She held up her glass to me. And I held up mine.

"To my knight in shining armor."

She clinked my glass, smiled, and took a healthy pull of the wine.

"So what on earth was that all about, Marshal Hitch?"

"Everett."

"I was just being formal for dramatic sake. Everett. What was that all about, Everett?"

"Just doing my job."

"But can't you expound?"

"I can, but I don't know it will make much difference or sense."

"Indulge me, please."

"Maybe indulge me first?"

"Certainly, by all means."

"How do you know Baptiste?"

"Henri?" she said with a French accent, making his name sound like "On-ree."

"Yes, Henri," I said.

"Well, I met him not long after I arrived here."

"The early bird."

"That's presumptuous of you."

"My apologies."

"No need . . . Are you jealous, Mr. Hitch?"

"You're being dramatic again."

"Everett."

"No. I'm not jealous."

"Well, good. You should not be. He's one of the people responsible for the theater opening."

"How did you meet?"

"The mayor of Appaloosa introduced us."

"What do you know about him?"

"At the time of the introduction, nothing."

"And now?"

"Well, he's charming enough, it seems, well spoken, educated. I appreciate educated men. He has good taste in wine and knows a great deal about the theater. He does, however, have a Napoleonic complex. Something that I personally have no issue with, but I suppose I understand it. Not every man is capable of carrying their bride over the threshold."

"He proposed to you?"

She smiled.

"Now I'm not being dramatic, just being . . . funny, isn't that somewhat funny?"

I smiled.

"I'm sure he's discussed the nature of his business and so forth?" I said.

"Yes, I know he is a wealthy man. I know about the gold . . . Now, how about you tell me? After all I was present, and perhaps in danger even, when you so gallantly arrested those two men."

"Well, he's part of — or, better put, is the owner of — one half of an outfit that is in opposition with another outfit, and they don't see eye to eye. So, as a result, they have it out for each other."

"That is the long and short of it?" she said. "No pun intended."

"Is."

"This has to do with gold, I take it?"

"Does."

She smiled.

"Gold makes people do things they otherwise might not do," I said.

"Are you sure you are not jealous?"

I shook my head.

"Not even a little?"

"Nope."

"Not sure I believe you."

"Did that one time," I said.

"Once?"

"Once. Didn't end good. Won't happen again."

She smiled and held up her glass to the waiter.

"Two more, please," she said.

Then she turned to me and smiled seductively.

"I like you," she said.

"Like you, too."

"I know."

"Figured."

"I saw you across the street from the theater," she said.

I did not say anything. I just stared at her as she stared at me.

"Romantic," she said. "Very romantic."

18

It was dark and late when the kid finally got to the house. He tapped on the door. A thin, elderly Negro woman opened up and let him in. He followed her down the narrow hall to a back room, where a shriveled man lay in bed. His lips were purple and his skin was pale, almost pink, with blue veins visible under his thin skin. He had a bald head and a long white beard. His eyes were closed, but he was breathing. The kid turned to the woman and spoke softly.

"That's him?"

She nodded.

"Don't look like him."

"It is."

"Damn."

"He bad."

"Always was."

She nodded.

"Can he talk?"

"He can. Not much."

"Ain't the glory-be mountain man he was."

"He not."

"You been taking care of him?"

"I have."

The kid watched the old man taking labored breaths, then shook his head.

"Miserable."

She nodded.

"He is."

"How long has he been like this?"

"All summer."

The kid turned to her.

"You with him," the kid said, looking her in the eye, "when he was upright, before he got sick?"

She nodded shyly.

He studied her, thinking about the two of them together, then looked to the old man.

"He don't need to be like this."

"Mayhaps he do."

The kid thought about what she said and nodded.

"You might be right."

"For all the grief he done gave," she said.

"Telegram said he was sick. I didn't know he was this bad."

"Worse ever day."

She moved to the bed and the kid followed.

"The boy, he here."

The old man did not respond. She took him

by the hand.

"The boy, he here, he come to see you."

The old man's eyes slowly fluttered open.

"He here," she said. "The boy."

He moved his eyes to the kid. The kid took a step closer.

"You hear me?" the kid said.

The old man nodded.

"I come up, all this way. Telegram said you wanted to see me."

"You growed," the old man said with a rasping whisper.

"What'd you want to see me for?"

"Fine how-do-you-do," the old man said.

"What'd you expect?"

The old man did not reply.

"Last time I saw you, you whipped me so hard I could hardly walk."

The kid gave a nod to the woman.

"Scars on my ass to prove it."

The old man met the woman's eyes and raised his withered finger toward the dresser.

"Get it," he said.

She nodded, moved to the dresser, opened the top drawer, and pulled out an envelope. Then she came to the bed with it and handed it to the kid.

"He said, in case he not here when you get here, to make sure that I give you this. And tell you the story."

"What story?"

The kid stared at the envelope, then met the old man's watery gaze.

"Open it," he said with a nod to the envelope.

The kid opened it and peered inside.

"Go on."

The kid took out a tintype photograph. It was a picture of a group of people standing in front of an old home place.

"Let me see it."

The kid handed it to him.

"Look here."

The kid moved to see what the old man was pointing at on the tintype.

"This here is my wife, Gertrude."

"What?"

The old man nodded.

"I never knew you had a wife."

The old man stared at him, then looked to the tintype.

"And that there is our oldest son, Elias. This here is his little brother, Ethan."

The kid got a sour look on his face.

"What are you saying?"

The old man nodded.

"Ethan is the husband of that woman next to him holding the baby."

The kid studied the photograph closely.

"That baby she is holding is you."

The kid stared at the old man. Then he

studied the photograph long and hard.

"Where did you get this?"

"I've had it."

"All these years?"

The old man nodded.

"And you never showed it to me?"

"No reason."

Tears welled up in the kid's eyes.

"What do you mean, 'no reason'?"

"No reason."

"Both my boys is dead. Fact they died not long after this here capture was taken. The boys died, your bitch mother left you with me and my wife, and Gertrude died of consumption not long after. All that was left was me . . . and you."

Tears were running down the kid's cheek. He glanced to the woman and shook his head in disbelief.

"And you thought it important that I not know?"

The old man's eyes drifted to meet the woman's eyes. She looked away.

The kid studied the tintype.

"How did they die?"

"They killed each other," the old man said. "They shot each other dead."

"Why, how?"

"Your daddy, Ethan, found out that he was not your father. He figured out that his older brother, Elias, was your daddy. So he got a pistol and went after Elias, but Elias was waiting for him, and they shot each other at the same time. Elias died straightaway and Ethan died a day later. That same day, your mother ran off. Then when Gertrude died I burnt the place to the ground and you and me went to the mountains."

"All these years I thought I was a goddamn stray, that I had no father, all these fucking years. I was feral and treated that way."

The old man stared at the kid. His eyes watered.

"I was ashamed."

"What?"

"I am your father, boy."

"What are you fucking saying?"

"Ethan had figured out wrong, ya see. And I don't think your momma had the gall or the gumption to have him figure things no different."

The kid stared at the old man.

"What?"

"That's right. I had her," he said and groaned. "I done her more than once, and you are mine."

The kid's face twisted up as he tried to contain his rage.

"After all this goddamn time," the kid said quietly through his teeth. "Why are you telling me this now, old man?"

The old man fixed his weary eyes on the woman. She nodded toward the boy for him to continue on with his story.

"Right after I took sick, I'd been traveling and was doing some trading here and there, had a few things I needed to unload. Right after I was fixin' to return here, there she was. I saw her."

"Who?"

"Your mother."

"What?"

The old man nodded.

"I did."

The kid's eyes darted around the room.

"I'm sure it was her. She looked like a refined woman. Hell, I don't know, maybe she was a refined whore for all I know. But she looked like she done well. The way she was dressed. The way she walked. The people she was with. She was kind of high-and-mighty-looking, not the dirty barefoot girl she once was. No. She was walking tall with some men on the street, and they was gentlemen. Dandies. They wore suits and derby hats."

The kid studied the woman's face in the photograph.

"How would you know a grown woman from this?"

"When I saw her, she did not see me. She

walked on past. And I called to her by her name."

The kid stared at the old man.

"She stopped, turned, and looked right at me. Looked me in the eye. That is why I knew I was goddamn right, that it was your momma I was looking at. Older, of course, but pretty like she was as a youngen. Just older. It was her."

"What happened?"

He shook his head.

"She . . . she turned and walked off."

The kid felt numb. He stared at the photograph. He saw his whole miserable life flash by. He was no longer crying. He was now only solemn.

"What is her name?"

"Helen."

"Where was this? What town?"

"Appaloosa," the old man said.

19

Naked as the day she was born, Martha Kathryn was reciting something. It sounded like Old World King's English. She stood balanced on one foot atop the bed in room twelve of the Hotel Windsor. Without wiggle or wobble, she stood with her hands pressed together in a praying position. They were tight between her breasts as she was performing.

I had no idea the origin of her monologue; she didn't say before letting loose with her grandiloquence. It sounded fancy, though, likely something from Shakespeare. But I could have cared less. There was no need to define or understand the source of her speechifying. It was nothing but a pleasant experience to simply watch her.

She was a sight, rising above me like that. Balanced on one leg, enunciating her words, using a unique combination of intense conviction and willful bluster. Her foot that was not planted on the bed was positioned firmly at the side of the knee of her standing leg, giving her the appearance of a tall heron or a flamingo.

Besides the fact that she was without clothing, Martha Kathryn seemed as refined as any woman I had ever met. An observation I made a point of sharing with her earlier after the second bottle of wine. When she was properly attired. The compliment prompted her to bring into question my worldliness and judgment.

Martha Kathryn was a thespian no doubt, through and through. Virgil had reminded me more than a few times. My last experience with a woman associated with a traveling troupe ended badly. But this was different. Martha Kathryn presented herself as a free bird. I had no expectations other than to enjoy her company while she was in town.

We shared a look that first time staring at each other in the mirror at Allie's shop. It was a look between us that defied unnecessary verbiage. But we did enjoy conversation with each other. The day was filled with a lot of subjects, from religion to politics to sex.

That topic got us up to her room for an evening of activity that Martha Kathryn referred to as "a go of it." We'd been doing just that, having *a go of it,* up until she decided to take a break and provide me with a spontaneous wine-induced soliloquy.

She was balanced on one foot, eloquently using an affected higher-than-usual pitch to her husky voice. She was also trilling every other word. The technique gave her quavering oratory a refined penetrating effect. She could have been addressing Congress.

"You're a damn good wordsmith," I said as I held up my glass. "I'm impressed."

She stood, willowy, with unblemished fair skin and a mane of unruly golden-colored hair that shimmered in the yellow glow of the lamplight.

Gold makes people do things they otherwise might not do, I thought, as I lay there watching her.

"An acrobat to boot."

"Shush," she said.

"What?"

"I'm not finished."

"My apologies," I said as I opened my arms wide. "By all means, carry on, please. I'm all yours."

So far in our short time getting to know each other, I could see that Martha Kathryn was not just a free spirit. She was livelier than most women I'd ever had the pleasure of dallying with. Besides being carefree, up to this point she had not been at all demanding or in the least bit needy. Never bringing up anything serious or off-putting.

She was her own woman and was smart as a whip. She said she lived in Boston when she was in her teens, where she attended school, but she was vague about her history. She seemed to be educated and well read on many subjects. My time at West Point, being in New York all those years, provided me a comfort with women of substance. But there was also something about her that made me think that she was a woman with a past. A woman not void of trouble.

But to that point, I liked women of trouble. I was attracted to them. I like, in general, the company of women, more than that of men, and had pretty much made a habit of having more women friends than men. Even if they were sometimes whores, I preferred the company of women.

Women were tougher by nature, because they had to be, to bear children and put up with ignorant men. The war left plenty of widows. I'd seen women through the years who'd mustered pure resilience and resourcefulness. A woman's basic will to survive never ceased to amaze me.

We had spent the final few hours of the night rolling around in bed, and now the clock was working its way toward a new day. And after the consumption of copious amounts of wine, the drunkenness added a stimulating bit of sass to her animated soliloquy.

I was also without my clothes. I was sitting up against the headboard with the bedding across my lap, watching her with a perfect bit of awe. As she was getting to what seemed to be the escalating end of her performance, there was a knock on the door.

Martha Kathryn stopped and we both looked at the door.

There was another knock.

I pulled my Colt out of its holster that was hanging on the bedpost.

20

The knocker spoke up.

"Very sorry to interrupt, but I'm looking for Everett Hitch."

"Book?"

"It is," he said. "Sorry, Everett."

"What is it?"

"Marshal Cole told me to find you."

"Hold on."

"Yes, sir."

I got up, helped Martha Kathryn down from the bed.

"Book?" she said.

"Deputy Daniels," I said. "When he's not doing law work he's got his head stuck in a book."

I pulled on my trousers and tossed her a robe.

"Not sure, but I think you might have been about to get to the best part of your one-leg oration," I said.

"What is it?" she said as she put one arm

and then the other into the sleeves of the robe. "Why would Marshal Cole be looking for you at this time of the evening?"

"Don't know," I said. "I suspect I'll find out soon enough."

"Must be important."

"Better be," I said.

I buttoned my trousers and pulled on my shirt. And as soon as Martha Kathryn got the robe tied on and settled, she opened the door. Hefty Book was standing there with his hands in his pockets and a glum look on his round face.

"Sorry, Everett."

"You said that."

His cheeks were redder than normal. He removed his spectacles and glanced over my shoulder to Martha Kathryn. He nodded at her and smiled.

"Virgil told me to find you right away."

"You found me."

Book nodded.

"What is it?"

"Got some shooting going on."

"Give me a minute."

Book nodded and I closed the door slightly.

"My goodness," she said.

"My apologies."

I sat and pulled on my boots.

"No, my gosh. I understand. It's just, well, this time of night. It is just so unexpected."

"It is," I said. "Be right back."

She nodded, then I stepped out into the hall with Book and closed the door behind me.

"Who's shooting who?"

"Not real sure what is what, but I think it's between the miners. The McCormicks and Baptiste."

"What makes you say that?"

"One of McCormick's men was shot."

"Dead?"

"No."

"What happened?"

"He was up on the north end at Lenora's place."

"Lenora's place?"

"The whoring place on the far north end," Book said.

"They got into a shootout there?"

"I guess so. Apparently one of McCormick's men had just got done with his business upstairs, and as he was on his way out, there were some words. He was shot by one of Victor Bartholomew's men. At least that is what he said."

"Where is he?"

"Doc Burris has him at the hospital," Book said. "He's gonna be fine."

"He was on his own? There at Lenora's?" I said.

"So he says," Book said. "Don't know all the particulars."

"No sign of Ed Hodge and the others?" I said.

"No," Book said.

"Hodge I'm sure will be on fire about this," I said.

"No doubt," Book said.

"Any idea where Victor's men are?" I said. "Where they went?"

"Boston House," Book said.

"How do you know?"

"The fella who was shot said he got on his horse and followed them there."

"He got shot and followed them?" I said. Book nodded.

"That doesn't make sense," I said.

"It wasn't bad. He got lucky. Bullet clipped his vest and caught a piece of flesh on his side. He was bleeding good, but he was okay."

"It don't make sense," I said. "For some-body to shoot someone, then just hang around."

"Bold of them," Book said. "No doubt."

"Stupid," I said, "and drunk."

"Better put," Book said with a nod.

"They staying at the Boston House?"

"No."

"What are they doing there?"

"In the saloon. Drunk, getting drunker, I imagine."

"Where is Virgil?"

"There at the Boston House."

"On his own?"

"No. Lloyd is with him and three deputies: Mark, Cory, and Merced. They are just keeping an eye on the place, making sure nobody leaves. Virgil told me he would wait on you before he confronts them."

"How many are there?"

"Four, it seems."

"Okay," I said.

Book nodded.

"I got your horse saddled for you."

"Good," I said. "Thank you, Book."

"And I got your eight-gauge. It's loaded and ready."

"Be right there."

I stepped back into the room. Martha Kathryn was standing with her arms crossed around the robe. I picked up my gun belt and buckled it.

"Intermission," I said.

21

The kid did not want to see the old man again, not ever.

"Not fucking ever," the kid said.

When he finished, he left the pillow covering the old man's face and walked out of the bedroom. He slammed the rickety door behind him so hard it busted from the hinges and broke into pieces.

"Goddamn it!" the kid said as he walked through the hall toward the front room. "Goddamn it!"

When he entered the front room, he started pacing. The woman was on a pallet in the corner packing her belongings into an old canvas bag. She lowered her hands to her lap and watched him as he moved back and forth.

"How come me?" he said. "Why me?"

She shook her head.

"Don't know," she said.

The kid continued to pace, all the while

focused on the tintype in his hand.

"The sonofabitch," he said, "the sonofabitch from hell."

"Him is," she said. "Don't think he coulda come from no other place."

"After all this goddamn time," he said.

She shook her head but said nothing as she continued to put her belongings into the bag.

"He's good and gone now. I sent the sonofabitch on his way."

She nodded.

"I figured," she said.

"Not that he deserved the goddamn relief," the kid said.

She watched as the kid paced a bit more.

"I did it for me," the kid said, shaking his head from side to side. "Not him. Me. I did it for me, you see? Not for him."

She nodded.

The kid stopped pacing and noticed for the first time what it was that she was doing.

"You're not staying here?" he said.

She shook her head.

"Lord, no. Not no mo'. Not one mo' night."

"Why'd you stay with him?"

"I don't rightly know."

"How long?"

"Three years off and on."

The kid looked around the room.

"You need help getting your things?"

127

"No," she said as she got up from the pallet and hoisted the bag over her shoulder.

"You got someplace to go?"

"I do," she said. "Nephew nearby. He be real glad to see me."

She crossed to the door and opened it. She took one last look around the room and shook her head.

"Go on, now," he said.

The kid followed her as she walked out the door. The night covered by clouds made it hard to see. But he could see her as she walked off up the street of the small town of Trinidad.

After she disappeared into the darkness, the kid stepped back into the house. He picked up a lamp off the table by the door and threw it against the wall over the pallet.

He stood there, watching the flames crawl. He found another lamp and busted it into the flames.

He watched and made sure the fire was going good, then backed out the door. He walked to his pony across the way, put the tintype into the envelope, and stuffed it into his saddlebags, then mounted up. He sat on his pony and watched the house, and waited, as the flames grew taller. He remained on his horse, watching, until the house was completely engulfed in flames. Memories of the old man came scorching in with the heat.

"Like father, like son," he said to himself.

He turned and rode away.

He rode for a while and thought of all that had happened in the past with the old man, the years in the mountains.

He remembered the day he left. When he was still a very young boy, after the old man beat him with barbwire. He remembered all the camps and towns in the Rocky Mountains. He thought about how the old man made him work, trapping animals and skinning them. And how he would ride with the old man, trading and selling hides.

Never knowing his place of birth.

"Or the goddamn year of it," he said out loud as he rode.

He never knew his name, other than Kid, that is what the old man called him. Kid is what the other mountain men in the camps called him, too. So he never knew much difference. After the camps he assumed names through the years, Leo, Ulysses, William, and Roy, but he could never settle on one, and none of those names ever stuck.

For some reason he remembered all kinds of details from those camp days as he rode away. All those times were playing like clunky out-of-tune hymns in his mind. He remembered the smell of blood, but he also remembered the trappers. The stinking, smelly, no-good trappers were always making fun of him. Talking about his skinny bottom, saying how they would make him their wife one day. And he remembered how he would loosen the men's cinches every chance he got. Or how he would steal from them, taking their food, whiskey, knives, and guns when they passed out.

Then he remembered the old man and the amount of killing that went on around him. He thought about having to set claw traps. About having to shoot and snare animals and how he would have to drag bloody carcasses from the woods to the camp. And he thought about the old man returning with scalps. He remembered how much the old man liked scalping Indians. How he would scalp Indians, then trade the scalps with other Indians and trappers. Something the kid never understood.

Blood and killing was something the kid had grown accustomed to, it was a way of life. His whole life was nothing but a goddamn bloody background. Death was all part of the living. He remembered having dried and frozen blood on his hands when he went to sleep and how he hated the cold weather.

And now, riding away from the fire, he thought about being in the tent under the covers in the cold with the dried blood. And how the old man would always come in drunk. The kid flashed on the vague memory of the old man trying to fuck him and something boiled up in his throat. But he could not remember everything; he had blank spots in his memory that worried him, that made him sick. That woke him up at night.

The kid leaned over in his saddle as he rode away from the burning house on the outskirts of Trinidad and threw up.

22

Virgil stood with Lloyd under the awning of a large coopering outfit on Main Street. They were across the road and down a ways from the Boston House. They moved out from the shadows of barrels stacked high on the boardwalk as Book and I rode up. Both Virgil and Lloyd had rifles in their hands.

"There you are," Virgil said as Book and I came to a stop.

"Virgil."

"Sorry to disrupt what you were doing," Virgil said.

"What have we got?" I said.

"Five of Victor's men," he said.

"Book said four."

"There were," Virgil said. "But now there are five."

"What'd they do? They shoot somebody, then act as if nothing happened?"

Virgil nodded.

"They don't likely have much in the way

of smarts, with all heads pitching in."

"Victor?" I said.

"He's not with them," Virgil said.

"How do you know?"

"I took a peek through the saloon window over there."

"How about the other two we saw with Victor?" I said. "Johnny and Wayne."

"Yep. They are in there," Virgil said. "That's how I was certain it was Victor's hands."

"What about the other three that are with them?" I said. "Know them?"

Virgil shook his head.

"Never seen them before."

"They all heeled?"

"Likely, but they're not showing leather," Virgil said. "None that I could see, anyway."

"But somebody has a gun," I said. "And they shot the McCormick hand?"

Virgil nodded.

"Yep."

"What are they doing?"

"Drinking," Virgil said. "Playing grab-ass."

Book and I moved our horses up and dismounted.

"Got our deputies posted around the place," Lloyd said, "just in case Victor's hands were to somehow slip out. Cory's up the street here, Jeff's down the street, and

Merced is in the rear alley behind the bar."

"Just want to make sure you and me have us a proper visit with them," Virgil said.

"You ready?" I said.

"Sooner than later," Virgil said.

I pulled my eight-gauge from its scabbard.

"You want Book and me to back you up?" Lloyd said.

"One of you sit by the front door and one by the side saloon door," Virgil said. "If for some reason they come out before Everett and me, I think it'd be safe to say you can kill each and every one of them."

"You sure you don't want us to waltz in there with you?" Lloyd said.

"I'm sure."

"You got it," Lloyd said. "Good to do as you say."

Virgil nodded.

Virgil and I crossed the street, walked up the steps, and entered into the main entrance of the Boston House Hotel. There were voices and laughter coming from the bar. The lobby was empty except for the young hotel clerk. He stepped out the door of the small room under the stairs and smiled.

"Can I help you?"

Virgil and I had been a fixture for coffee, dining, and drinking at the Boston House.

Ever since our first day in Appaloosa, it was a place we visited. But we'd never seen this clerk, and he'd never seen us.

I moved to him and showed my badge.

"Just remain quiet," I said. "Fact, just go on and close the door behind you."

Without a word, the clerk did what he was instructed to do.

Virgil and I stepped through the doors and into the bar without anyone paying us any attention. As usual, even as late as it was, the place was busy. The room was full of smoke, and it was noisy. Everyone was engrossed in his or her own world, talking, laughing, and enjoying their drinks. There was not an empty seat at the bar, and the card tables were active.

We stood just inside the door and looked for the gun hands in the crowd.

"See 'em?"

Virgil shook his head some. He moved into the barroom through the tables and I followed.

When we got close to the bar, we could see into the side billiard room off the main barroom.

"There they are," Virgil said.

Wayne and Johnny were perched on stools. Next to them was another man. He was big and he had a chubby saloon gal in his lap.

They were all watching two other men playing pool.

None of them, at least for the time being,
noticed us.

"Reckon that is all of the covey?" I said.
"The three of them there and the two with
the sticks?"

Virgil nodded.

"Most likely," he said.

We moved on and entered the billiard
room.

Johnny and Wayne saw us at the same time
and lifted off their stools. The big man by
their side stood, too, and the chubby gal in
his lap fell to the floor.

"Which one of you shot the fella at Lenora's place?" Virgil said.

"Don't know what the fuck you're talking
about," Wayne said.

"How about you, Johnny," I said. "Do you
know what the fuck we are talking about?"

"No, *señor,*" he said.

"All right, then," Virgil said.

"All right what?" Wayne said.

Virgil smiled.

"You boys can all go down to the jail with
us."

"Bullshit," Wayne said.

"Not bullshit," Virgil said.

"Who the fuck are you?" the big man with

136

the chubby gal said as he took a staggering step toward us. He glanced to Wayne and Johnny.

"Who the fuck are these guys?"

"I'm Marshal Virgil Cole and this is Deputy Marshal Everett Hitch."

The big man laughed and moved closer to Virgil and me.

"Oh, yeah," he said. "I heard of you. Glad to get an eye on you. Do you know who I am?"

"Nope," Virgil said. "Everett?"

"I do not," I said.

Everyone in the billiard room started drifting to the side of us. Headed for the main barroom.

"I'm Noah Miller," the big man said.

"Did you shoot the fella at Lenora's, Noah?" Virgil said.

"You best get on about somebody else's business before you get my temper up," Noah said.

"He the one?" Virgil said to Wayne and Johnny.

Noah made a gesture to the other two men playing pool to make ready. They set their sticks on the table and stepped apart like they was ready to shoot.

"You best move on," Noah said as he

adjusted his jacket to show the butt of his pistol.

One of the pool players did the same. He, too, showed a pistol tucked into his belt. He was a beady-eyed fella with a slouch hat snugged low on his head. He took a step toward us.

"Like he done uttered," the beady-eyed man said. "You all best get."

By now everyone in the room had cleared out.

"Was it you?" Virgil said to the beady-eyed fella. "You shoot the fella at Lenora's?"

"What if I did?"

"Have to take you in."

"You ain't taking me nowhere."

"You do it?" Virgil said.

"Well, if I did, I'd be a right smart dumbass to tell you," he said with a crooked smile. "Wouldn't I?"

"You pull on me, you will die."

He laughed.

"There are five of us here," he said and sneered.

"I can count."

"If I wanted to kill him, I would have," the beady-eyed man said. "Just like with the both of you. The choice is y'alls to make."

"No reason for any of you to die. You can come with us," Virgil said. "And you, too,

138

Noah, seeing how you are heeled."

"No," Noah said, followed by an arrogant laugh. "I will not do what you want me to do. It's you that best move on."

"Wayne, Johnny," Virgil said. "You boys heeled, too?"

Before Wayne and Johnny could answer, the beady-eyed fella went for it and Virgil shot him before he had his gun out of his belt.

Virgil had his Colt pointed to Noah's head. Noah froze without touching his pistol handle.

I had my eight-gauge up and leveled at the second pool player with both hammers back.

Gun smoke hung around the lamps over the pool table.

Wayne and Johnny put their hands up.

Noah held his hands away from his pistol.

"You sonofabitch," he said.

"Little late for name calling," Virgil said.

"You won't get away with this."

"Little late for that, too."

"You'll regret this," he said.

"Not as much as you."

"We'll see about that," Noah said. "You'll need to keep an eye out for some unexpected visit."

"Right now," Virgil said, "you get to make an unexpected visit to the local jail."

23

We locked up the four hands that worked for Baptiste next to the two McCormick hands that we'd locked up the day before. When we were done it was a quarter past two in the morning. Regardless of the hour, I decided to return to the Hotel Windsor.

I knocked lightly on her door. She did not respond. I tapped again and waited. I turned to move, but then she answered.

"Who is it?"

"It's me . . ."

"Everett," she said, with a lift to her voice.

I leaned on the doorjamb and waited. After a few seconds she unlocked and opened the door.

"Did I wake you?"

"No," she said. "I wish."

"Apologize for the late hour," I said.

"That's okay."

"I was enjoying your one-legged performance," I said. "When we were rudely interrupted. That's not what you were planning to perform for Appaloosa Days, is it?"

"God, Everett," she said as she opened the door wider, grabbed me by the arm, and pulled me into the room. "Come in here."

"I should go."

"No," she said.

She closed the door behind her, leaned her back against it, and folded her arms tightly across her waist.

"I'm so thankful you are okay," she said. "My gosh, and I'm of course very glad to see you."

"Good."

"Yes."

She was still in the robe that I'd handed to her earlier. It fell open some, revealing her long body underneath.

"I expected you'd be asleep."

"Seriously?"

"Glad you're not."

"I have been worried."

"You shouldn't."

"Well, of course I should. It's not every day one gets called in the night to . . . to respond to shootings."

"What we do."

"Well . . . of course but I was concerned and . . ."

"Deputy Book could have been less de-

142

scriptive."

"Nonetheless," she said.

"Here I am," I said.

"Thankfully. I was worried, seriously."

"I been doing this business for a long time."

"I know," she said. "And I know we have just gotten to know each other but . . ."

"But?"

"Well, I care for you," she said. "How could I not?"

"I'm pretty irresistible," I said.

She smiled.

"Yes, you are."

"So I've been told."

"I don't know how Ms. French, Allie, handles it."

"Law work?"

"Of course the law work, if you want to call it that."

"What else would you call it?"

"Dangerous."

"At times," I said.

"I just met you, and you have . . . well, I have been face-to-face with what you are doing. What you are about."

"Just work. Not necessarily what I'm about."

"You know what I mean."

"I do. Don't mean to make light of it."

"My heart has been just racing."

"And to be honest, Allie doesn't handle our marshaling all that well, so I know what it is like. How you feel. Even though we don't know each other all that well, I know, I do. Allie is anxious most the time."

"I'm not surprised."

"I think she has gotten better about it since she has her own business."

"What does that have to do with it?"

"Security," I said. "Something happens to Virgil, she knows she will be able to make a living. Take care of herself."

She picked up a bottle and showed it to me.

"Well, I was nervous enough, I moved on from the wine to bourbon," she said. "Care to join me?"

"Sure."

She poured us a drink.

"What happened?"

"Just some drunks, being stupid. Shooting at each other. That sort of thing?"

"I take it that this sort of thing has to do with the gold?"

"In part."

"Was . . . anyone hurt, Everett? Was anyone killed?"

I didn't want to say, but I really had no reason not to answer her honestly.

"There was."

"Oh my God. Someone died?"

"One."

Her eyes went wide.

"Really?"

"Yes."

"Who?"

"A gun hand. He was drunk and he did something stupid."

"So, can you tell me? I mean what . . . what happened?"

"He got out of line and got shot."

"By you?"

"No."

"Thank God."

"And the others?" she said. "You said there were other drunks?"

"We locked 'em up."

She stared at me, then set down her drink. She took the glass out of my hand and put it on the table next to hers. Then she put her arms around me, rested her head on my chest, and held tight. She remained holding me for a long time without a word. When she pulled away and gazed up at me, her eyes were wet. We stared at each other. Then I leaned down and kissed her softly. Her lips were warm and tender. We continued to kiss and then she kissed me harder. We continued to kiss, long and hard, until I could feel the heat rising between us. Then she took my hands and slid them inside her robe. She rubbed my hands over her body. First on her breasts, and then slid my hand below. Then she closed her eyes.

24

The kid had been in the saddle for too long. In the morning he passed a number of houses leading up to a wide iron bridge. A sign let him know it was the Rio Blanco. He rode his pony across, looking down at the deep river valley.

"Whoa. How about that?" he said to his pony. "Long damn way down there, huh?"

He continued riding and soon arrived at a small town built in a cluster around a train depot. There were two streets running the opposite direction of each other and crossing in the middle.

His stomach was aching and he was hungry. It'd been a day since he had anything to eat. He found a hotel with a café. He ate some ham, cheese, and bread. After breakfast he found a room at a boardinghouse. He slept through the heat of the day.

He considered riding on, but instead settled in at a small saloon across the street. He played some cards with a group of fellas about his age. After some beers he learned they were section-line workers. They traveled with the trains and did maintenance up and down the tracks.

The kid was doing most of the winning until a strong older fella, a teamster, sat at the table.

He got the kid's attention right away. He was a big, handsome fella. He wore a leather shirt that was open, revealing necklaces made of beads and animal teeth. He had a head of thick curly dark hair and a long beard. His forearms were as big as the kid's thighs.

After a few hands, the kid could feel the teamster's eyes on him. The teamster leaned in his chair and took a glance under the table.

"Them Mexican spurs you're wearing?"

The kid peered at him over the top of his cards.

"They are," the kid said.

"You don't look like a Mexican," the teamster said.

The kid eyed the pot on the table, then studied his cards. The teamster glanced to the other card players and smiled.

"You a Mex?" the teamster said.

"I'm not," the kid said.

"You from Mexico?"

"No."

"How come you dress like a Mexican?"

The kid shrugged.

"Beats being like every other swinging dick."

The teamster laughed to the other card players, then grinned wide, showing his straight white teeth.

"So it's your call," the teamster said.

"I got no idea," the kid said with a chuckle.

"Well, if you don't, then nobody does," the teamster said.

The other card players laughed as the kid bit the inside of his jaw, studying his cards. They were all older than the kid, but not by much.

"Think I'll fold."

"Now, hold on," the teamster said.

One card player, a young fella with a head full of gray hair that was out of his scalp before it should be out, shook his head.

"You can't just fold on us," he said.

"Sure I can," the kid said. "I'm doing it."

"Okay," the teamster said. "Fellas?"

The others showed their hands, then the teamster smiled, showing his teeth again.

"You are one lucky teamster," the gray-haired player said as he scooted away from the table. "I'm goddamn done."

"What?" the teamster said. "It's early."

"I got enough money left to get properly drunk before I got to go to work tomorrow," he said. "So that is exactly what the hell I am gonna do. I'm gonna get drunk."

The others around the table agreed, saying the same thing, and moved away as the teamster raked in the pot.

"Suit yourselves," the teamster said.

He watched as the card players moved away, then rested his eyes on the kid.

"You want to play a hand between just the two of us?"

"Sure," the kid said. "But why not try me straight-up?"

The teamster stared at the kid and the kid smiled.

"Between you and me," the kid said.

The teamster studied the kid.

"You caught on quick," he said under his breath.

The kid glanced at the other card players standing by the bar.

"I could feel the cards," the kid said. "I know what you are doing. I just wanted to see how good you were doing it."

He turned his head to the side and grinned at the kid.

"You are kind of scrawny for that kind of talk."

"I can take care of myself."

The teamster appreciated the kid's gall.

"You have any skills of the trade?"

"Me? Naw."

The teamster smiled.

"You're full of shit."

"Me? No," the kid said.

"You got some skill, I know it."

"Naw."

"Shit," the teamster said. "So. Can you deal seconds and not get caught."

The kid smiled.

"Better than you," he said.

The teamster smiled as he regarded the other card players. They were now all leaning on the bar with their backs to them. The teamster handed him the deck.

"Your deal, show me."

The kid picked up the deck. He glanced inside the deck. Then shuffled it with grace, moving short stacks and reshuffling. Then he dealt a blackjack hand. Then the kid set the deck on the table and nodded to the teamster's cards he'd dealt.

"Nice hand you got there," the kid said.

Showing was the jack of spades. The teamster stared at the kid, then turned over his face card — an ace.

"Dice is best," the kid said.

The teamster leaned back and smiled.

"You got your own?" the teamster said.

"Dice? No, I'm just good."

"Let me ask you again: Do you have your

own dice?"

"That is a good way to end up on a spit," the kid said.

The teamster nodded.

"So you do? You got your own sets of loaded devil dice?"

The kid said nothing.

"Have I seen you in here before?"

"No," the kid said.

"You live around here?"

"No."

"Where?" the teamster said.

"Nowhere."

"Meaning?"

"I just got here."

"Where did you just get here from?"

"Down Mexico way."

"That explains it."

"Just in, seeing the place, really. This is my first stop. Need to work. Need to make me some money."

"You got work."

"At this point in time, no, I don't."

"No . . . you got work."

"You mean doing this?" The teamster nodded.

"I don't count on it," the kid said. "Good way to get your nuts cut off."

"Better than shoveling shit."

The kid nodded.

"I try not to make a practice out of it," the kid said. "Or shoveling shit."

"What do you practice?"

"I don't mind working. I do all kinds of things. I'm a pretty good all-around hand. Hell . . . I like work, keeps my mind busy."

"From doing?"

"Things I ought not, I reckon."

"Like get your nuts cut off?" the teamster said.

The kid nodded and smiled.

"Like that," the kid said with a nod and a grin. "What about you?"

"What about me?"

"This your home?"

"This is my home as a matter of fact," the teamster said. "We like it here."

"I don't even know the name of this place," the kid said.

"Don't make any difference, does it?"

"I suppose not."

The teamster laughed.

"Chester."

"How far is Appaloosa?"

"Fifty miles."

The kid looked around the room, thinking.

The teamster said, "I live here, but I'm gone a lot. I haul to and from the mines and up and down the river, and move goods to ranchers and other towns, Yaqui and Appaloosa. I keep my work normal. This work is on the side. I like it here. A train stop and there are always new folks passing through . . . Where you staying?"

The kid shook his head.

"No place, just yet."

"Let me help you out then."

"Really?"

"Sure. You can stay with us if you like."

"Who is 'us'?"

"My wife and me."

"Don't want to put no one out."

The teamster smiled. He liked the kid.

"Fuck you," he said.

The kid smiled.

25

We questioned the four Baptiste gunmen that we'd locked up about the missing miners. We talked with each one separately, and with the exception of Johnny Rodriguez, they were all tight-lipped. And their stories were all the same: they knew nothing and told us nothing about the miners. Johnny also said nothing about the missing miners, but he let us know where they were all boarded and that their job was to do what Victor Bartholomew told them to do. And so far, according to Johnny, they'd just been riding back and forth between Appaloosa and the gold mines.

We knew it would be only a matter of time before we would have to deal with the McCormicks' lead gunman, Edward Hodge. Same with Baptiste's lead gunman, Victor Bartholomew. What we did not expect was how we would have to deal with them.

Virgil and I sat with Lloyd on the porch

of the sheriff's office as the sun was setting. We were listening to one of Lloyd's Texas Ranger stories when we heard a horse galloping. It was Skeeter, Book's young deputy. He rode his stocky roan fast around the corner and came straight up to us. He pulled to a hard stop, kicking up a swell of dirt in front of the office.

Skeeter was a scrappy and small Mexican fella. He was the youngest of Book's deputies, but tougher than most men twice his size. Skeeter was also a smart fella with a good head for law work.

"The gold-mining man," Skeeter said, breathing hard. "McCormick. He has died."

"Which one?" Virgil said.

"The taller one," Skeeter said. "The younger one."

"James?" I said.

"*Sí,*" he said. "James."

"How do you know?" Virgil said.

Skeeter pointed.

"I saw him. I saw it happen. In front of my eyes."

"Where?" Virgil said. "Where did you see this?"

"In front of a home, over on Fourth. I was patrolling on Fourth Street when I see him."

"You sure he's dead?" Virgil said.

"*Sí.*"

"How?" I said. "How did he die?"

"I am not sure how."

"Murdered?" I said.

"I do not know," Skeeter said.

"What did you see?" Virgil said.

"I came around the corner there, off Raines Street onto Fourth. Then I see at the far end of the street a man. He's walking wobbly down the steps of a house. Then he falls into the street. A woman, she comes out of the house and runs to him and I ride over to them. I got off my horse to help them, to help her, to see what was wrong, and the woman yelled at me, 'My husband is dead.'"

"You hear any gunfire?" Virgil said.

"No."

"Did you see if he was wounded?" I said. He shook his head.

"I don't know how," Skeeter said. "Or know what has happened. I did not see blood."

"What did his wife say?" I said.

"She just yelled at me to get help. To get lawmen. This much is all that I know."

"Did you notice anyone else there at the house," Virgil said, "or nearby?"

"No, sir," Skeeter said. "I see a few of the people come out of their homes to see, they hear the woman yelling at me."

Virgil glanced at me and shook his head.

"That was it," Skeeter said.

"Is this McCormick's house?" Virgil said.

"I think so," Skeeter said.

"And you sure it was James McCormick?" Virgil said.

"*Sí.*"

"How do you know for sure?" Virgil said.

"Well, I saw him before, when he came here to talk with you," Skeeter said. "He is James."

Virgil shook his head.

"Here we go," I said.

I stepped into the office and got my eight-gauge, and as I gathered it and the shells, I looked through the open door leading to the cells. And I could see Bartholomew's gun hands, Noah Miller, Johnny Rodriguez, and Wayne. They were all leaning on the bars. They obviously overheard Skeeter.

"You need anything from us, Deputy Marshal," Noah said with a smirk, "just holler. We'd be happy to show you what to do and how to do it."

They started laughing. I answered Noah by closing the big door that separated the hall to the cells from the front room. But I could still hear them laughing as I walked out onto the porch.

"I tried to tell her," Skeeter said. "I tried

to tell her that I was the police and she just yelled at me louder. She yelled at her neighbor to stop looking. She was yelling at me and yelling at everybody who came close, just yelling. She is mad."

26

Johnny Rodriguez had provided us with information as to where the Bartholomew gang was staying, a bunkhouse hotel called Dag's near the depot. And up to this point in time, we had no real reason to knock on Victor's door at Dag's, other than to question him about the men who were missing. And knowing Victor like we knew Victor, that line of questioning without some kind of evidence would go nowhere. But now with this news about James McCormick falling over dead in the middle in the street, I figured it might be a good idea that we pay Victor a visit before too much time passed.

Skeeter was still talking with Virgil when I stepped out with my eight-gauge.

"How about Skeeter and I have a look-see at Dag's," I said. "Maybe talk to Sandy. Maybe the old man that is there all the time? See what they know. Maybe see if anybody might be doing something that they might not ought to be doing. Like leaving town in a hurry after killing someone."

Virgil nodded.

"We'll just take a peek," I said.

"Only one other gun hand beside Victor that's not locked up," Virgil said.

"We'll see what they might do," I said.

"Victor's a snake," Virgil said. "Careful."

"We'll come right to you after," I said.

Virgil moved to his horse.

I mounted up and turned my horse.

"Come on, Skeeter."

Skeeter and I rode with some pace. We crossed the tracks and turned uptown toward Dag's. When we got to the hotel we slowed.

"Let's pull up right here," I said.

We stopped shy of the place and sat our horses.

"What are we looking for?" Skeeter said.

"Just watching," I said. "Just to see if anyone is coming in or going out."

After a short time watching the place, I stepped out of the saddle.

"Let's tie up here."

Skeeter followed and we tied our horses on a fence across the road.

"When we get in here, Skeeter, you keep your gun in its leather unless I tell you otherwise, *comprende*?"

"*Sí.*"

Dag's was a grungy place Virgil and I had been in a few times, looking for one miscreant or the other. It normally housed mining crews. But it also attracted those types prone to lawlessness.

The main room smelled of tobacco spit, smoke, and whiskey. It was a narrow, high-ceiling space packed full of café tables and barrels for chairs. Spittoons were under the tables, and, as always, the stuffed buffalo was the only thing on the wall. It sported a pink bonnet.

The one person in the room was Sandy, sitting behind the counter. Sandy was the same caretaker that greeted us every time Virgil and I had been in the place. She moved her heavyset frame to the edge of the counter and smiled, showing her missing teeth.

"Well, what did I do to deserve the pleasure?" she said with a slight whistle.

"Hello, Sandy," I said quietly, then put my finger to my lips as we neared her.

She nodded.

When Skeeter and I got closer, she raised her eyebrows and whispered, "Hello, Marshal Hitch."

"Sandy."

"What are we whispering for?"

"Victor Bartholomew here?"

Her eyes narrowed.

"Victor who?"

"Skinny man with the bullwhip?"

"Oh, him," she said, shaking her head. "No, he ain't, that no-good shit."

"He's not here?" I said

"Nope, not no longer. The spindly fuck," she said. "He said his name to be Ben Davis, but I knew he was lying. 'Course damn near everyone that walks through that door lies about who they are. Except for lawmen like you. Always giving a name other than the name they was given. But I don't need to tell you that. That all you are interested in?"

She batted her eyes.

"For the time being," I said, "Sandy, it is."

"There was others with him staying here for a while, but them others been gone the last few days. Not sure where they took off to. I suspected them all to be up to no good."

"When is the last time you saw him, Victor, the Ben Davis fella?"

"This morning," she said. "But they took off."

"Know where?"

"I don't," she said. "All of them had their horses stabled across the way there at Deek's. Maybe he knows something."

"You said 'they,' " I said. "Was there someone with Victor this morning?"

"Yeah, they. It was him and another fella was still staying here with him," she said. "But, like I say, they took off. Took what few things they had and left."

"What can you tell me about the other fella?"

"Real tall like a goddamn giraffe and skinny as bale wire. Mean eyes. Him and that other fella Ben Davis or Victor whatever that you are looking for look sort of like brothers."

I nodded.

"They are," I said.

27

James McCormick's body was being loaded into the ambulance by a few of Doc Burris's men as Skeeter and I approached. It was past dark when we neared, but I could see Virgil. He was standing with Doc on the tall porch of James McCormick's stately home.

Seated on the porch were James's brother, Daniel, and two women. One a slender pretty woman I figured to be James's wife. The other woman was older, tougher-looking, and I figured she was likely the wife of Daniel.

Skeeter and I came up the street from the south. When we pulled to a stop, Hodge and three of his men came riding in fast from the north. I thought they were likely the other gun hands Daniel had told us he hired. The four horsemen reined to a halt in a waft of rolling dirt in front of McCormick's house.

"I am damn sure sorry to hear what has happened here," Hodge said.

Daniel got to his feet and took a few steps toward the edge of the porch.

"What has happened here?" Virgil said.

"What?" Hodge said with a sharp look at Virgil.

"Who told you?" Virgil said.

"None of your goddamn business," Hodge said.

Virgil took a step toward the porch edge, looking down at Hodge.

"It is," he said.

"No trouble, please," Daniel said.

"I was at your damn office. I come to see you, like you asked me to do. And your boy there, Lawrence, and them other fellas in the office was all crying about this. Said you left. Said your brother had died in front of the house, in the street here. That is how we know."

The other horsemen nodded.

"That your brother, James, is dead here at his home, died in the damn street . . . Now has come the time for us to do what we came here to do."

"I appreciate your sentiment and your intention, Mr. Hodge," Daniel said. "But now is *not* the time."

"In all goddamn due respect, it *is* the

time," Hodge said. "Them boys shot and wounded one of my men and now they done this. I goddamn know what happened here and I aim to make things right."

"Mr. Hodge, please," Daniel said. "We don't actually know what has happened to James."

"*You* might not *actually* know. But I do, and we aim to do what we were hired to do."

"I understand your feelings," Virgil said.

"Goddamn good to know," Hodge said.

"But feelings will get you killed," Virgil said.

Hodge shook his head.

"Your law work is what you do," he said. "But what we do is something else altogether different."

"We already got two of your hands locked up," Virgil said. "So unless you boys want to join them, you need to turn around and skedaddle."

"Fuck you," Hodge said as he jerked the reins of his dun. "Let me tell you something —"

"Enough," Daniel said. "We don't even know the cause of my brother's death here."

"Bullshit," Hodge said.

Hodge turned his dun and rode close to the ambulance. He leaned down, trying to see inside through the curtain-covered glass. But it was too dark to see anything. The faint outline of James's body covered with a blanket was all that was visible. Hodge, full of bluster and bravado, was trying to make a point. He turned his horse and moved toward the porch.

"You telling me he died out here in the street, all by his self, of natural causes?"

"I'm not telling you anything," Daniel said. "Other than I want you and your men to go, please, just go."

"You hired us to —"

Daniel interrupted. "I know why I hired you."

"Then let us do what we were hired to do."

"This is not the place or time for this sort of brouhaha," Daniel said.

Hodge nodded but did not seem too convinced. "Just go," Daniel said. "I need you to respect me and my family at this most unfortunate time."

Hodge shook his head, then turned his horse away.

"This ain't over."

"It is," Virgil said.

I moved up on my horse and Skeeter followed me.

Hodge turned back to Virgil.

168

"This is war," he growled.

Hodge reined his horse around and rode off, with the other men following him. After the sound of the rider's hooves faded away, an odd silence remained. No one said anything. Then, after a minute, James's wife stood up. She was an elegant, slender woman with auburn hair. She walked stoically past Virgil and Daniel and came down the steps to the street.

"Bernice," Daniel said.

But she paid him no mind. She kept walking. She moved past Skeeter and me, then walked up to the ambulance. She stared at James's body behind the curtains covering the glass sides of the carriage.

Doc held up his hand, signaling the ambulance driver not to move.

"I told him something like this would happen," she said. "I knew when this gold was found that something like this would happen. I did not know what or how exactly, or when. But I knew."

She was not addressing anyone in particular.

"Filthy gold."

The older woman got to her feet and walked to the edge of the steps.

"Bernice, dear," she said. "Let's go inside."

"I never wanted to move here in the first place," Bernice said. "I was perfectly fine where we were."

"Bernice," the woman said again.

Bernice remained looking at her dead husband for an extended time. No one said a word. Then she turned and stared at all of us who were watching her. She was not crying. Nor did she seem particularly upset now. She was just matter-of-fact.

"What is it about greed?" Bernice said.

"I don't know, dear," the older woman said.

Bernice started walking toward her house. She walked up the steps past Virgil and Daniel and the other woman. She entered the house and closed the door behind her.

28

The teamster had a small homestead over the bridge with a large barn surrounded by corrals and trees. There were chickens and pigs and goats and a stable full of mules, with a garden next to the house.

Right away the kid was awestruck by the teamster's wife. More than awestruck. He thought her magnificent. He'd never seen a woman anything like her before in his life. She was a big striking woman. She reminded him of photographs he'd seen in books of ancient Greek gods. She was as tall as the teamster. The kid figured she was likely as strong as the teamster, too. She was dark, with mounds of dark curly hair piled atop her head and dark, penetrating eyes under eyebrows that touched in the middle. She smoked a long pipe and spoke with a thick accent. An accent the kid had never heard before.

She fed the kid food like he'd never tasted. It was a spicy meal of tomatoes, carrots, and lamb rice with oil, creamy sauce, and fried bread. After the meal, the three of them sat outside in front of the house under the stars. The night was clear and bright, with a near full moon that hovered above the eastern horizon.

Every word that the teamster's wife said that started with the letter *W* sounded like a *V.* And every word that ended with *ing* sounded like *ink.*

"Where are you coming from?" she said.

"Down Mexico way," the teamster said with a smile.

She threw her hand at her teamster husband like she was flicking something at him.

"He can speak for himself, no?"

The kid smiled.

"Can you?"

"I can."

"Where in Mexico?"

"Border towns, for the most part, Nuevo Laredo, Juárez, and some places in between."

"You are a little brown, but you are no Mexican."

"No."

"Blue eyes," she said.

"Sí," he said.

"My husband tells me you are a good card player?"

He laughed.

"I have some skills."

"Tell me, where do you come from?"

"I just come from Trinidad."

"Trinidad? What is this Trinidad?"

"Colorado."

She nodded as she puffed on her pipe.

"Your home?"

"No."

"What was there in Trinidad?"

"Turned out my father was there."

"And your mother?"

He shook his head.

"No, she was not there."

She puffed on her pipe some more as she gazed up to the stars.

"So Trinidad is your father's home?"

"It was."

She looked to him.

"He's not there anymore?"

"No."

"Where is your mother?"

"I'm not sure. I aim to find her."

"So where are you going to find her?"

"I'm pretty much there, now."

"Chester? Your mother is here?"

"Appaloosa. I hear tell she's in Appaloosa."

"Appaloosa," she said with a scoff, and then spit.

"What's the matter with Appaloosa?" the kid said.

"One too many people in Appaloosa."

"I have never been," the kid said.

"But you think she is there?"

The kid nodded.

"That is what my father told me," the kid said.

"You will see," she said. "Too many people."

"I don't mind people."

"But with people comes too many horses. Too many horses, means too much horseshit. Too much horseshit brings too many flies, summers especially."

"I'm used to the heat. Horseshit, too, I reckon. Like your husband said, I come from the south. I like the south. I like the Mexican way of living."

She nodded.

"Do you like tequila?"

"I do."

She turned to the teamster and tipped her head toward the house. He got up without a word and went into the house.

"You move gracefully," she said.

He smiled.

"Like a dancer."

He laughed.

"I am a good dancer."

She nodded, staring at him.

"But it has not been easy for you," she said.

"What makes you say that?"

174

"Because I know these things."

"Easier than some," he said. "Harder than others, I guess."

The teamster came out with a bottle of tequila and handed it to his wife. She took out the cork and took a pull. Then she passed the bottle to the kid. The three of them shared, drinking directly from the bottle.

"Where did your father go?" she said.

"Go?" he said.

"You said your father was not any longer in this town . . . this . . . Trina . . ."

"Trinidad," the teamster said.

She stared intently at the kid.

"Oh. No, he left when I left."

She nodded like she knew what happened to him.

"Where did he go?" she said with a smile.

"Hell," the kid said. "He went to hell."

She grinned and offered a nod to her husband.

"I knew something like this," she said to her husband, then turned her attention to the kid. "And how did he get there? To hell?"

"I sent him," the kid said, looking her in the eye. "I sent him up in flames."

She nodded, then turned to her husband.

"What did I tell you?" she said.

"She told me you danced with fire," the teamster said.

She leaned in, staring at the kid as she puffed on her pipe.

"I see things like this," she said.

"She does," the teamster said.

The kid did not know what to say.

"What do you expect from her?" she said.

The kid stared at her long and hard.

"You don't know?" she said.

"Not exactly," he said.

"Do you want her love?"

The kid didn't say anything.

"Do you want to harm her?"

The kid stared at her.

She nodded.

"Maybe I can help you."

"How?"

"Help you to know what it is that you expect of her."

He said nothing. And no one spoke. Silence set in. The kid tilted his head back and took in the night sky full of stars.

She remained staring at the kid, then lifted out of her chair. She stood, and she, too, gazed up at the stars with the kid.

"He will sleep with me tonight," she said to her husband. "You will sleep in the barn."

29

After the ambulance departed, Virgil and I stayed and talked with Daniel McCormick on the front porch of James's home. Now that the women had gone inside, Daniel was shaking. It was as if he hadn't allowed his emotions and feelings to surface until now. He appeared weak as he turned, looking for a place to sit.

"Gentlemen," he said, lowering into a porch chair, "I don't know what to say. I . . . I have no words for any of this."

Virgil waited before he spoke.

"We need to figure out what happened here," Virgil said. "Who did this and how."

"No," Daniel said. "I understand that, I do. Indeed, I do."

"The sooner we get onto this," Virgil said, "figure out what exactly happened here, the better."

"Well, you don't have to look too far for who killed James. That is obvious," Daniel said. "Goddamn obvious."

"How was it you were here?" Virgil said.

"Well, my wife and I live just there."

He pointed to a house a few doors down and across the street.

"Bernice came rushing over."

"You were home?" Virgil said.

"No, my wife sent our housemaid to come and collect me. I was at the office. That is obviously how Mr. Hodge knew about this, from my employees there."

"What do you know?" Virgil said. "Did James's wife offer any explanation of how this happened or who did this?"

"I don't know much more than you do," he said. "She said nothing to me, really. Except that she was out on the back porch and she heard James enter from the front here. She said she heard a crash, then she came inside the house to see a vase had fallen; it was broken on the floor. The door here was open and James was staggering away."

"Mr. McCormick," I said. "Right now we need to speak with her, your brother's wife. Bernice, is it?"

"Yes, Bernice," he said.

He removed his hat and pushed his hand through his hair as he stared at the floor.

"I'm obviously shocked and devastated

with all this. And Bernice as well, more so perhaps. Though I'm not sure that is possible, as I'm frankly goddamn sick. But if it is all the same to you, I think it best we give her, and me, the evening to let this . . . I don't know, let this sink in. And let us see you in the morning and talk then."

I glanced at Virgil.

He nodded.

"We'll have deputies here," Virgil said. "Watching out. Make sure no one tries anything they should not."

Daniel nodded.

"Thank you. Now, if you will excuse me," he said as he got to his feet. "I would like to be with my wife and Bernice."

Virgil nodded.

"Let her know we will need to talk with her tomorrow," Virgil said.

Daniel offered a weary smile.

"And for the time being we will keep this silent," Virgil said. "Less talk, the better."

"I understand," he said, then entered into the house, closing the door behind him.

Virgil and I walked down the steps.

"So what in the hell did happen here?" I said.

"He was shot all right," Virgil said. "One shot in the side toward his back it seemed. Not a lot of bleeding."

"And nobody saw anything, nothing?"

"No," Virgil said, "nothing more than what you heard and what Skeeter told us."

"Hard to believe nobody came forward," I said. "No neighbors claiming they heard a shot or saw anything?"

"No," Virgil said. "Nothing. Everyone stayed away. As far as the folks that live nearby know, he just fell dead in the street."

"My stop to Dag's turned up a few things," I said.

"Victor Bartholomew was already gone," Virgil said.

"That's right."

"And his big brother, Ventura Bartholomew, was seen with him," Virgil said.

"That's right, too," I said. "How'd you know?"

"I didn't," Virgil said.

"Where there is smoke?" I said.

"Yep," Virgil said.

"Double the trouble," I said.

"Don't suppose anybody has any idea where they are," Virgil said. "Where they went, where they were headed."

"No," I said. "The gal there at the hotel, Sandy, said they had their horses stabled at that livery, Deek's, across the tracks there from Dag's hotel. Maybe somebody there might have some idea as to where they took off to."

Virgil nodded.

"Baptiste and Eugene Pritchard likely know where they are," Virgil said. "They had to find them in the first place."

"Maybe the Bartholomew hands we have locked up, Johnny, Wayne, Noah Miller, and the other one," I said, "maybe they could point us in the right direction."

"Could," Virgil said. "But then what? We just lock them up, too. Ol' Hodge might be right," he said.

"That this is war?"

"That's right," Virgil said. "Both sides of this are itching."

"Seems so," I said. "We got a good portion of them behind bars, though."

"That we do," Virgil said.

"Might not be a bad idea to let them fucking go," I said, "and let them sort it out."

"Might not," Virgil said.

"Might make things easier for us in the long run," I said. "Let them whittle on each other."

"Might," Virgil said.

"Hodge was damn sure convinced that James was murdered," I said.

"That he was," Virgil said. "Has every

right, too."

"Don't think there'd be too many to disagree on that assumption," I said.

"No," Virgil said. "I don't, either."

30

Virgil and I got deputies lined up to keep watch on the home of Bernice McCormack. Then we got our horses and headed for the hospital.

As Virgil and I rode, we crossed Appaloosa Avenue, a half-block away from the theater.

I thought about Martha Kathryn. I was trying to determine the timeline of the play. Playing it in my mind as to what act they were currently in. Somewhere between the dancing cow and the spewing whale, I figured.

Duncan Mayfield, a reporter from the *Appaloosa Star,* met us when we entered the hospital lobby.

"Marshal Cole. Marshal Hitch," he said. "Dr. Burris would not allow me back there. And he told me any news about James McCormick would have to come from a source other than himself. Told me I would have to talk with you or someone in law enforcement."

He was a thin, pimple-faced fella who wore spectacles and was always in a wrinkled suit.

"So I'm asking," he said. "What can you tell me?"

Duncan was the last person Virgil would want to see. We'd dealt with Duncan before. He was kind enough, but the nature of his job, asking questions, rubbed Virgil the wrong way.

"I just heard about it after the fact and was too late to make it to the house. This is a tragedy no doubt involving McCormick. No doubt. So. What can you tell us?"

"Nothing," Virgil said as Duncan followed us toward the hall to the back rooms.

"I'm just doing my job," Duncan said.

"Good," Virgil said.

"The fact that you are here at the hospital tells me there is more to the story of James's death than just falling over dead in the middle of the street."

As we got to the door that separated the lobby from the hallway that led to the operating rooms, Virgil turned to face Duncan.

"We will get to the story one way or the other," Duncan said. "But hearing the details from you would allow me to get the

184

story out in a factual manner. How did he die? Was he murdered?"

"The one thing you need to know right now is this," Virgil said. "If we get up in the morning and find you have written something that pisses me off, I will make certain you wish you had thought twice or maybe three times about it."

Virgil turned and pushed through the door, leaving Duncan in the lobby.

"I'm pretty certain he means what he's saying," I said.

"Just trying to do my job," he said.

"I know," I said. "Us, too."

Duncan nodded. Then I pushed on through the door and followed Virgil down the hall.

A few minutes later, Virgil and I stood over James McCormick's body. He was laid out facedown on his table in the hospital. Doc Burris was looking over his body with one of the night nurses.

There was some dried blood around the bullet hole high up on the left side of his back.

"Looks like he was shot just this once," Doc said. "And not a lot of bleeding."

Doc wiped the dried blood free from around the wound and studied it closely.

"Small-caliber," I said.

Virgil nodded.

"Not much bigger than a .22," he said.

"It's a bit bigger," Doc said.

Doc nodded to his nurse.

"Hand me that magnifying glass."

Doc took the glass and leaned in. He looked at the hole closely and shook his head.

"I'll get into this and let you know what I find," he said.

"What are you thinking?" I said.

"A .32, maybe," Doc said. "I could be wrong. God knows I have been wrong before. Married and divorced three times to prove it. But I'll get the bullet out and let you know."

Virgil and I looked closer at the wound.

"Let's turn him over," he said.

Doc and the nurse rolled the body over. Then Doc looked the corpse over carefully. He looked into the ears, then nose and throat, then raised his eyelids. He leaned in and looked through the magnifying glass into James's dead eyes.

"Give me some time and check back with me."

We thanked him and walked out of the room and down the hall toward the lobby.

"What do you figure?" I said.

Virgil shook his head.

"Don't know," he said. "Not many fellas carry pea shooters."

31

Virgil and I made a trip to Deek's livery, where the Bartholomew hands had their horses stabled across the tracks from Dag's Hotel. Deek was an old-time resident of Appaloosa who Virgil and I knew somewhat and had visited with on occasion.

According to Deek, the horses belonging to Victor and Ventura Bartholomew were gone. The brothers had picked them up earlier in the day. The horses belonging to the hands we had locked up were still stabled and were grazing in a pasture behind the livery. But the Bartholomew brothers had saddled up and vamoosed, and Deek had no idea as to their whereabouts or destination. The only other information Deek had to offer was that he didn't much care for the lanky brothers. Shitheads, he called them.

When we got to the office, we interrupted one of Lloyd's stories. He was telling Skeeter about meeting Custer and his wife, Libbie, when Custer and his battalion once dispatched to Houston, Texas. I often wondered how much of the Texan yarns Lloyd spun was factual. But Virgil and I did not really care, and the deputies anticipated his stories. Law work was often monotonous. Having colorful pieces of history told by a good storyteller, even if he was a tall-tale Texan, kept the days from being boring.

We had Lloyd open up the door leading to the cells. All of the hands that were locked up stirred when they saw us, wondering what was going on. The two McCormick hands were separated from the Bartholomew gunmen. Bartholomew's big man, Noah Miller, got up off his bunk and moved to the bars as we entered.

"We getting out?" Noah said. "You letting us go?"

Lloyd ignored Noah's question with the seasoned insolence of a lawman.

"Johnny Rodriguez?" Lloyd said.

Johnny was asleep facing the wall on a corner bunk. He turned and looked to us.

"Qué?" he said sleepily as he looked back over his shoulder with his eyes narrowed, trying to focus.

"Get up," Lloyd said.

He seemed confused, then slowly swiveled

around and put his feet on the floor.

"*Sí?*"

"*See, see, see,*" Lloyd said as he unlocked the cell. "Come on."

Johnny gazed around.

"*Vámonos,*" Skeeter said, "*no tenemos toda la noche.*"

Johnny got to his feet.

"*A donde?*" Johnny said.

"*Donde* on out here, Johnny," Lloyd said. "Let's go. Step on outta there."

"What for?" Noah Miller said.

"You don't look like no Mexican Rodriguez to me," Lloyd said. "I'm talking to Johnny see, see, see Rodriguez here."

"What's going on?" Noah said.

Johnny stepped out into the hall and Lloyd locked the door behind him.

"Where we going?" Johnny said.

Johnny walked to the office with Virgil and me. Lloyd closed the door to the hall behind him.

Virgil pointed to a chair.

"Sit down there, Johnny," Virgil said.

Johnny sat. His clothes were wrinkly and his long, bristly hair was sticking out in every direction. His round face was covered with thick whiskers that were closing in on the length of his quarter-'til-three mustache.

"Got a few questions for you," Virgil said.

"What kind of questions?"

"Just answer," Virgil said. "Try not to think too hard."

Johnny smiled, showing his missing front tooth.

"Cigar?" Johnny said.

Virgil looked to the desk.

"Sure," Virgil said as he got a half-spent cigar out of the ashtray. He handed it to Johnny. Johnny turned his nose up at it, then took it and put it in his mouth. He smiled.

"Got a match?" he said.

Virgil handed him a match and Johnny pulled the tip across the bottom of the chair and lit the stub. Once he got it going good, he smiled.

"How can Johnny help you, Marshal Virgil Cole?" he said.

"Any of you boys carry a small-caliber pistol or rifle?" Virgil said.

"Like a .22?" I said.

"A .22?" Johnny said.

"That's right," Virgil said. "Rifle or pistol."

"No, *señor,*" he said.

"No time to bullshit here," Virgil said.

"No," he said. "No one has a .22. Not that I know about."

"Did Victor or Ventura ever get any instructions from the *jefe* you boys was working to harm or kill any of the miners? I

191

asked you before and you said no."

"I know nothing about no miners," he said.

"How about harm or kill the McCormick brothers?" Virgil said. *"El jefe?"*

"No, *señor.*"

Skeeter leaned against the front doorjamb with his arms folded in front of him, shaking his head.

"Mentiroso," Skeeter said.

"Fuck you," Johnny said. "I am not lying. I do not know nothing about no miners."

He turned to Virgil, shaking his head slowly.

"Nothing."

32

After more tequila, she led the kid down the hall toward her bedroom at the rear of the house. He was warm from the alcohol that was thrusting through his veins. He was feeling feral. He thought he might be unsteady after so much drink, but he was not. She carried a single lamp through the narrow hall that led to the room.

The interior of the room was like nothing the kid had ever seen before. It was painted completely white. The ceiling, walls, and floor were all white. Thin white curtains covered the windows, and white fabric draped over the rafters throughout the room. And there were mirrors. More mirrors in one room than imaginable or understandable to the kid. He watched her move. She glided rhythmically and without effort, like a magnificent creature.

"You sure about this?" the kid said.

She said nothing as she closed the door and set the lamp on a table next to the bed.

"I can sleep elsewhere," he said.

"No," she said.

The bed, covered in fur hides, shimmered from the lamplight, giving the impression that the bed was a living creature. The hides were all patched together and appeared to be a breathing mixture of beaver, fox, and coon. All animals the kid had skinned in this youth. He knew these creatures. Creatures that made the nighttime their active time. He ran his hand through the hair, feeling the pelts' softness.

Then he turned and watched her as she moved about the room, lighting candles. Many candles. Years of wax had built up under the snowy mounds.

It all reminded the kid of winter, of his time living in the mountains. It made him think of the snow-covered tents in the camps, where he was raised.

Then, when she was done lighting the candles, she moved toward the kid. He stood frozen, watching her. She towered over him. He stared up to her. He felt as if he was about to be eaten.

"Sit," she said.

He did just that and sat on the bed. She pushed his chest and laid him flat on the bed. Then she removed his boots. He cut his eyes to the door. Thinking he heard something. And it crossed his mind that he might just be sacrificed tonight. Was this it? Was this his last day on earth? It kind of felt like that to the kid, but she spoke as if she were listening to his thoughts.

"You are not afraid," she said.

"I don't know fear," he said.

She smiled.

"Yes," she said. "I know."

"I have no reason," he said.

"This, too, I know," she said.

"Sometimes I wish I had," he said.

"Wishes are for fountains," she said.

The candlelight reflecting in her dark eyes made her seem even more mysterious.

"I am here for you," she said.

He nodded.

"Perhaps I have been waiting for you," she said.

"Well," he said. "I'm here."

She nodded and smiled.

"Yes, you are," she said.

"We will go places we've never been," she said. "But they will be familiar."

Then she unbuckled his belt.

"Because we have, in another time, within another animal, been there before."

"I have seen you before," he said.

She nodded.

"I know."

He smiled as she stared at him.

"You have every reason to be everything that is within you, and everything that you can harness within me," she said.

"I don't have a choice about that," he said.

"This, too, I know about you," she said.

She pulled down his trousers.

"To do the things you need," she said.

He stared at her.

Then she pulled her dress over her head. And she was muscled and naked before him.

She untied her hair that was piled atop her head and let it fall. The dark twisting locks appeared violent and alive. Everything about her seemed somehow otherworldly to the kid, prehistoric even.

"My God," he said.

"God has nothing to do with it," she said.

33

Johnny remained sitting in the chair in the sheriff's office and continued to insist he knew nothing regarding the miners who had gone missing. But he was becoming more and more agitated from Virgil's questioning. Like Skeeter, Virgil, Lloyd, and I were thinking that Johnny had something to hide, but getting to it was another matter. So Virgil offered him another cigar, this time a fresh, clean one. After Johnny got it going good, Virgil stayed on the course of his interrogation.

"Are you a killer, Johnny?"

"Me?" he said. "No."

"Mentiroso," Skeeter said.

Virgil glanced over at Skeeter. Skeeter held up his hands, a gesture to say *sorry,* and stepped out on the porch.

"I done told you before, *señor,*" he said.

"Where is Victor and his no-good brother?" Virgil said.

197

"The hotel by the tracks over there," he said.

Then he pointed his finger in the direction of the hotel he'd been staying at before he was arrested.

"You know the one. I told you."

"They're gone," Virgil said.

Johnny raised his eyebrows.

"Where to?" Johnny said.

Virgil smiled.

"I'll ask the questions, Johnny, and you'll answer," Virgil said. *"Muy bueno?"*

"Sí, señor."

"Any idea where Victor and his brother have gone off to?" Virgil said.

He shook his head hard.

"No, *señor.*"

"Where were you boys before you got here?" Virgil said.

"Before we come here, to Appaloosa?" Johnny said.

"Sí," Virgil said.

"Santa Fe," he said.

"How about Victor's brother, Ventura?" Virgil said.

"What about him?"

"He come here with you from Santa Fe?"

"No, *señor.*"

"Where'd he come from?"

"He was in Las Vegas," Johnny said. "He

met us here. One week after we got here."

"How did he know you were here?"

Johnny shrugged.

"Victor sent him a wire," he said.

"Why?" Virgil said.

"Said there was money to be made," Johnny said. "I don't know for sure, but that would be my guess."

"Doing what?" Virgil said.

"I did not ask," Johnny said. "I just do what it is that Victor tells me to do."

"So what did he tell you to do?"

"So far we have done nothing other than ride around between the mine and here."

"You know of any other people here in Appaloosa that Victor or Ventura know?"

"What do you mean?" Johnny said as his eyes narrowed from the sting of the cigar smoke wafting.

"Just that," Virgil said. "Answer me. Do Victor or Ventura have any friends here that you know about?"

"No, *señor,*" he said, shaking his head. "Don't think so."

"Everett and me stopped by Deek's livery," Virgil said. "Didn't we, Everett?"

"We did," I said. "You know Deek's, Johnny? That's the livery there by Dag's Hotel. Where you boys have your horses stabled."

"Sí," he said.

"Your horse is the pinto?" Virgil said.

Johnny's eyes lit up.

"Sí," he said. "Jasper."

"The good news is Jasper is still there," I said. "Not been sold off, seeing how you are locked up."

"Sold off?"

"That's right," I said.

"Do you want to get your horse back?" Virgil said.

Johnny sat up.

"Sí, señor," he said.

"Maybe get out of jail?" Virgil said.

"Sí."

"Give me some information," Virgil said.

"I don't want Jasper to get sold," he said, with tears welling.

"No," Virgil said. "I don't imagine you do."

"What do I say?" Johnny said.

"Did Victor kill those miners?"

"No," he said.

"How about them boys you been locked up with?" Virgil said. "Did any of them have a hand in those miners who went missing?"

He shook his head.

"Tell me about Ventura," Virgil said.

Johnny's eyes swiveled between Virgil and me.

"Did Ventura have a hand in what happened with those miners?" Virgil said.

Johnny stared at Virgil, then down at the floor. He turned in his chair to the door separating us from the hall, leading to the cells. Virgil glanced to me.

"Did he?" Virgil said. "Tell me, Johnny."

Lloyd's eyes turned to me. Then Skeeter lingered into the doorway. We were all waiting on what Johnny had to say.

"Tell me what happened," Virgil said.

Johnny shook his head.

"Ventura did it," he said.

"You see him do it?" Virgil said.

"He said he would kill us if anybody ever found out."

"You see Ventura kill those miners?"

He nodded.

"Sí."

"How?"

He shook his head.

"Tell me."

"Shot 'em. He just shot them."

"What about Victor? Him, too? Did Victor do it, too? He pull a trigger, too?"

"No. He was not there, either time."

"Where was he?"

"Every day they kind of took turns," Johnny said.

"Doing what?" Virgil said.

201

"Riding to the mines. That was our job, to make ourselves seen. And that gets kind of *no bueno* after some time. Ventura, he was all the time mad being just seen. So he killed them. He just did it. Both times."

"What about the other men?"

"We tried to stop him. I swear to you we did, but he's . . . he's colder, meaner than any *hombre* that I have ever known in my life."

Virgil's eyes moved to Skeeter, then Lloyd, then me, then rested on Johnny.

"Where, Johnny? Where did he kill them?"

"The shortcut trail, off the main road. Between here and the mines."

"Both men?"

"*Sí.*"

"Where are the bodies?"

"Arroyo," he said. "Off the trail."

"And their horses?"

"Ventura sold them."

"To who?"

"That I do not know."

"Let me ask you again. Since Victor and Ventura are no longer in the hotel there by Deek's livery, do you have any idea where they are?"

Johnny puffed on the cigar as he stared at Virgil. He glanced toward the closed door again. Then he leaned in and spoke softly.

"You will let me out?"

"Answer the question. You bullshit me, *no*. You don't bullshit me, *maybe.*"

"I have told you so much already. So much to get myself killed by one or both of the brothers, so why maybe?" Johnny said. *"Maybe* is *no bueno."*

"Better than *no,*" Virgil said.

Johnny chewed on the cigar and tipped his head toward the cells.

"They cannot know," he said. "Any of what I have said."

"Answer," Virgil said.

Johnny leaned closer and his eyes narrowed.

"What will happen with Ventura and Victor?"

"Johnny?" Virgil said.

Johnny leaned in even closer.

"There is a whore that Ventura knows. He is sweet on. He could be there, Victor, too, maybe."

Virgil glanced to me.

"I am not bullshitting you. He has been staying there. Sleeping there."

"This at Lenora's place?" I said. "The whorehouse where you boys got in the shit with the McCormick hand?"

He shook his head.

"No, *señor.*"

"What's this whore's name?" I said.

"I do not know her name," he said, shaking his head. "But I think I can find her place."

Johnny smiled a little at Lloyd and nodded.

"Don't look at me, you prickly cactus," Lloyd said. "Only thing I can offer you is to keep your good-for-nothing ass locked up until I'm told otherwise."

"You say you think you can find the place?" Virgil said.

"Sí, I can show you where she is. I do not know if that is where Victor and Ventura are, but I can show you."

"Here?" I said. "The north end?"

He nodded.

"Sí. I will have to go there with you and show you. I do not know which whore place it is to tell you."

"Es falso," Skeeter said.

"Fuck you," Johnny said. "I am not lying. Fuck you!"

"You would like to, I know," Skeeter said. *"Maricón."*

Johnny stared hard at Skeeter. He wanted to charge Skeeter. But it was clear. Johnny was seeing an opportunity. That if he played his cards right, he could get out of jail.

"I do not have to tell you, you know. There

are many whorehouses there on the north end of town," he said with a point. "Between all the places, I am not sure. But when I see it I will know . . . I was only by there one time. But I will remember. You will see I can show you."

"You've seen this whore?" Virgil said.

"No, *señor.* I never was inside. I only know the house. We waited there for Ventura before."

"Don't bullshit me," Virgil said.

"No bullshit," Johnny said.

Virgil turned his head toward Lloyd and me.

"Worth a try," I said.

Virgil nodded.

34

We picked up Johnny's horse, Jasper, from
Deek's livery. Virgil, Skeeter, Johnny, and I
mounted up and rode to the north end. We
kept Johnny's hands shackled and left the
bridle off his horse in case he felt like trying
to hightail it. I towed Jasper with Johnny in
the saddle by a lead rope. We rode up
through the twisty roads leading to the hilly
section of the north end.

One thing for certain that Johnny wasn't
bullshitting about was the quantity of
whorehouses. With the growing number of
businesses in and around Appaloosa and up
and down the river, the north end was in
full bloom. Most of the houses were cheap,
small, two-story structures. Every place appeared to be only a slightly different version
than the next. And the way the streets were
laid out in this area of town — twisting and
turning this way and that between brothels,
saloons, and card houses — made navigat-

ing and searching for criminals damn near impossible. So finding what Johnny was looking for proved, for a time, to be a task without end. We stopped in front of a number of places before Johnny pointed out a two-story building that caught his attention.

"There," Johnny said. "I think that is the one."

"You think?" I said.

"This is the place," he said.

Like most of the north end places, it was dimly lit. The sound of piano music came from within. But it was nearly drowned out by the noise coming from the rowdy card house across the way.

"You are sure?" Virgil said.

"*Sí,*" he said. "This is it."

"You see Victor or Ventura's horse?" I said.

He swiveled around in his saddle, checking out the horses on the dark street. Then I rode in a circle, pulling Johnny on Jasper so he could get a real good gander at all the animals hitched on both sides of the street.

He shook his head.

"No, *señor,*" he said. "Victor and Ventura both have big brother horses, gray gelds. I do not see their horses here. I am sorry."

I nudged up next to Virgil.

"What do you figure?" I said.

Virgil shook his head.

"*Mentiroso,*" Skeeter said under his breath.

"Fuck you," Johnny said. "You are the liar. *Estoy contando la verdad, hijo de puta.*"

"*Maricón,*" Skeeter said. "*Maricón.*"

"Maybe I can find the gal Ventura is sweet on in there," I said. "Maybe she knows a thing or two. Have some kind of idea where he might be?"

"Maybe," Virgil said.

I handed Virgil Jasper's lead rope.

"But what about me?" Johnny said. "It is not my fault they are not here."

Virgil did not respond.

"Skeeter," I said. "Let's you and me step inside there and visit with the girls."

I slid off my horse and pulled the eight-gauge from its scabbard. And Skeeter jumped off his pinto.

When we entered the place it was dark and it had the smell of roses working hard to cover up some kind of unpleasant stench. An out-of-tune crank piano wedged in the corner was playing "Camptown Races." A short gal with a round figure and painted face came right up to us. She was damn near close to busting out of her tight dress.

"You are lucky, fellas. Two-for-one special tonight," she said. "That's the two of you, and smidgen me."

Skeeter narrowed his eyes at me and shook his head a little.

"Or," she said, "you can choose one of the other lovely ladies here, if you prefer. Have a look. Take your pick. But with them it's only one of you. With me, you both get to ride for one price."

There were three other whores sitting at a table in the corner, playing cards. They all smiled in our direction. Each of them turned in their chairs and flayed their legs seductively toward us, showing us their goods.

"Appreciative but not interested," I said. "Right now, I just have a few questions for you."

"Okay, handsome . . . let me see if I can answer. But I have to warn you, some answers might require a small fee."

I slid open my lapel.

"Or not," she said, focused on my badge.

"We are trying to find Ventura and Victor Bartholomew," I said.

Her eyes did a quick dart up. Skeeter caught her look, too.

He cut his eyes to me, then looked up the stairs.

"Who?" she said. "Victor and Ven . . . Ventura, who?"

I pulled back both hammers on my eight-gauge. And nodded to Skeeter.

Skeeter pulled his Colt.

"What?" she said. "What's going on?"

"Hush," I said.

Then I took a few steps and looked up the stairs.

35

"Is he here?" I said. "Up there?"

Her eyes moved back and forth.

"Is he?" I said.

"I have no idea who you are talking about," she said.

I put my finger to my lips and pointed to a chair.

"Sit right there. One word other than answers to my questions and I will lock you up."

She nodded, then took a seat as she stared at me.

"How many rooms up there?" I said.

"Three," she said.

"Are both brothers here?"

She said nothing.

"Are they?"

"No," she said. "Not both."

"Which one? And do not lie to me."

"Ventura. Just Ventura is here."

"Which room?"

211

She pointed.

"The room facing the street."

"How many windows to that room?"

"Just the one facing the street."

"And doors?"

"Just the one into the room. At the end of the hall."

"Closets?"

"No, no closets."

"Any other men up there in the other rooms?"

"No. No other men."

"Do not lie to me."

"I'm not. Just Ventura. He is in the front room with Karla?"

The piano stopped playing and everyone was staring at me.

"One of you start that piano up again," I said.

One of the gals got up and walked to the piano and gave it a crank. And it started up again.

"Good. Now sit, and all of you stay seated and do not talk. Okay?"

They all nodded. I turned to Skeeter and pointed to the door.

"Gonna let Virgil know," I said.

Skeeter nodded.

I opened the front door and eased out to the porch. I motioned to Virgil to move up some. He nudged his horse and moved closer to the porch.

"What do you got?" he said.

"Ventura is here," I said, pointing up. "In the room facing the street here."

Virgil looked up.

"Be damned," he said.

"See what I say," Johnny hissed.

"Shut up," Virgil said.

"I'm just going to go up and ask him if he'd like to talk," I said. "I will let him know we got him covered up, down, and around. And see what he does."

Virgil nodded.

"Don't imagine he'll want to visit none," Virgil said.

"I'll be ready if he don't," I said. "This window up above here is one of his two ways out. If he feels like trying to leave without talking first."

Virgil looked at me and nodded.

"I'll move out of view a ways," Virgil said.

I nodded.

"You good?" Virgil said.

"I am."

"Watch out," Virgil said.

"Will," I said.

I stepped inside and moved next to Skeeter standing at the bottom of the stairs.

"You stay down here," I said. "If for some

reason I don't come down the stairs here and a tall *hombre* does, you shoot him, okay?"

"I can go up, too," Skeeter said.

I shook my head.

"No. Stay here. Make sure none of these ladies get to talking and such."

"We ain't saying nothing," the chubby gal said. "Right, girls?"

They all nodded.

"Stay here," I said to Skeeter.

He nodded and I walked up the stairs. When I got toward the top, I moved very slowly. Doing my best not to make noise. I could see through the balusters. There was a short hall that led to a single door to the room facing the street. I stood still, then took one step at a time. All the time I kept my eye on the door.

When I was on the landing, I moved slowly to the door and stood off to one side. I knocked.

"Ventura," I said. "It's Marshal Hitch. We got you surrounded. Got plenty of lawmen out here. We would just like to ask you some questions. Come on out. Let's have a friendly talk. As of now, we have no reason to arrest you, unless you do something to give us a reason."

"No," a woman from behind the door

214

screamed. *"Ventura, no!"*

Then the door exploded with shots fired from within, six shots in all, as Ventura unloaded his six-shooter. Then, I heard some commotion, and then a shot from outside, and the woman in the room let out a blood-curdling scream.

"Ventura! No!" she cried. "Oh my God . . . No."

I stepped back and kicked the door open.

Ventura had obviously made a move through the window and got shot by Virgil. He was shirtless and bloody, with a wound to his shoulder. He shoved a round into his pistol.

"Drop it," I said.

He pointed the pistol at me, but I pulled both triggers, and the blast of the barrels and the double-ought buck blew Ventura out the window.

The half-naked woman, Karla, ran out of the room, holding her ears and screaming as she exited. I moved to the window and looked out below.

Ventura, crumpled, was dead in the street.

Virgil looked up to me.

I leaned out and said, "I asked him if we could have a friendly talk."

36

The kid waited outside. It seemed like forever. He paced back and forth under the tall clock tower. Then he saw her. The men followed her out of the building. He was amazed at how tall she was and how beautiful.

The wind came through and lifted some trash that swirled down the boardwalk.

The beautiful woman with the men crossed the street, and the kid followed them. He knew from the tintype that she was his mother — it had to be her. But he had no idea who the men were. Like the old man had told him, they were dandies wearing derbies.

She had on a long, tight-fitting silk dress with a matching hat. She was making the men laugh as they walked. The kid wished he were not wearing his Mexican clothes. For the first time ever, he felt like he was in the wrong clothes. He wanted her to be impressed with him. But it had been so long and he was anxious for the reunion. He had no time to change.

They stopped at a busy street, waiting for buggies to pass. He was getting close to her now. He hurried up behind them. His heart was beating hard in his chest. And when he was close, he stopped and took a deep breath.

"Helen," he said.

She remained looking straight ahead.

"Helen," he said again.

She turned to him. The men wearing the derby hats also turned to the kid.

"It's me," the kid said. "Your boy."

She laughed and shook her head, then turned away from him.

"Mother?" he said.

She turned to him and shook her head.

"What did you say?"

"Mother."

She laughed, and the men laughed with her.

"I'm sorry, young man, but I'm not your mother."

"Hold on," the kid said as he held up his finger.

"Go away, kid," one of the men said.

"Please just wait, let me show you something."

"Go on, now, boy, do as I say," the man said.

The kid had the tintype with him. He opened the envelope and pulled it out to show her.

"Please, here, look at this. You will see."

"Go on, boy," another one of the derby men said.

"Please. You have to see this."

She smiled and shook her head.

"I'm sorry, but I must be moving on."

She turned and stepped into the street, not seeing the massive horse and buggy barreling toward her.

"Look out!" the kid said.

Then he sat up.

Somewhere a rooster crowed. The kid was unsure where he was. Then he felt the naked body of the teamster's wife next to him. He lifted his head and looked around. His mouth was dry and he could feel the effects of the tequila he'd drunk.

It was still dark out. There were a few candles burning that offered some dim light. He turned to her. Her large, dark eyes were closed and she was sound asleep. Her wide, fat lips were open, and he thought about how she smothered him with kisses that covered his mouth. He marveled at her muscles and the size and strength of her. He thought if she were without woman parts she could easily be a man, a pretty, muscular man.

He thought about what had happened through the evening. For a period of time, he wondered if he were not some kind of sacrifice. It went through his mind that the teamster might come in and grab him and nail him to a cross or something. Or set him afire and burn him up like he had done to the old man. But here it was, it was close to sunrise, and he'd made it through the night without horrific incident.

He lifted up in bed and put his feet to the floor. He sat there, trying to feel stable enough to stand. Then she moved behind him. He felt her hand on the back of his neck. She slid her large hand around his neck. Her long fingers spread across his neck and chin, and she pulled him to face her.

"What did you see?"

"What?" he said.

"In your dreams?" she said.

"I . . . I'm not sure."

"Remember," she said.

"I don't know."

"Sleep is more telling than waking hours," she said.

He looked at her, thinking, trying to remember his dream.

"I was waiting. I waited for her."

"And?"

"I . . . I saw her."

"Where?"

"On the street."

He thought, trying to remember.

"I remember a big clock."

"What was she doing?"

"She was turning away from me," he said.

"What time?"

"What?"

"What was the time on the clock?"

He shook his head.

"I don't remember."

"What else?"

"She was in danger," he said.

"What did you do?"

"I tried to help her."

"What else?" she said.

He shook his head, squinting, trying to remember.

"I don't know. I don't know."

She pulled him in and kissed him. Again, her wide mouth took in his mouth fully.

Then she pulled his head back to see his eyes. He was close to her, face-to-face, and her eyes were as dark and deep and as big as anything he could imagine.

She seemed like an animal, a fierce bloodthirsty creature ready to devour him. But instead she smiled and retreated into the pillow, with a lusty expression. A soft take-me look. And that is what the kid did.

Later, the kid followed the teamster in the corral as he gathered mules for a trip.

"You'll be my swamper," the teamster said.

"What's a swamper?"

"My helper. Helping me move a heavy load down the road."

"What are you hauling?" the kid said.

"Picking up sticks of bell and spigot iron pipe at a factory on the river and taking it to Appaloosa. You will be with me. You will get to see Appaloosa."

"Yeah. Well, I figured on moving on, just going there on my own. You know. Settling in."

The teamster glanced over to his wife, who was standing behind the kid.

The kid turned. He had not seen her. He did not know she was there. Her long, dark hair was down and blowing in the wind. She was wearing a thin white cotton dress, an interesting vision, the kid thought, the white of her dress next to the dark of her skin. And it, too, was blowing. Again, she reminded the kid of something wild.

"You can help me," she said. "I can help you."

"Help me?" the kid said.

"Yes."

"With what?"

"Your future."

The kid grinned.

"I don't think anyone has ever helped me do anything."

"You will see."

The kid looked to the teamster as he led the mules toward a long flatbed next to the barn.

37

After Ventura got himself shot dead, Virgil unlocked Johnny and sent him away. Virgil let Johnny know that if we saw him again in Appaloosa, we'd lock him up for good.

The following morning, Virgil and I were sitting on the front porch drinking coffee when we got word from Doc Burris's assistant. He let us know Doc was up through the night, treating a family with a handful of sick children, and that he would not be able to follow up on the examination of James McCormick's body until later in the day.

The news of Ventura Bartholomew's death had yet to be reported.

But the morning news of James McCormick's death was all over town. By way of Duncan Mayfield's article that came out in the *Appaloosa Star.* He was able to get enough information about what happened from neighbors to cobble together an account. The article included a description of Bernice screaming at a Mexican deputy to get help. But the story did not allude to the notion that there was foul play involved or that James was murdered. Duncan knew better than to report something like that. He was warned. And he knew he would have to deal with the wrath of Virgil Cole if he reported any unsubstantiated account of James's death.

Virgil and I sat in Daniel McCormick's office. With us was Daniel; his wife, Irene; and James McCormick's widow, Bernice. She was not happy about the account of her actions in the paper. But for a woman who the night before had lost her husband, Bernice seemed well put together. She appeared fresh and clean, as if she had recently bathed. She wore a form-fitting rose-colored dress with a high collar that accentuated her long neck. Her brown hair was neatly fixed atop her head. She sat upright on the edge of her seat with her chin up and her shoulders back.

After a few words of condolence, the door opened. Lawrence, Daniel's office manager, entered, pushing a rolling cart with a coffeepot and cups. Without a word, he poured us each a cup of coffee. Then he left the room, closing the door behind him.

Daniel's wife, Irene, was a striking but harsh-edged woman with intense dark eyes and a narrow face. She was also nervous and talkative. She seemed uncomfortable and intolerant of silence.

"This is just awful," Irene said as she reached out and took Bernice's hand. "Just awful. I don't think I slept an hour straight last night. I'm sure you didn't, either, dear."

Bernice remained stoic and did not say anything.

"I'm sure you know just how hard this is for us, for Bernice."

"We do," I said.

"I'm sure you will find the men responsible," Irene said as she scooped spoonful after spoonful of sugar into her coffee. "Won't you, Marshal Cole, Marshal Hitch?"

Virgil nodded.

"We'll do what we can," he said.

"Yes, I told Bernice that is exactly what you would do." Then she turned to Bernice. "Like I told you, dear. Like I told you. Justice will prevail."

Virgil put his coffee cup on the table and leaned in with his elbows on his knees, in front of Bernice.

"What can you tell us?" he said.

His manner was thoughtful, gentle.

Bernice shook her head.

225

"She does not know what or how this even happened," Irene said. "She was out back."

"Let Bernice answer, Irene," Daniel said.

"Well, of course, dear," Irene said. "I'm sorry. I'm just trying to be helpful in this most difficult time." She turned to Virgil. "I'm sure you understand."

"We do," he said.

"I apologize, dear," Irene said to Bernice. "Go on, of course. Please."

Bernice offered a weak smile and adjusted in her seat before she spoke.

"I don't know what happened and I don't think I can offer any details other than what Daniel told you. Nothing that you don't already know."

She summoned up a feeble smile to Daniel.

"Just give them an account of what you know," Daniel said. "What we talked about. What you told me."

She nodded.

"I was just outside, on the back porch. I'd been out there for an hour, I'd say."

"Doing?" Virgil said.

"I was reading."

"And James?" Virgil said.

"He was not home, I was home alone. Well, Netta, our housemaid was home with me. She was upstairs at the time."

226

She paused and shook her head.

"I heard the front door open. Then I called out and asked if it were James. But he did not reply and I did not think much about it. I thought it might have been Netta at the door, going in and out for whatever reason. Then I called to Netta but did not hear her respond. Then I heard a crash. Something breaking. And I thought, *My gosh, what on earth, what could that possibly be.*"

Virgil nodded.

"Then what?" he said.

"Well, I got up. I went inside and the first thing I saw when I entered was a broken vase. It was there down the hall, shattered near the front door. The front door was open wide, and the vase was just there on the floor. A few other things had fallen, too, a few books, a carved box, a small candelabra, and so forth."

"Poor dear," Irene said.

"Irene," Daniel said.

"What did you do?" Virgil said.

"Well, I moved to see what was the issue, what happened," she said. "As I got near the entry, I saw Netta as she came walking down the stairs."

"She see anything?" I said.

Bernice shook her head.

"I asked her what happened, and she said she did not know. She said she just heard the crash, too. Then out the open door, I saw him."

"You hear gunfire?" Virgil said.

She squinted at her hands in her lap then closed her eyes and shook her head.

"No," she said.

Virgil glanced to me.

"And where was James?" Virgil said.

"On the porch," she said.

"You saw him?" Virgil said. "That's when you saw James?"

She nodded and opened her eyes, looking at Virgil.

"He had his back to me. He was holding on to the post, at the top of the stairs. I called his name, but he did not turn to look to me. He just stumbled off down the stairs."

She stopped talking and stared blankly at nothing for a full minute doing her best not to cry. Then she met Virgil's eyes.

"I ran out after him," she said. "And he collapsed in the street. Right there in front of me."

"And that's when you saw the deputy?" Virgil said.

"Yes," she said. "I did not know he, the young Mexican man, was with law enforcement. I just asked . . . actually screamed at him to get the authorities. I was rather hysterical, I'm afraid."

"Well," Irene said. "My goodness, who would not be under those circumstances."

Virgil nodded, then glanced over to me.

"Is there anything else you remember," I said. "Was there anyone else around other than you and the deputy?"

"No," she said. "Well, there was Netta came out after me, behind me. But there was no one else even on the street until I began to yell at the young deputy to get help."

She looked to Daniel. He nodded.

"That is all I can tell you," she said. "Then I sent Netta to get Irene here, and the next thing I know is my husband was dead. Just dead there in the street."

"And no gunshot?" I said.

"No," she said.

"Where had he been?" Virgil said. "Where was he coming from?"

"He'd been with me at the office," Daniel said.

Bernice nodded.

"I expected him home. We had planned an early dinner and we were going to the theater after."

Virgil nodded, then turned to Daniel.

"What happens to James's portion?" Virgil said.

"Of our company assets?" Daniel said.

Virgil nodded.

"Well, they belong to Bernice," he said.

"So you and Bernice are now partners?" Virgil said.

"Well, yes," he said. "In a sense."

"What do you mean by that?" Virgil said. " 'In a sense'?"

"Well," he said. "I mean, Bernice will, of course, inherit James's portion of all our holdings, including the gold mine, but she would have no need to do anything. I can handle the work, and the profit will go to her as if it was James. She'll be taken care of in that respect."

"What would happen," Virgil said, "if something were to happen to you?"

"Well, my wife, Irene, would receive my portion," he said.

"And who would run the company?"

He shook his head.

"Well, I have in my will that they can carry on with the business as they see fit or they could liquidate. All assets could be sold off and the proceeds would be divided between them, Irene and Bernice. That is, if that was their choice."

Virgil smiled and nodded.

"Good enough," Virgil said.

Virgil gave a sharp nod and we got to our feet.

"Appreciate you taking the time," Virgil said.

"If we have any further questions," I said. "We'll get in touch with you."

Virgil moved to the door and I followed. He turned to the trio before opening the door.

"Do not talk to anyone about this," he said. "Nobody. The less others know, the better."

The three exchanged nods with each other.

"Of course, Marshal," Daniel said. "Of course."

The women nodded, too. Virgil opened the door and we left. We walked out past Lawrence and a handful of other young men who were busy shuffling papers. They all stopped their work to watch us as we exited.

38

After we left McCormick's place, Virgil and I walked a ways on Appaloosa Avenue before Virgil stopped and pulled a cigar from his pocket. He bit the tip, then fished a match. He lit the cigar, shook the match, then worked on making sure it was going good.

"What do you figure?" I said.

"Don't know. Don't make good sense."

"It doesn't. Not completely."

Virgil puffed on his cigar as we watched traffic.

"Think it's time to pay Baptiste a visit?" I said.

Virgil looked up to the Appaloosa Avenue sign above his head and nodded.

"We're here," he said.

We started toward the office of Henri Baptiste.

"For some reason it's hard to think James's murder was the work of the Bartholomew brothers," I said.

"Is," Virgil said.

"The motive and the pay would be there," I said. "But the way James died, seems like somebody else might have had a hand in it."

"Hard to say," Virgil said. "Baptiste could have hired someone else to do this."

"Or done it himself?" I said. "Or fucking Pritchard?"

Virgil nodded.

"Don't seem like the type to do it by themselves," he said. "Hire another killer, maybe, but not do the blood work. Everybody is capable, though."

"Obvious motive points to the gold," I said.

"If Daniel McCormick were to wake up dead," Virgil said, "and the mines were sold, Henri Baptiste would swoop in and have it all."

We walked a bit more, thinking.

"One thing for certain. If it was them, if the Bartholomew brothers did the killing," I said, "there is just one brother left for us to sort out about it."

"Yep," Virgil said.

"Might be the meaner of the two," I said.

"Might," Virgil said. "You offered to talk to Ventura instead of shooting him."

"You shot him first," I said.

"I did," Virgil said. "He pointed his pistol out the window at me."

"The fact that he reacted like he did," I said, "bodes well toward guilt, though."

"It does," Virgil said.

"Why else would they get out of the hotel like they did?" I said.

"The Bartholomew boys have been guilty and moving, and guilty and moving, since the day they was born," Virgil said. "Being quick to shoot and move goes with the territory."

"Don't imagine Victor will be none too happy to hear about his brother," I said.

"No," Virgil said. "He goddamn won't."

"But they were hired by Baptiste to do such things," I said. "Can't forget that."

"That's right," Virgil said. "Ventura killed them miners, sold their horses."

"What's your thoughts of how this murder happened?" I said.

"Don't goddamn know."

We walked without talking. We passed Allie's shop. It was still early, and Allie had yet to open up.

"So, James McCormick walks home from their office on Appaloosa Avenue, turns a few blocks this way and that," I said. "Gets shot on the way, I guess, before he gets home?"

"That's right," Virgil said. "And nobody hears the shot?"

"Then he comes up the stairs to his house," I said. "Enters the house and knocks over a bunch of stuff on the entrance table on his way in. Then stumbles out the front door."

"Or maybe he was inside and on his way out when it happened?" Virgil said.

We walked, thinking about that for a bit.

"Then he staggers and falls into the street and dies?" I said.

"What she said," Virgil said.

We were met at Henri Baptiste's office by one of Baptiste's young freckle-faced bookeepers. He told us Mr. Baptiste and Eugene Pritchard had left earlier that morning to spend the day at the gold mine.

By early afternoon Virgil and I saddled up and rode out to pay them a visit. There was a shortcut that riders took when traveling north in and out of Appaloosa, a tree-covered path that curved through a wooded valley. It crossed over a rocky rise before reconnecting to the main road. It was too narrow for wagon travel, but horsemen who knew about it always used it to save travel time.

When we came to the high point on the path and started down, we were met by three riders.

39

As we got closer it became clear that the riders were Edward Hodge and his two men. They were a good fifty yards in front of us, riding in our direction. Hodge stopped his big dun horse and his men did the same. The manner in which they stopped on the narrow path gave us the impression they might likely have notions of blocking us from passing.

We pulled to a stop.

"None other," Virgil said under his breath.

"Well, well," Hodge hollered.

Then he pulled a rifle from his scabbard and laid it across his lap.

"Don't look pleasant," I said.

"No," Virgil said, "they don't."

Hodge said something to his men and they pulled their rifles and laid them across their laps.

"Look who in the hell we got here," Hodge said loudly.

Virgil pulled his Winchester and rested it on his saddle horn. I pulled my eight-gauge from its scabbard and turned my horse slightly to the right. Then I put the barrels on the left side of my fork and pulled both hammers back.

Hodge nudged his horse closer. The two men flanking Hodge did the same.

"Imagine that," Hodge said.

We moved closer.

"What brings you fellas out this direction?" Hodge said.

"Be a good idea that you boys don't fuck around and get yourselves killed," Virgil said.

"We ain't fucking around," Hodge said.

"Good," Virgil said.

"Being out here," Hodge said, "makes things a little different, don't it?"

We continued slowly and moved closer yet. The whole time I kept my horse angled to the right.

"How so?" Virgil said.

Hodge laughed.

"For starters, the first thing is, there are three of us against two of you."

"Against?" Virgil said.

"Goddamn right, *against*. You got a problem with that?"

"Got no problem. Fact is you choosing to

238

get yourself and your friends killed or not, is more your problem."

"Listen to mighty Virgil Cole . . . I offered you our help."

"Don't need any help."

"I would not be too sure of that."

"Sure enough," Virgil said.

"These sumbitches have gone way too far and you know it."

"I know what I know."

"Well, that's real good," Hodge said.

"What's the other?" Virgil said.

"What's that?" Hodge said with a sneer.

"You said for starters, the first thing is, there is three of you and two of us," Virgil said. "What's the second thing?"

"Good to know you can count," Hodge said. "The second thing is we ain't within the town limits. In case you ain't noticed."

"There is not much not to notice about you," Virgil said.

"Oh, you think?"

"I do," Virgil said.

"Don't matter," Hodge said.

"It matters," Virgil said.

Hodge nodded to his rifle but left it lowered.

"Got no rules out here for us to follow, do ya?"

"Oh, there are rules," Virgil said.

Hodge and his men rode closer and we moved closer still. Now we were within pistol distance.

"Your rules?" Hodge said.

Virgil nodded.

"That's right."

Hodge smiled.

"I don't much care for you, Virgil Cole. Or your fucking rules."

"That's okay."

"Yes," Hodge said. "It damn sure is."

"But you'll do best not to test me," Virgil said.

"Just funnin'," Hodge said with a nasty grin, "Just funnin'."

"That right?" Virgil said.

Hodge smiled and turned to his men.

"Put your guns away."

The two sidekicks smirked and the three of them slid their rifles into their scabbards. Then Hodge moved closer and stopped. His men followed.

"No worry, though," Hodge said, focused on Virgil. "We will have our day."

Virgil said nothing. Hodge stared at him then moved his horse off the trail.

Virgil glanced at me and rode on. Once he was twenty feet behind Hodge and his men, he stopped and turned his horse to face me. Then I rode on.

Once I got to where Virgil sat his horse, I turned to face Hodge and his men, who had all turned their mounts slightly to face us. Hodge laughed but said nothing. Then he turned his horse and rode off, with his men following.

"Think he's right?" I said. "That you and him will have a day?"

"If he keeps it up," Virgil said. "I suspect so."

"In their heads, Baptiste has got a leg up in the tally," I said. "Baptiste has only lost the one Bartholomew hand who pulled on you. And McCormick's group has lost two workers and now James McCormick himself."

Virgil nodded.

"One thing for certain, Hodge is dead set on intimidating you," I said.

"He is," Virgil said.

"Think it's working?"

Virgil smiled.

"Not really," he said. "You?"

"No," I said.

We turned and continued on up the trail.

"They no doubt came out here looking for what's left of the Bartholomew clan that's not locked up," I said.

"They did," Virgil said.

"Think they found them?"

"I don't," Virgil said. "You?"

"No. For some reason, I don't either."

"They didn't seem satisfied," Virgil said.

"No, but they're damn sure gonna keep after it," I said. "Until they are satisfied."

"Or dead," Virgil said.

40

When we got to the mine we stopped short and sat our horses under a stand of white pine trees across from the office. We figured we'd observe the comings and goings, thinking we might see Victor Bartholomew. There was nobody but the miners moving about, though, going this way and that, doing their mining business.

"Guess that buggy there belongs to Baptiste," I said.

Virgil nodded.

"What say," Virgil said, "we go in and say hello."

We rode up to the side of the office. I pulled my eight-gauge out of its scabbard, and we dismounted.

Virgil and I entered. Eugene Pritchard was sitting at the big desk with his feet draped over the edge. The *Appaloosa Star* was held out in front of him. He peered at us over the paper. Then he laid it flat on the desk and leaned back in his chair. Henri was sitting in the chair opposite the desk. Their foreman, Frank Maxie, was in a corner chair, drinking a cup of coffee.

They did not seem to be too startled when we entered. It seemed as if they were expecting us.

"Well," Henri said. "Marshals."

"Look here," Eugene said.

Frank Maxie smiled.

"Virgil," he said with a nod. "Everett."

Virgil smiled at Frank.

"Wasn't too long ago," Henri said, "that we were paid a visit by the McCormick men."

"That right?" Virgil said.

"They were most unpleasant," Henri said.

"Don't think that is the word for them," Eugene said, with all the unfriendliness he could muster in his voice. "Good thing we have guards out here."

"What'd they visit you about?" Virgil said.

"As if you don't know," Eugene said.

"Tell me," Virgil said.

Eugene bristled. Henri nodded to the newspaper.

"We read about the account of James McCormick's passing in the newspaper," Henri said. "What on earth happened to him? It doesn't say there in the paper."

"And so we know goddamn good and well why you are here," Eugene said.

"Why?" Virgil said.

"Goddamn obvious, Cole," Eugene said harshly.

"Eugene," Henri said with a sharp look.

"Tell me," Virgil said.

"You got no right coming out here," Eugene said. "Acting like we are responsible for this."

"Responsible for what?" Virgil said.

"Tell you what," Eugene said, getting to his feet. "I will tell you like I told the others. Just turn your ass right around and go back to where you came from."

"Eugene, please," Henri said.

"Ever since I've been in Appaloosa you two have been full of yourselves. You don't scare me, Cole. And you neither, Hitch."

"You said you know why we are here?" Virgil said.

Eugene moved around the desk.

"Please, just hold on, Eugene," Henri said. "What can we help you with?"

Virgil smiled and glanced to me.

"Where were you yesterday afternoon?" I said.

"So he was murdered?" Henri said. "James McCormick was murdered. Is that it?"

"Where were you?" I said.

"None of your goddamn business," Eugene said.

"It is," I said.

"Bullshit," Eugene said.

"Where?" I said.

"Don't say anything," Eugene said. "We don't need to say a thing to you."

Henri raised his palm up to Pritchard.

"Please," Henri said. "We were in town yesterday."

"Leave it be," Eugene said. "That is enough."

"Both of us were in town," Henri said.

"And Victor Bartholomew?" Virgil said.

"I do not know," Henri said.

"You hired him," Virgil said, "and you don't know where he is?"

"No," Henri said. "I don't know where he is."

"That's enough, Henri," Eugene said.

"No, it's okay," Henri said. "Look, we needed protection, not trouble. And what happened with his men at the Boston House, getting arrested, was not part of our agreement."

"I asked you before," Virgil said, "about Victor's brother and you said you did not know him, know about him."

"And I did not," Henri said. "Not when

246

we spoke. He was not with Victor and the others when we hired them. I don't know much about him other than Victor demanded I pay him, too. Which I did."

"Henri," Eugene said.

It was clear Eugene Pritchard was boiling up.

"They've wanted to do things their way," Henri said. "And that is not acceptable."

"How not acceptable?" Virgil said.

"You don't need to tell them anything more," Eugene said.

"I wanted the Bartholomews to forget our business," Henri said. "But they seem to have a mind of their own. I wanted them to move on. But they insisted they stay and do what they were hired to do. So I acquiesced and agreed they continue."

"And you don't know where they are?"

Of course, we had inside information on Ventura's whereabouts. We knew he'd moved on for good, but had no need to show our hand to Baptiste.

"Not at this time," Henri said. "No."

Virgil nodded.

"There anybody to vouch for you?" Virgil said. "Where were you two yesterday afternoon?"

"Vouch!" Eugene said.

In a huff, he came charging around the

desk as if he were going to do something he should not. "Vouch for us?" he said. "Get the fuck out of this office, now!"

He was red-faced and shaking his fist toward Virgil, who did not flinch. Easily and without much effort I stopped Eugene's forward movement. I jabbed the butt of my eight-gauge hard into Eugene's belly.

"No," Henri said. *"My God."*

Eugene coughed, then doubled over and dropped to his knees. Frank stood up and I turned the double barrels of my big gun toward him.

"Hold on. I got nothing to goddamn do with nothing, Everett," Frank said. "I just do like I told you before, I take care of the men here and the rock they break. That is it."

Eugene stayed down on his knees, trying to catch his breath. He put one hand on the corner of the desk to stabilize himself. He glared up at me.

"Goddamn you," he said. "Coming in here, acting all . . ."

"Stop," Henri said.

"Don't say nothing more to them," Eugene said. "We got nothing to do with James McCormick."

"We for sure have people to vouch for us," Henri said. "Indeed we do. You can check.

Eugene was in the office, going over books with our other accountants."

"And you?"

"I was at the Appaloosa Theater," Henri said.

"Doing?" Virgil said.

"I was there in one of the dressing rooms. Backstage."

"Doing?" I said.

"Visiting an actress," Henri said. "A lovely actress."

Virgil looked at me, but I didn't meet his eye.

41

The kid rode with the teamster in the long buckboard. He was impressed at how well the man worked the team. His gee and haw commands were effortless. He drove the mules without the crack of a whip. They traveled a well-rutted road for ten miles or so until they came to a huge Bessemer steel outfit by the river.

There they picked up the sticks of pipe, then headed for town. It was a rough ride, but it was pleasant enough, the kid thought. They talked about all kinds of subjects on the journey. The teamster carried on about the loads he carried and the mules. They talked about the teamster's days in the Army and about horses and about the weather. They talked a lot about gambling. They carried on about the nuances of playing seven-up and faro and three-card, and stiff-arming dice. They'd been traveling for the whole day. And they talked about all kinds of things, except for something that was gnawing at the kid. So he figured he'd bring it up.

"So, I've been wanting to ask you something."

"What's keeping you?"

"Nothing, I reckon."

"So ask."

"You don't have no problem with me, do you?" the kid said.

"What kind of problem?" the teamster said.

"Well, I don't got to point it out, do I?"

"You mean you sleeping with my wife?"

"Something like that," the kid said. "Yeah."

"You didn't have any problem with it, did you?" the teamster said. "With her?"

"Problem?"

"Yeah?"

"Well, no. But . . ."

"You liked it, didn't you?"

"Well . . . yeah. I mean . . ."

"That's good," the teamster said.

"How could I not?"

The teamster laughed. But the kid could not tell just where the laughter was coming from.

"She took a liking to you," the teamster said.

"I just never. Well, I never had no man's wife ask me to do such thing," the kid said. "Not with the husband right there next to me noways."

"You're not complaining, are you?"

"Complaining? Hell, no. I'm just . . ."

"What?" the teamster said.

"Just a . . . wondering how you feel about it."

"I didn't throw a shoe, did I?"

"No."

"If it bothered me, I'd let you know."

"It don't?"

"She knows things I don't. See's things I don't see," the teamster said. "She's special."

"I'll say."

"There is no beginning and no end to her."

The kid thought about that.

"I think I know what you are saying."

"Like she came down from the stars," the teamster said with a slight laugh.

"Where did she come from?"

"I found her in Death Valley."

"Doing what?"

"She was young, her father had been recently killed, and she was left with a group of crazy gypsies. She was in a wagon train with a string of them, the gypsies there in the Borax Flats. After a few nights together, she told the others she was staying with me. That was that."

"And you married her?"

"You could say that," he said. "She married me. Been five years thereabout. She likes that I don't take bullshit. Likes that I can take care of her, see to it she is free to be the woman she needs to be."

"This sort of thing happen often?" the kid said. "Like with me, last night?"

"No," the teamster said.

They rode in silence.

"But it's happened before?"

"No," the teamster said. "As a matter of fact. You're the first."

The kid stared at the teamster. The teamster met his eyes. He stared hard at the kid with a serious expression.

The kid was unsure. Then he noticed a slight grin and realized the teamster was ribbing him. The teamster laughed and the kid joined him in the laughter.

After the teamster and the kid dropped off the load of pipe in the city's construction yard, they continued on, traveling west as the sun set.

It was early evening when they approached the town. The kid felt a sensation he'd never felt before as they got closer. He was excited, thinking this would one day soon be his home. He whistled through his teeth when he saw the glow of lights in the distance.

"Hot damn," he said. "Is that it?"

"Yep," the teamster said. "There she be."

The kid was fighting back his emotions. Tears were coming up, hankering to spring from his eyes.

"I'll be damned," the kid said. "Appaloosa."

Two riders came out of a path to the right and rode up just behind the buckboard. They were riding at a pace and in no time moved around it. They were handsome, rugged-looking men on fine-looking horses with shiny oiled tack. One of them was dressed in a black suit and vest with a crisp white shirt and a ridged brimmed black hat. He had a bone-handled Colt showing under his coat. The other was wearing matching shades of dark greens. He had a wide hat with a curled brim and high military-style boots that were polished. As they came alongside of the buckboard, they gave the kid and the teamster the once-over. They both had that kind of penetrating eyes. The kid knew the look. So did the teamster. Though they could not see badges, it was clear to the kid and the teamster that the riders were lawmen. One of them, the man in the shades-of-green clothing, nodded and tipped his hat a little as they passed. The kid noticed the tall butt of a huge nickel-plated shotgun sticking out of his scabbard. It appeared bigger than the average shotgun, bigger than a twelve-gauge, the kid thought, bigger than a ten-gauge even. After the two men passed, the teamster and the kid watched them as they moved on up the road, distancing themselves from the buckboard. The kid shook his head.

"That might have been a goddamn eight-gauge in that Johnny lawman's scabbard," the kid said.

42

It was her night off performing Evangeline, and Martha Kathryn and I were invited to dinner at Virgil and Allie's house. As arranged by Allie, I stopped by the Hotel Windsor to escort Martha Kathryn. When I knocked on her room door, I was not displeased to see she had yet to dress.

"Hello," I said.

"Well, hello to you."

"You want me to wait downstairs?"

"Why?"

"So you can dress," I said.

"Are you shy?" she said.

"A little."

"Why do I get the feeling you have never been shy about anything?" she said.

"Don't know," I said.

"Perhaps it's because it's never happened."

"Perhaps."

"Or . . . Maybe it's because you are only

accustomed to watching women *undress*?"

I nodded.

"Maybe," I said.

She smiled and pulled me into the room. She closed the door and pushed me up against it. Then she kissed me. It was a sweet, full kiss. With meaning and intention, she kissed me long and hard. But then she pulled away and did a pirouette in the room, which made her robe flair, showing her long legs.

"But," she said, "not for the time being."

"No?"

"No, for the time being, I will dress."

"Okay," I said.

"You're not disappointed?"

I smiled.

"I am disappointed."

"Good," she said with a giggle. "Good."

"You want me to suffer?"

"I do," she said.

Then she let the robe fall to the floor. She stood there with her arms covering certain locations on her naked body, shyly feigning modesty.

"How do you feel?"

"Suffering."

"Yes. Good, Everett. But we of course don't want to be late, do we?"

"Of course not," I said.

She took a few sensual strides toward me with that look in her eye and smiled.

"It just would not be appropriate," she said.

"I agree."

"Good," she said. Then she laughed, turned, and opened the armoire. She pulled out a blue satin dress.

"It's the actress in me," she said. "Punctuality is the key, timing is everything."

"I won't disagree with you there," I said.

"No?"

"No," I said.

She held the dress in front of her.

"What do you think?"

"Nice," I said.

"Glad you like it," she said as she checked it out in the mirror.

"Look better on the floor," I said.

She smiled, walked to me, and kissed me again.

"I shall dress," she said.

I bowed, then took a seat in the corner chair and watched her. Once she was properly attired, it was everything I could do not to reverse the course of the action. She fitted her silk hat above her hair, then turned and smiled.

"Like to ask you something," I said.

"Okay," she said.

"Henri Baptiste?" I said.

She paused as she adjusted her hat in the mirror.

"What about him?"

"When did you last see him?"

She turned and cocked her head.

"Why?"

"I just need to know."

"You're jealous?"

"We already covered that territory," I said.

"Seems like we're on it again," she said.

"No," I said. "Just business."

"Business?"

"Yes."

"Really?" she said.

I nodded.

"Really."

"He came to the theater."

"When?"

"Yesterday."

"To see the show?" I said.

"Yes."

"Did you see him before the show?"

"Yes. He stopped by my dressing room, prior to curtain."

"For?"

She stared at me.

"He brought me some flowers."

"And after?"

"I did not see him after. I had a late dinner with my cast. Why?"

"I can and will explain at some point. I just needed to know. Nothing personal."

"Business?" she said.

"It is," I said.

She walked up to me eye to eye. Then she leaned in and kissed me.

"Shall we?" she said.

I nodded.

"Let's," I said.

And we were out the door. We walked without talking for a few blocks. The night was warm and we moved along at an easy pace, her arm in mine.

"You know, Everett, as much as I like you — and you know I do — you must know that I do have admirers."

"I would be surprised if you didn't."

"But," she said. "In seriousness considered, I could get used to this, Everett Hitch."

"Used to what?"

"Do I need to spell it out for you?"

"Are you proposing?" I said.

She walked for a ways, smiling.

"But I'm a vagabond," she said.

"With admirers," I said.

"A few thousand," she said. "But a vagabond."

"Oh," I said. "Well, you do have a profession."

"You know what I mean," she said. "I'm all over."

"Everybody has to be someplace," I said.

"Are you intentionally making it easy?"

"Let me think about that," I said.

"Are you?"

"Maybe I am."

She smiled and squeezed my arm.

"We do what we do," I said.

"That is true," she said. "But everything has a beginning and an end."

We thought about that as we walked. We both realized that comment could easily fit into a start or a finish.

43

Since Appaloosa had been on a constant growing spree, more and more money was being made. It seemed everyone who was doing well and getting ahead had extra help around the house. Virgil and Allie were no exception.

Effie, Allie's housemaid, opened the door when Martha Kathryn and I arrived. Her eyes lit up.

"Come in this house, Mr. Everett."

She smiled wide at Martha Kathryn with her fists planted on her round hips.

"And just lookie here," she said.

"This is Martha Kathryn," I said.

"Well, of course she is. Come in. Come in."

Effie closed the door behind us and circled Martha Kathryn like a buyer studying her confirmation.

"Just look at you."

"Martha Kathryn," I said. "This is Effie."

"How do you do," Martha Kathryn said.

"Miss Allie was not making up nothing," Effie said. "When she go telling me about you. You as perdy as they come."

"Thank you, Effie," Martha Kathryn said. "But I'm afraid you are mistaken."

"How so?"

"You're the one that is as pretty as they come."

Effie grinned wide.

"Well, listen to you," Effie said. "You hear that, Mr. Everett. We got three perdy ladies in this here house."

"Obvious as the day is long, Effie," I said.

Effie, a seasoned housemaid with a personality bigger than a circus, was as round as she was tall. Ever since the demands of Allie's dress-shop business, Allie had little time to take care of chores around the place, and Effie was now in charge of the house. And she let everybody know about it. Including Virgil.

"Let me get your hat and shawl," Effie said as she helped Martha Kathryn with her removal.

Effie took care of everything from fetching groceries to cleaning, cooking, and laundry. Since she had been working with Virgil and Allie, I don't think I'd seen Virgil without his suit and shirt cleaned and pressed and his boots polished.

She had no problem speaking her mind, either, and she did so often. She was originally from the south of Georgia, and though she was a slave in her younger days, she had been a freedwoman most of her life.

She was always with a smile and spent most of her waking hours talking. And though Virgil didn't appreciate her constant babbling, he was happy for her cooking, which was far more accomplished than Allie's.

But Allie's cooking was way better than it used to be. Partly because of the Appaloosa ladies' social, an organization Allie helped found. The social was good at providing recipes, and for the most part Allie had grown accustomed to following them.

"Well, hello," Allie said as she came out of the kitchen.

"Allie," Martha Kathryn said. "What a lovely home."

"Why, thank you," she said. "So happy you are here."

"My pleasure."

Allie was wearing an apron. And like normal when she was cooking, she was covered with remnants of what she was working on.

"Something smells good," I said.

"Roast," Allie said.

"Yum," Martha Kathryn said. "I'm famished."

"Where's Virgil?" I said.

"Out in his shed," Allie said. "Where else."

"What can I do to help you?" Martha Kathryn said.

"Not a thing," Allie said.

"She said the same to me, Martha Kathryn," Effie said. "Normally I do the cooking, but . . ."

"I insisted," Allie said, "and let's hope we don't all regret it."

"I'll leave you folks to your carryings-on," Effie said. "If you need anything, just holler, Miss Allie." She turned to Martha Kathryn. "A sure enough pleasure."

"All mine," Martha Kathryn said.

Effie smiled and started away.

"Everett," she said, "you might oughta get yourself a ladder and a faster horse to keep up with this one."

Effie turned the corner and was gone.

"How 'bout a drink?" Allie said as she moved to the hutch behind the dining table. "Wine, Kentucky whiskey, brandy."

"Whiskey," Martha Kathryn said with a childish grin.

"Everett?"

"I'll have the same."

Allie poured us a drink, and after we toasted I walked out back to find Virgil.

"What are you doing out here, Virgil?"

He was sitting on a tall stool at the far end of the shed, smoking a cigar. The smoke was drifting up into the light of a lamp hanging overhead.

"Thinking."

"About?"

"Doc Burris stopped by earlier."

"And?"

"James McCormick was not shot."

"What happened to him?"

"He was stabbed," Virgil said.

"Stabbed?"

"Yep."

"Goddamn," I said.

Virgil nodded.

"Ice pick, he figured, or the end tine of a pitchfork, or some other sharp instrument."

"What do you make of that?"

"Don't know."

I shook my head, thinking about it.

"That ain't all," Virgil said.

"What?"

"Doc wasn't real sure, but he thinks he also might have been poisoned."

"Might?"

Virgil nodded.

"What would make him sure?"

"He said he was going to do some testing in the morning and he'd let us know."

"Son of a bitch," I said.

Virgil nodded.

"Yep."

44

They drank some beer. That was the first order of things. Once they got a good bellyful, the kid and the teamster wandered the streets on the north end of town. The kid had never seen so many whores in one place. They went from brothel to brothel. Some had dirt floors and some were fancy, with velvet furniture. A few places, the nicer, more elegant establishments — the ones west of First Street — tossed them out before they could get across the threshold.

They were not looking for her, though. They were only seeing all there was to see. The teamster wanted the kid to get a good lay of the land.

The kid did not think about coming face-to-face with her. Not here in this part of town. But it crossed his mind for sure. What if she was a whore? *She could be,* he thought. *She very well could be.* He laughed to himself. He figured he would have to be careful what woman he might spend his earnings on. Wouldn't that be something, he thought, to bed down with his mother?

But they were looking, not sampling. For the time being, they were on a reconnaissance mission. That is what the teamster called it. He said they were going about things under the looking-around rule and not the whoring rule of business. It was all a carnival to the kid, complete with Indian whores in the dirtier places and fancy painted women in the places with draperies and tablecloths and furniture. The kid was fascinated. He felt as though he'd entered another world. That he'd crossed a line into another place in time and there was no going back.

They stopped at an open saloon. There were no walls or tent coverings. It was a board atop two barrels, where two wide-chested men served cheap beer in tin mugs. That was it.

They got beers and sat on a bench. The kid rolled a cigarette and lit it. They watched and talked about the different characters passing by as they drank beer. The kid was feeling the alcohol. It made him feel warm and he was happy. But he was also edgy, blunt, and direct.

"Hi," he said to an older cowhand walking by.

"Howdy," the cowhand said as he passed,

tipping his hat to the kid.

The kid was feeling his oats. Even though he'd been in town only a short time. He felt like for some odd reason he was accepted here, and that was something he had not really experienced before.

The kid shook his head.

"Hell," he said. "I might not even ever find her."

The teamster wiped the beer froth from his mouth with the back of his hand and eyed the kid.

"Wasn't that long ago," the kid said, "that I never, ever even, thought about her. Never even knew about her."

"You might not," the teamster said.

"Good chance of it," the kid said. "That I won't find her. Not ever."

"Lot of goddamn people in this town," the teamster said.

The kid nodded.

"Might not even be here," the kid said.

"Might not," the teamster said.

The kid smoked his cigarette as he thought.

"You might not want to find her," the teamster said. "You ever think about that?"

"Yeah, I thought of that," the kid said. "What if she is a goddamn whore?"

The teamster shrugged.

"Everybody has to do what they have to do," he said.

They drank their beer in silence for a minute. Then the kid belched loud.

"You ever get to Mexico City?" the kid said.

"No."

"Me neither," the kid said. "Always wanted to. Been meaning to, but just never did. A long way down."

The teamster nodded.

"This place is big enough for me," he said.

"Never seen nothing like it," the kid said.

"I'll give you that," the teamster said.

"I like it," the kid said.

"This is just the north side," the teamster said. "We'll go south later, I'll show you."

"What's that way?"

"You didn't think this place was just this, did you? Whores and beer and whiskey and cards?"

The kid laughed.

"No. I reckon not."

"This up here on the north side is what I call the doing part of town. The south is the thinking part of town."

The teamster nodded, then took a pull of his beer.

"I have a place there in the south where we can stay, good bedding," the teamster said as he stood up. "But let's right now find us a good

271

game of chance. How about it?"

That is what the teamster was looking for. That is what the rule of the moment called for. The kid stood.

"How about it?" the kid said with a skip in his step.

On the far reaches of town, they settled into a lively card parlor that had dice walls, faro tables, and bowling lanes. There were long pits out back where a boisterous crowd of miners, cowboys, and city workers gathered, throwing horseshoes. And everybody was drinking and most were drunk.

Inside, they found an open game. They played five-card with some easy fellows who thought they were good players. But the teamster and the kid had a system and took them for all that they had.

They went out and walked the streets some more. A few shadow teams of no-goods were hanging about here and there. The teamster and the kid came across three fellas who appeared rough and unsavory, fellas who might want to jump them, try to rob them.

But walking with the teamster was like having a canon by his side, the kid thought. On his own, the kid had always needed to be cautious with the shadows and alleys he'd enter. But there were no worries with the teamster. The teamster made most men back up a little, if not a lot.

The teamster and the kid were drunk. It was getting late by the time they got to the south section of town. They searched for a saloon, but the ones that were open refused to serve him. The kid knocked on the door of one closed saloon, and the man on the inside yelled at him to go away before he called the police and had him locked up.

Then everything became a blur. The kid realized he was alone, that he'd lost the teamster. The last thing the kid remembered was the gnaw of hunger, and then eating something.

Things now were spinning. Then he sat up. He was glad to see the teamster sleeping in the bunk next to him. But he was in a place he did not remember getting to. And now he needed to move. Quickly.

He pushed out through a door and was in the street. He stumbled and fell off the edge of the boardwalk and lost what food and slosh he had in his gut. The food he'd eaten exploded out with a load of rancid beer. He heaved and heaved until there was nothing else to vomit. After some time on all fours, he rolled onto his back and closed his eyes. When he opened his eyes. Rising above a building across the street was the blurry image of something familiar. He lifted his head, focusing.

It was the clock tower from his dream.

He was sure of it.

And it was midnight.

45

Allie's dinner turned out to be better than good. Her roast was tender and cooked perfectly. After, Virgil, Allie, Martha Kathryn, and I enjoyed a lemon cake that Allie made. It, too, was good, even if it was chewy. We'd spent the evening around the dinner table talking about a little bit of everything. Including Allie's interrogation into Martha Kathryn's adventures. Martha Kathryn was happy to expound on her life and times and on her wayfaring. She described what life was like as an actress on the road, the training, the shows she had been in, and the actors she had worked with. It was only when Allie asked what Martha Kathryn's early family life was like that Martha Kathryn felt the need to change the direction of the conversation. "Enough about me," she said, and she turned the direction of the talk to Allie and her history. But that line of interrogation was also

275

derailed. Allie insisted her story was boring and lacked the color and adventures of Martha Kathryn's. That statement prompted Virgil to glance in my direction and smile.

For the most part, we had avoided a discussion about the death of James McCormick. Allie brought it up once, saying it was odd that a man of his age just dropped dead in the street. But Virgil shortened the notion of the conversation by suggesting it wasn't an appropriate discussion to be having over such a delicious dinner.

Later, the four of us sat in the living room, playing dominoes well past midnight. And after we were close to polishing off the Kentucky whiskey, Allie felt the need to reengage Virgil on the subject of James McCormick's death. And though it was late, and Allie was feeling the effects of the Kentucky, she did her best to give the topic of James McCormick's passing a sensitive and delicate approach.

"It was nice to see Dr. Burris this afternoon," Allie said.

Virgil glanced at me.

"It was," Virgil said.

Allie stayed focused on the dominoes.

"Though brief as it was," she said.

Virgil nodded.

"What was it he wanted?"

"He didn't want anything," Virgil said.

Allie thought a second, placed a domino, then smiled at Virgil.

"Well, why was he here?"

"Just a friendly visit."

"Not a business visit?"

"Friendly with an inch of business, nothing else," Virgil said.

"What kind of inch of business?"

"Legal business."

Allie smiled at Martha Kathryn.

"Virgil's stonewalling me."

Virgil hesitated before he spoke.

"Not stonewalling you, Allie."

"Does Doc's visit have to do with James McCormick?"

Virgil studied the dominoes as if he didn't hear her.

"Virgil?"

"I hear you, Allie."

"You can't stonewall me forever, Virgil."

"Allie," he said.

"I don't interfere with your business, Virgil," she said. "You know that."

Virgil nodded.

"That's true," he said, "you do not. For the most part."

"But this is different."

"It's not."

"Oh, but it is."

"Law work, legal business is boring, you know that, Allie."

"And you know that I'm very respectful of your legal business, Virgil."

"And I appreciate it, Allie."

"But. You know, Virgil. I know Bernice McCormick."

"I know you do."

"You know that she's a member of our social."

"I know."

"And you know that she has pitched in, financially, with Appaloosa Days."

"Yes, and that is good."

"Which, I might add, the event is right around the corner."

"I know."

"She's new to the social. And I would like to at the very least let her know that we care for her, that we are here for her. I can't be so crass to hope this . . . this tragedy won't be a damper on the event."

Virgil was doing his best to keep Allie from carrying on, but he was running out of options.

"I understand," he said.

"So I don't know why you don't want me to pay her a visit yet."

Virgil leaned back in his chair.

"Don't think that is a good idea."

"But why?"

"Just 'cause."

" 'Cause there is an investigation going on right now?" she said.

Virgil looked to me.

"I knew it," she said.

"Well, we don't know all the facts about what has happened is all, Allie."

"You haven't even told me how he died."

Virgil swiveled in his chair and crossed his arms.

"Help me out here, Everett," Virgil said.

"He was murdered," I said.

"Oh my God," Allie said. "Sweet Jesus. I knew it. He was too young to drop dead in the street of a heart attack or some such."

"My goodness," Martha Kathryn said.

I nodded.

"Appaloosa is not without its own brand of drama," Martha Kathryn said.

"Murdered?" Allie said. "By who?"

"We don't know all the details regarding his death," I said.

"But he was murdered?" Allie said.

"And until we do know the details," Virgil said, "we have to treat everyone as a suspect."

I nodded.

"Including Bernice?" Allie said.

"Nobody is excluded," Virgil said.

"Well, my word," Allie said with a scoff. "Surely beautiful Bernice is not a suspect?"

"We don't know who did this, Allie," Virgil said.

"Beautiful or not," I said.

"We need to be quiet about this until we know more," Virgil said. "That is all."

"Well, it has to be the bad men, the gunmen, the men we saw in the Boston House, of course. Don't you think?" Allie said. "And this all started with the two McCormick miners who were missing. And now this."

"In a situation like this, Allie," I said, "we have to be careful not to jump to conclusions."

Virgil nodded.

"Not until we know what is what," he said.

Allie was wide-eyed.

"We will get to the bottom of it," I said. "Rest assured."

"The gold," Allie said.

Martha Kathryn cut her eyes to me.

"This," she said. "The questioning earlier?"

I nodded.

She shook her head.

"Just need to keep this quiet, Allie," Virgil said. "Last thing we need is to have the ladies' social talking about this all over town. Just move forward with your Appaloosa Days and let us do our job."

"Gold makes people do things they otherwise might not do," Martha Kathryn said.

"Does," Virgil said.

46

The whole trip home the kid was sick to his stomach. Along the journey he had to ask the teamster to stop a few times so he could puke. It'd been only in the last few hours that he was beginning to feel better. But as they neared the house, the kid was alarmed by the sound of gunshots.

"Son of a bitch," he said.

"It's okay," the teamster said.

But the kid whipped around and grabbed his Winchester from behind the seat of the buckboard.

"It's nothing," the teamster said.

"What?" the kid said as more shots rang out.

"It's her."

"What? What do you mean, 'it's her'?" the kid said as he chambered a round in his rifle.

"It's my wife," he said.

"What?"

"Gunfire. Shooting guns is normal around our place."

"Shooting what?"

"She's likely sighting in a long rifle."

The kid sat back, resting his Winchester in his lap.

"She collects and trades all kinds of fire-arms," the teamster said. "And shoots them. Constantly. Part of her universe."

When they rounded the corner and the homestead was in sight, the teamster pointed to a hill behind the house.

"There she is."

More rifle reports echoed. And puffs of gun smoke kicked up from where a figure was positioned. As they got closer, it was clear to the kid that it was the teamster's wife shoot-ing the rifle. Her dark skin was glowing with sweat and it was shiny in the late-afternoon sun.

"Guns are a big part of her life."

The kid just watched but said nothing as they neared the house and she continued to fire.

"Like most things she touches," the teamster said. "She's good with them."

The kid thought about that. Thinking about her touching things and being good with what she touched.

"Mostly rifles," the teamster said.

The kid just stared up at her.

"She has a dead eye," the teamster said.

"She's fond of shooting. She picked up an old Sharps rifle at an auction the other day. Looks like she's sighting it in on horse apples. But she prefers moving targets."

"I'll be damned," the kid said.

"She likes keeping her skills sharp. She says you never know when they might come in handy."

"Handy for what?"

"Fuck if I know."

The teamster pulled the buckboard to a stop near the barn. They sat and watched her.

"Never seen no woman wise on guns," the kid said.

"There's one right there," the teamster said with a laugh as he jumped down from the buckboard.

"She has passions, they run deep in her."

"Don't I know," the kid said.

"You don't know the half of it," the teamster said. "She has her clothes, and her foods, and her oils, and her potions. She concocts different types of potions."

"What kind of potions?"

"She makes different kinds that do different things. Some are calming, some curing kinds. Most all of them are potions that alter your perspective."

"Perspective?"

"Your outlook, your angle on things."

"Oh, yeah," the kid said. "I know about that kind of loco stuff."

"You do?"

"I come on a Mexican witch doctor's camp near Juárez where they did that sort of thing."

"You did it?"

"Not myself," the kid said. "But I seen folks crying and laughing there. Some running around like chickens with their heads cut off. All the time talking to things that don't talk back. Heard about people trying to fly and end up dying. Run right off the side of a cliff."

"She says it's to keep you from getting too comfortable with yourself."

"What's that mean?"

"Hell if I know."

"You do it?"

The teamster scoffed.

"No, never. She said I did not need it. Wasn't right for it. Said I was already uncomfortable with myself enough."

"Maybe she thought you might want to fly?"

The teamster nodded and chuckled.

"Maybe," the teamster said. "May . . . be."

The kid remained seated, watching her.

"She likes weapons way better than people, I can tell you that," the teamster said. "She appreciates the fact weapons have a point."

She stopped shooting when she saw them. She held her hand over her eyes, blocking the sun's glare.

The kid waved but felt foolish for doing so. He glanced at the teamster to see if he had noticed.

But the teamster was busy with his mules. When the kid turned to her again, she was on the move, working her way down from where she had been perched. The kid watched her. The manner in which she was moving, quickly and surefooted, with her dark skin and her dark hair blowing in the wind, made him think of an Indian brave.

After the kid and the teamster got the rigging and the mules squared away, they walked toward the house.

The teamster's wife stood over a washbasin on the front porch, washing the dress that she had been wearing. She looked naked. Her thin white underwear clung to her sweaty body. She finished scrubbing her dress as we walked up. The teamster moved up behind her and kissed her neck. She turned to him and kissed him back. Then she proceeded to hang the dress on a clothesline that was tethered from the porch to a post near the garden.

"You haven't been doing much shooting of late," he said.

"I was in need," she said. "I felt it was time."

"I was telling him about your shooting. About your guns."

The kid nodded.

"Said you were a dead eye," he said.

She turned from the clothesline with her full body facing him.

"Said you liked your guns better than people."

She stared at the teamster.

"They do not lie," she said.

She picked up the Sharps that was leaning against the porch post. Then moved closer toward the kid.

"This is a truth," she said as she looked to the rifle in her hand. "Guns have no-nonsense."

Then she turned, with the rifle barrel angled toward the teamster.

"There is nothing unclear about a gun," she said.

The teamster smiled.

"They have no bullshit," she said, "and no fat. No unimportant or unnecessary moving parts."

The kid looked back and forth between the teamster and his wife as she continued to speak.

"And if used correctly," she said, "they provide a desired end result, a final outcome that's a function of their design."

She raised the rifle up, pointed it at the teamster.

The kid took a nervous short step.

"Um . . ." he said.

But she continued and raised the rifle and pointed it to the teamster's head.

"They have a particular point of their purpose," she said.

The teamster smiled. Unafraid. Then cut his eyes to the kid.

"But there is a point when they are completely worthless," the teamster said.

Then he looked to his wife again, who held the gun pointed at his head.

"Without ammunition," the teamster said with a smile. "They are completely worthless. Isn't that so?"

She stared at him, unsmiling, and pulled the trigger.

47

Virgil and I were on the porch of the sheriff's office with Book, Skeeter, Lloyd, and two of the newer deputies. Summer bugs were more active than they'd been in the last few evenings. The warmth of the day was lingering later than it had been, keeping the moths and late june bugs active. They were swirling around the sconces on both sides of the door to the office. The lamps inside also had swirls of bugs and flies enjoying the light and the heat.

Virgil leaned on the post just in front of the office door, looking out into the street as he smoked a cigar.

As usual, we were listening to one of Lloyd's stories. This one was about a run-in he had in the Indian Territory with the Cherokee outlaw Ned Christie.

"We chased him all over the goddamn place. Up across the Red and the Arkansas River, right up through the Choctaw coun-

289

try. Then followed him north right into Cherokee land. It was just about midmorning when we come upon him. Same time of year as this — August, it was. It was hotter than a witch's teat. We was weeks following the sonofabitch. And now we closed in on him, we had Ned in the palm of our hand. And we chased him over a goddam lil' ol' rise on the horizon just in front of us. We had the sonofabitch! Had him. And then we come over that rise and we saw him. He was stopped and facing us. He rode right into the middle of thousands of Indians. It was like he wired ahead to have every Indian in the Indian Territory gathered up there to scare us off."

The deputies were all staring at him, wide-eyed.

"No shit," Lloyd said. "Spread out in front of us was a wall of Indians as far as the eye could see. There we were, facing what seemed like every Indian that was ever fucking born. There was twelve of us. And we was looking at a goddamn red sea."

"What did you do?" Skeeter said.

"Well," Lloyd said, "we by God knew right fast that we had no goddamn business being there."

Lloyd paused as he took a sip of coffee. The deputies were hanging on his words.

"So what happened?" Book said.

"Well," he said. "Needless to say. We were scared off. We smiled and slowly and very quietly turned and moved away. And when we got below the rise, out of their sight, we fucking run off as fast as we could goddamn gallop those tired horses."

"You vamoosed?" Skeeter said.

"Vamoosed like a bunch of goddamn barefoot kids that just poked a fucking hornet's nest with a stick," Lloyd said. "Never even took a gander behind us for fear I might wet my saddle. We ran like hell."

"And?" Book said.

"Well," Lloyd said. "I don't know, we likely gave them a good laugh, is about all that happened."

"What's funny about that?" Skeeter said.

"Texas Rangers, running," Lloyd said. "If that ain't funny, I don't know what is."

"Where did you run to?" Skeeter said.

"Texas," Lloyd said with a scoff. "Where all big, bad Texans hide, where else?"

Virgil glanced to me and smiled.

"Hell. Just being alive is laughable," Lloyd said. "I look back on so much that we did. Hell, I'm lucky to be sitting here on this porch and talking about it. Instead of being up there and looking down on it."

"Up? Cielo? Looking down? Infierno?"

Skeeter said with a wide grin. "From all we have heard you would be down in Infierno and be looking up to Cielo?"

"You ain't too old for me to put you across my lap," Lloyd said. "And give you a whippin'."

"Like to see you try," Skeeter said, then laughed and moved off the porch and out of Lloyd's reach.

Virgil turned as he took a pull on his cigar. He blew out a roll of smoke, then focused on Lloyd and me sitting on the bench in front of the office window.

"I been thinking," he said.

"About?" I said.

"About those gun hands," Virgil said. "Locked up in there."

I glanced over my shoulder toward the jail.

"You want 'em out?" I said.

Virgil nodded.

"All of them?" I said. "Baptiste hands and the McCormick hands?"

"Yep," Virgil said.

"You don't want them to face the judge?" Lloyd said.

Virgil puffed on his cigar and shook his head.

"Nope," Virgil said. "Don't think there is much that they can be held for. Firearms will be a fine, and they have already spent enough days against the fine."

"Nothing for them to be convicted for, really," I said. "Maybe Noah Miller for facing you in the Boston House. But fact is, not likely, though, because he never touched his pistol. And neither did the McCormick hands I locked up."

"But keeping them behind bars does keep the hostile bullshit between the miners at bay," Lloyd said.

Virgil nodded.

"Does," Virgil said. "And I'm not sure that is a good thing."

"You thinking maybe the quicker all this comes to a head, the better," Lloyd said.

"That'd be my thinking," Virgil said.

"Can't really force them to leave town, can you," Lloyd said. "Seeing how they did time and are let go."

"We can ask them polite-like," I said.

"We can," Virgil said. "But they will stay as long as there is pay."

"That what you want to do?" Lloyd said.

Virgil blew out a roll of smoke and nodded to Lloyd.

"Now?" Lloyd said.

Virgil nodded.

"Now," Virgil said. "Speed the plow."

48

"You thought she was gonna fucking kill me, didn't you?" the teamster said with a laugh.

"Well, hell," the kid said.

"You did," the teamster said.

There had been no talk about the Sharps incident during the dinner. Again the kid ate foods like he'd never experienced. Spicy things. Hotter than the chilies in Mexican foods he was fond of. After the table was cleared the teamster and the kid settled into the outside chairs in front of the house and smoked cigarettes.

"Didn't you?"

The kid glanced toward the house and he could see her. She was lifting a steaming pot that was sitting on the big iron stove.

"There was little time to think, really," the kid said. "But it goddamn rabbited across my mind for a split second, you bet."

"You mean until the hammer dropped and the Sharps clicked," the teamster said, "instead of going boom."

The kid nodded.

"You mean instead of watching your god-damn head explode," the kid said. "That's a goddamn .50-caliber."

"That it is," the teamster said.

"That would have took your fucking head right off," the kid said.

"Yes, it would," the teamster said.

"That damn thing is meant to drop buffalo, elk, and bear at two hundred, three hundred yards," the kid said.

"She don't want me dead," he said.

The kid shook his head.

"Well, she sure is different," he said.

"I'll raise you on that," the teamster said.

"How did you know, though," the kid said. "That there was not a fucking round in front of that goddamn hammer?"

"I didn't," the teamster said.

The kid stared at him, then shook his head. "She's done that before?"

"No."

"Well, you're goddamn a flip side of most fellas under the gun. Holy hell."

"How so?"

"Well, hell, you know, you seen it in your soldiering days. Surely you seen it?"

"Some. I've seen it some."

"Some? Bullshit," the kid said. "You have

seen it more than some."

"What makes you say that?"

"I can tell these things," the kid said. "You been further around hell and back more than most folks have dug around in a potato sack."

The teamster laughed.

"I ain't no killer, though," the teamster said.

"Well," the kid said. "I seen a good number of men in front of a barrel pointed at their head, but I've never seen one smile like you done."

"No?"

"No, hell, no," the kid said. "Mostly they cry or pray or beg. Begging, mostly. Carrying on about their mothers or their youngens. Begging, trying to get sympathy."

"Got no kids," the teamster said. "No mother, either, my mother died long ago."

"Pee or puke or mess themselves is common," the kid said. "They do that, you know?"

"You would know," the teamster said. "You are a killer."

"I've had to do what I've had to do," the kid said.

"Oh," the teamster said. "You have done more than that."

"What do you mean?"

"You have it in your blood," the teamster said. "It's instinctual. It comes natural to you."

The kid stared at him.

"It's okay," the teamster said. "She saw it in you and you have inspired her."

"Inspired her?" the kid said with a glance to the house. "Inspired her to do what?"

"I can't say for certain," the teamster said. "But I have noticed her shifting. Changing. The targeting of the Sharps and other things."

"What other things?"

"Fucking you, for one."

"Whoa," the kid said, "I . . . I thought . . . ?"

"It's okay, kid," he said. "It's okay . . . You remember when she was telling you about Appaloosa and all the horses and horseshit and all the people?"

"I do."

"Well, she meant something altogether different than having a problem with all the horses and horseshit and people."

"What kind of different?" the kid said.

"That is why she said there is one too many people there," the teamster said. "There is one person in particular that she has on her mind and in her sights. I thought she maybe had forgotten about it. But I don't know."

"Don't know what?"

"I might be wrong, but I think you have inspired her, given her a newfound need."

"For what?"

"To kill."

"Kill who? Somebody in Appaloosa?"

The teamster nodded as he turned his eyes to the house.

"You remember I told you her daddy was killed before I found her traveling with the goddamn crazy fucking gypsies in the Borax Flats?"

"I do."

"He had a vendetta," the teamster said.

"Her daddy?"

The teamster nodded.

"What kind of vendetta?"

The teamster leaned in a little.

"Well, her daddy did some bad shit. He was really a no-good sonofabitch, as far as I can tell. But she feels he was taken away from her. Said he got worse and worse. One thing led to another and he got himself shot through the throat by a lawman. Damn near killed him, but it didn't, and he was sent to prison. Years later he broke out and set out to kill that lawman that shot him and sent him to prison, but the lawman killed him instead."

"And this lawman is in Appaloosa?"

"He is."

The kid shook his head.

"And you think I have fucking inspired her to kill him. Kill a lawman?"

The teamster shook his head and pointed at the kid.

"What?" the kid said.

"You," the teamster said.

"Me?"

The teamster nodded.

"You think she wants me to kill him?"

The teamster shrugged.

"She has not said . . . but."

"But what?" the kid said.

"I don't know for sure," the teamster said.

"Thought she wanted to fucking help me?"

The teamster said nothing.

"She's the one with the guns," the kid said. "She's the fucking sharpshooter."

The teamster nodded. "But is she a killer?" he said.

The kid did not take his eyes off the teamster.

"Her old man was a killer," the kid said.

The teamster nodded.

"But is she a killer?" the teamster said.

"She's capable, I say," the kid said. "And what about you?"

"What about me?"

"You're her husband," the kid said.

"What difference does that make?" the teamster said.

"You know killing," the kid said. "You are no stranger to that."

He shook his head and smiled broadly at the kid.

"I am a teamster," he said. "A workingman. I

play some cards and I make a little money off of saps in town and up and down the road. But that is it. Nothing more."

The kid stood up and walked out of the spilling light into the darkness and relieved himself. He lifted his chin and closed his eyes up as he wetted the ground.

"Nothing more," the kid scoffed. "Everybody is a killer . . . Circumstances bend and break all the rules of yours and everybody's so-called . . . nothing more."

She pushed open the shutter and called out. She said something to the teamster in a language the kid did not understand.

The kid buttoned up. Then walked toward the teamster.

"What'd she say?"

"You are needed," he said.

"What for?"

The teamster shook his head.

"Good goddamn," the kid said.

He moved past where the teamster was seated and walked to the house. She met him at the door. He looked up to her. She appeared extra-tall standing before him in the doorway. She stepped to the side.

"Come," she said, and pulled him inside.

Then she spoke to the teamster. She said something, again in another language, and pointed toward the barn. The teamster lifted his hat and nodded. Then she looked to the kid.

"Take off your clothes," she said.

"What?"

"Off," she said.

"Right here?" he said.

"Yes," she said.

She pointed to a bath basin full of water with steam rising above. The kid looked out the door to see the teamster was watching them.

"I want you clean," she said, as she started unbuttoning his shirt.

He turned his gaze from the teamster to her. He watched her hands undoing the buttons on his shirt, then he considered her magnificent face.

"You want me to kill."

She met his eye. Then she looked out the door to the teamster. He was staring at them. She closed the door and the kid kicked off his boots.

49

The gunmen we had locked up were all released. The McCormick gun hands walked one way and the Baptiste gun hands went the other. Book and his deputies stayed with them, watching them. The Bartholomew hands all went to Deek's livery. They wasted no time getting their horses, mounting up, and riding out of town. The deputies followed them for a few miles until they were out of sight and turned back. The others, the McCormick gun hands, walked to a rooming house where Hodge boarded.

Book kept two deputies posted at the rooming house through the night, and had two deputies on the road out of town where the Baptiste gun hands had departed. Virgil's instructions were only to see what happened. Don't interfere with any of their comings and goings, but keep an eye on them just the same.

The night proved to be without conflict.

And morning, too, was quiet. The McCormick gunmen went to a café for breakfast
and did nothing other than linger about.
They drank coffee and rolled smokes as they
piddled around on the front porch of the
hotel.

Midmorning, Virgil and I met up at Doc
Burris's office. He had just delivered a baby
and was washing up when we entered.

We followed him into his office. He
dropped into his chair behind his desk, and
without a word he swiveled around, pulled
out a bottle of rye and three glasses from a
hutch behind his desk, and poured us each
two fingers.

"I have to ask you to join me in a toast,"
he said. "In the face of never-ending notions of impending peril, I have to raise my
glass to the miracle of every new one that
comes into this world. Plus, it's the only
time my wife allows me to indulge. And,
please, gentlemen, if you don't mind."

We nodded and held up our glasses.

"To Davis Christopher Ridenhour," Doc
said. "Out with the old, in with the new,
cheers to his future, to the good he will do,
and may all his dreams come true."

We toasted and drank. And Doc quickly
refilled our glasses.

"Hear, hear," he said.

He drank down his second shot and refilled his glass. Then he removed his spectacles and set them on his desk in front of him. Leaning back in his chair, Doc leveled a serious look at Virgil and me. He smiled and took a sip of his drink before he spoke.

"James McCormick had poison in his system," he said.

Virgil glanced to me and shook his head.

"You're sure?" he said.

"I am," Doc said. "Likely strychnine. But maybe something milder or a diluted-down version of strychnine."

"You can tell by . . . ?" I said.

"Yes, for certain. What I saw under the scope and by a close examination of this body. His tendons."

"You can see poison in the body?" I said.

"No, not exactly, but actually, when I first saw James McCormick there in the street and then when we loaded him into the ambulance, I noticed things. And I thought it odd and a possibility then, but I of course was not certain."

"What did you notice?" I said.

"Well, he didn't piss himself, for one," Doc said. "But also just the way his hands were drawn in some toward his wrists and his neck was arched, with his chin raised up like it was. But I didn't mention it. I needed to be sure, to take a closer look."

He took a sip.

"What did you see?" I said.

"A few things. Let me show you," he said. "Poison gets right to these tendons."

He turned to a life-size skeletal diagram on the wall behind his desk. He pointed with a pointer to show us what areas he was referring to as he spoke.

"There is a contraction that occurs," he said. "Hence what I saw in the hands and neck. And after having a good look under the microscope, I'm certain. There is evidence of poison throughout his body."

"Is there a way for you to determine how he was poisoned?" I said.

Doc shook his head.

"No, not really," he said. "I mean, I just can't say for certain. But I did have a look into his digestive system. Just to see what was there."

"And?" I said.

"Well, he had some traces of food, digested earlier in the day. And there was some alcohol in his system, too."

"Early in the day," I said.

Virgil nodded.

"He didn't strike me as a daytime drinker," I said.

"His wife and brother said he was at his office before he went home," Virgil said. "Maybe that is where it happened."

"Or maybe he stopped someplace in between the office and home?" I said.

"That could have happened, right, Doc?" I said. "He could have been poisoned in town, then walked to his home?"

Doc nodded.

"If I may," Doc said. "And let me say before I do that I am of course no officer of the law. But my deduction might be — and it falls in line with your thinking, Everett — that the poison did not do the job as intended."

"And?" I said.

"And thusly, the murderer or murderers perhaps panicked and decided to finish him off, so to speak. By stabbing him."

Virgil stared at Doc, then nodded. He got up and walked to the diagram on the wall. Thinking as he studied it, then turned to me.

"What do you figure, Everett?" he said.

"Well," I said, "it damn sure doesn't seem like the Bartholomew brothers' way of doing things."

"It don't," he said.

"They'd just put a bullet in him and leave it at that," I said.

306

"No matter," Virgil said. "We still have to find Victor."

"After what happened to Ventura," I said, "Victor will be wanting to find us, I'd imagine."

"He will," Virgil said.

"He's not done here," I said.

Virgil shook his head.

"Not by a long shot," he said.

"One thing we know for certain," I said. "There is one great goddamn good reason for someone to kill James McCormick."

"Sure the hell is," Virgil said.

Virgil downed his rye and set his glass on the corner of the desk.

"Appreciate it, Doc," he said.

"Well, of course," he said. "Just let me know if you boys need anything else."

"Will do," Virgil said. "And let's make certain this here business goes no place else."

"Goes without saying," Doc said. "Goes without saying."

Virgil smiled, then nodded me toward the door. I drank down the rye and got up.

"Thanks, Doc," I said.

I followed Virgil. Doc moved out from behind the desk and strolled with us into the lobby.

"So . . . tough," Doc said. "If you don't

mind me asking."

We stopped at the door and turned to Doc.

"What is it?" he said. "What's the great goddamn good reason? For his murder?"

Virgil smiled at me.

"Gold," I said.

Virgil nodded.

"Makes people do things they otherwise might not do," he said.

Doc nodded, followed by a shake of his head, and we pushed out the door into the hot afternoon air.

Virgil walked halfway down the steps and stopped, staring off across the street. I followed his look. Sitting on a bench under the shade of an awning was Hodge. He was staring at us. Then he got to his feet and walked off down the boardwalk like he was on a Sunday stroll.

"Fluffing his feathers," I said.

"Showing his ass," Virgil said.

50

The kid helped the teamster hitch up the mules to the buckboard for another trip. The teamster told the kid this delivery was a standard supply run. A trip he made monthly, picking up grains and sundry feeds from a river store and taking the supplies up to a string of manufacturing outfits along the river.

"I'll be ending in Porterville," the teamster said. "A town north, up the river. The opposite direction of Appaloosa."

"You sure you don't want me to go with you?" the kid said.

"I am," the teamster said.

The kid followed as the teamster pulled two more mules from the barn and walked them toward the buckboard.

"I don't mind," the kid said.

The teamster smiled to himself as he walked.

"Now, don't tell me you're scared of being alone with her . . ." he said. "Are you?"

The kid gave a furtive glance around before he spoke.

"Heck, no."

"Good," the teamster said.

"No reason," the kid said.

"She has her hooks in you," the teamster said.

"Now, hold on," the kid said.

"She does," he said. "And that is okay."

"She don't belong to me," the kid said.

"No. She don't belong to you, or anybody else, for that matter."

"She belongs to you."

"She belongs to nobody, including me."

"Well, she's your wife. You married her."

"We did, and that is that."

"I don't plan on making a habit of being the one in her bed," the kid said. "You can bet your bottom dollar on that."

"You complaining?"

"Well . . . no."

"Good."

"It's just . . . that . . . well . . ."

"I know," the teamster said. "Hard to put her into words. There ain't nothing quite like her in that way."

"Um . . . well. No," the kid said. "I will have to agree with you there. There ain't nothing quite like her."

"So you ought enjoy it while it lasts."

"I do, I mean I am. It's just that she's, well, goddamn it, she is your wife."

The teamster stopped rigging the mule and turned to the kid.

"She has other plans for you," he said. "Don't you see that?"

"Like what?"

"Appaloosa," he said. "She said she will help you find your mother, and that is what she will do. She's traveling with you."

"What?" the kid said. "When?"

"Right soon," the teamster said, then continued harnessing the mules.

"What about you?"

"What about me?"

"Why ain't you coming?"

He shook his head.

"Not my business," he said. "You will go with her on your own."

"Well, fuck," the kid said.

"You don't want to?" the teamster said.

"No," the kid said, "it's not that, it's just . . ."

"You'll be in good hands," the teamster said.

"I reckon."

"You reckon?" the teamster said. "You are okay with that notion, ain't you?"

"Well, sure," the kid said. "That was my plan all along."

"Good, then," he said.

"I just never planned on traveling with no

woman," the kid said. "Not sure how this happened."

"Stars lined up for you, kid."

"Be good if you was there," the kid said.

The teamster shook his head.

"I have my own way," he said.

"We can wait till you return."

"No. It will be a while," he said. "I won't be back for a while."

"Just don't seem right," the kid said.

"You're headed there to find your long-lost mother. And my wife will help you."

"But the thing is, I ain't got no goddamn interest in gunning down no lawman."

The teamster nodded.

"I understand that," he said. "A man has to do what a man has to do."

"That's right," the kid said as he pressed his shoulders back, making him feel slightly taller than he was. "That is right. A man has to do what a man has to do."

"But you need to keep her satisfied," the teamster said as he snugged the girth band under one of the mules. "You don't want to disappoint her."

The kid didn't say anything and the teamster turned to face him.

"You know what I mean?" he said.

"I do," the kid said.

"Good," the teamster said, then turned to

the mules again. "She has traveling money. Good money. You will be taken good care of and you will take good care of her."

51

Much-needed rain rolled in from the north and settled in for a few days. It continued on and off, offering slow showers and a light drizzle, but so far we'd had no real downpours. And by the look of things, it appeared the brief bit of rain was clearing out. It was dark out in the late afternoon, but pieces of sun were breaking through the waning clouds in the west.

"Wasn't much," I said.

"Not enough," Virgil said.

At the moment it was nothing but a light mist where Virgil and I sat our horses under a big oak tree. We were overlooking the Catholic cemetery. Below us, the funeral of James McCormick was under way. A good-size crowd gathered around the gravesite. Most of them were huddled under umbrellas. Bernice was standing with Daniel and Irene. Behind them stood the others gathered to pay their respects, including Allie and a half-dozen other women from her ladies' social. Standing off to the side and behind the crowd without umbrellas were Hodge and the two hands I had locked up for following Baptiste. After the priest said his final blessing, everyone bowed for a prayer.

"That's that," I said.

"Is," Virgil said.

When the prayer was over, the priest nodded to a small man with bagpipes who was standing off a ways. He lifted the pipes and played some tune that sounded familiar. As the pipes continued, the undertaker turned a crank that started lowering the casket into the grave.

"Whiskey?" I said.

Virgil nodded.

"Why not."

We watched for a while longer. Then, as the crowd began to disperse, we moved on.

The days leading up to the funeral had been uneventful. We had Book, Lloyd, and the deputies keeping an eye out for Victor as they patrolled about town, but there was no sign of him or any of the hands of his we released. Hodge and his men had done nothing more to stir up any kind of trouble. All seemed quiet.

Virgil and I put our horses away and

walked to the Boston House saloon. It was early and the place was not yet full of drinkers and gamblers. There were a few older fellas sitting at a corner table, but nobody else at the bar. And none of the working-women appeared to ply their trade.

When we ordered a second whiskey from Wallis, Victor Bartholomew walked in the side door. At first I did not recognize him. He'd cut his long hair and shaved his beard. He was wearing a nicer hat and clothes than normal with a starched white shirt.

"I'll be goddamn," I said under my breath.

Virgil followed my look to Victor.

He stood still, staring at Virgil. Then he walked over and took a seat at the far end of the bar.

"Whiskey, the Kan-tuck good stuff," he said. "And your best beer."

He turned to us without expression.

"Been looking for you," Victor said. "But then I found you."

Virgil leaned back, looking past me to get a clear view of Victor, but said nothing.

"And I think you been looking for me," Victor said. "How 'bout that shit?"

Victor took his hat off and set it on the bar. His hair was cut tight to the sides of his head but was long on the top. Strands of hair fell in front of his eyes. He pushed the hair out of his face and grinned.

"Yep," he said. "You looking for me and me looking for you. Funny, ain't it?"

"Not really," Virgil said.

Virgil stopped looking at Victor.

"Well, I'm right here," Victor said.

He opened his coat.

"And I ain't heeled."

Wallis placed the whiskey and beer in front of him. Then moved away from Victor quick-like. As if Victor might be some kind of creature that might bite.

"I damn sure should be heeled, but I ain't."

He downed the whiskey, then slid off his stool as he picked up his mug of beer. He sauntered in our direction.

"No matter," Victor said.

Virgil remained looking forward as he spoke.

"No," Virgil said. "It matters. If you was heeled, I'd have to lock you up."

"That's funny," Victor said.

"No," Virgil said. "It's not."

"What do you think, Everett?" Victor said. "You think that is funny."

"No," I said.

Just then two of Victor's hands, Wayne and the big man, Noah, walked in the side door. I picked up my eight-gauge and had its

317

hammers back with the barrels pointed in their direction as Wallis dropped quickly down behind the bar.

52

They stopped a few steps in and stood side by side, looking at us. Noah smiled, holding his hands away from his body.

"They ain't heeled," Victor said. "Show 'em?"

Noah and Wayne nodded and opened their coats.

"I'll be damned," Noah said. "We meet again."

"And I got to say it is a real pleasure," Wayne said.

Virgil glanced at them, then turned his attention to Victor.

"What do you want to tell me about James McCormick?" Virgil said.

"Know he's dead," Victor said. "I just watched him get put in the ground while ago."

I leaned away from the bar so Virgil could have a clear view of Victor.

"Newspaper said he died of natural

causes," Victor said.

"You have something to do with those natural causes the newspaper wrote about?" Virgil said.

Victor laughed.

"I know that is why you and the dumbass Appaloosa deputies are looking for me. What were you gonna do if you found me? Got nothing on me."

Virgil stared at him.

"Did you?"

"You killed my brother," he said. "And you have the goddamn gall to ask me that question?"

"I know telling the truth is not part of your way of being," Virgil said. "But I'm giving you the benefit of the doubt."

"You fucked up," Victor said.

"But I won't be in the giving mood much longer," Virgil said.

"I know exactly what happened," Victor said. "I talked to his whore, she told me what happened."

"Good," Virgil said.

"You killed my brother."

"He had a chance and he chose not to take it," Virgil said. "And now you have the same chance."

"You threatening me?"

"Just giving you the facts."

"Sounds like a threat to me."

Virgil shook his head.

"Everett?"

"Might sound like a threat to you, Victor," I said, "but Virgil don't threaten anybody. Warning's more like it."

"I had fucking nothing to do with James McCormick getting his ass buried, but why should you believe me?"

"That's a damn good question," Virgil said. "Don't you think, Everett?"

"I do," I said.

"Where were you?" Virgil said. "Last Friday in the afternoon?"

"Why, I took the train to Yaqui," he said.

"For?" Virgil said.

"None of your business," he said.

Victor grinned, then fished a ticket out of his breast pocket.

"Got my ticket right here. Just so you law dogs can have a look-see at my departure from Appaloosa and my return to Appaloosa. Nice place, Yaqui."

He walked closer and tossed his train ticket on the bar near me. Then he backed away to his seat. I picked up the ticket, read it, then put it in front of Virgil.

"What about your brother?" I said.

Victor downed his beer, then set the mug down hard on the bar.

"What about him?" Victor picked up his hat off the bar. "Fact is, he's dead. And of course James McCormick died of natural causes, so there is nothing to really be concerned about there, nothing to discuss. Least that is what the paper said."

He dropped a few coins on the bar.

"Since you like Yaqui so much," Virgil said, "you might ought to do yourself a favor and go back there. Think you might find it a better place for you and yours."

"No," he said. "I like it here better."

He tipped his head toward his men.

"And we have ourselves a job here, don't we, boys."

They nodded and smiled.

"We do," Noah said.

" 'Sides that," Victor said, "I understand there is a big town get-together shindig coming up. Appaloosa Days. We damn sure don't want to miss that."

Victor sneered, then started for the door. He walked extra slow. And I kept my eye on him, but Virgil did not. Victor stopped at the door and turned to face me.

"Let me tell you boys something. You done lit the fuse. This is the beginning of hell to pay. And know this . . . that is not a goddamn threat to either one of you, or a warning. It's a rock-solid promise."

Victor turned and walked out. Wayne and Noah considered us a second, then followed him out the door.

"Pesky no-good fucks," I said.

Virgil leaned forward, looking at the cigar boxes behind the bar that were lined up under the mirror.

"Wallis?" he said.

Wallis was leaning on the backside of the bar with his arms folded. It was his "I ain't listening" pose.

"Yes, sir," he said.

Virgil pointed to the cigar boxes.

"Let me have one of those Julietas there."

"You bet."

Wallis got a cigar from the box, cut the tip, and handed it to Virgil. Like magic, he held out the flame of a stick match. Virgil leaned in to the fire. When he got the cigar going, he nodded.

"Couple more whiskeys for me and Everett," Virgil said.

"You bet."

Wallis poured. Then he left the bottle with us and moved away. He was good like that. Knowing when to give Virgil and me privacy.

"He didn't do it," Virgil said.

I thought, then shook my head.

"No, he didn't."

I picked up the ticket.

"And he didn't need to show us this to know that," I said.

"No," Virgil said. "He did not."

"He wouldn't even be back here," I said.

"Ventura didn't do it, either," Virgil said.

"No," I said. "I don't think he did, either."

"He didn't," Virgil said.

I nodded.

"Yeah. Victor leaving town," I said, "and Ventura doing that on his own with the poison and the stabbing all the while he's shacked up with that whore up there on the north end. That did not happen."

Virgil shook his head as he puffed on the cigar.

"No," he said. "Didn't."

We thought about that.

"Maybe James fucked over somebody we don't know about, some bad business dealings," I said. "And they come back for revenge."

"Could be."

"We ruled out Baptiste and Pritchard, and the Bartholomew brothers," I said.

"And the other Baptiste gun hands were locked up," Virgil said.

"So who the hell did kill James McCormick?" I said.

"Damn good question," Virgil said. "Someone damn sure knows something."

"What do you think Victor meant about the rock-solid promise of hell to pay?"

"Guess we'll know soon enough," Virgil said.

53

The teamster's wife was saddled on a lean and muscled buckskin, and the kid was on his pinto. He was towing a small mule with packed panniers. They were mostly full of her gypsy clothing. She rode up ahead of him as they made their way toward Appaloosa. They passed the turnoff that led up toward the gold mines. When they got to the shortcut trail, she turned off the main road.

"Where we going?" the kid said.

She turned in the saddle, placing her hand on her horse's rump, as they rode. She stared at him briefly, then turned forward again.

It was getting late as they traveled the narrow passageway through the canopy of trees. The sound of cicadas was overwhelming. Finches and sparrows moved quickly as evening approached, squeezing and separating the birds from their daylight.

"I have made plenty of trips through here," she said as she watched the birds darting about. "Many times before, I have come through here."

The sun was slanting through the trees. It was shining directly on her. It was as if she was in the light by some kind of magical design. Like it was her personal divine ray leading her. He watched her backside moving sensuously with her horse's gate. The sexual rhythm made him want her. He wanted to stop and take her there on the trail in the woods, but he did not say anything. He just watched her as they rode on.

She did not wear a hat or a bonnet. Her dark, violent hair was up, piled high atop her head. She wore a black dress that was loose but fitted and clung to her strong frame. And she wore sandals that laced up her muscled calves. She resembled something one of the old master painters might have painted. He had seen images of Michelangelo before and she reminded him of something biblical. He knew a little bit about God and the scriptures. Not a lot, but he knew some. He knew the difference between the Old Testament and the New Testament, and he'd seen plenty of biblical paintings in the Catholic churches in Mexico. And he prided himself on his imagination. He had a good painting in his head as to what women folk like Delilah or Jezebel or Salome might look like. And he thought this magnificent creature riding in front of him would fit perfectly in an old painting created by masters.

Her dress was open about the neck, and her dark skin and parts of her shoulders and chest shined in the light. She wore strands and strands of beads around her neck. Strange necklaces made of shells, small animal teeth, bones, and shiny stones. Polished stones that he figured were valuable. They were bright blues and dark greens. And she wore bracelets. Silver bracelets. There were many of them, and they made noise when she moved about.

"Why?" the kid said.

She glanced to him.

"Why have you made trips through here?" he said.

She rode some before answering.

"At another time, when I was very young and with my tribe, my travelers, we made and sold things," she said. "Traveled all through here from Santa Fe to Yuma to Yaqui to Appaloosa. And from here we made trips to the ocean."

"I've never seen the ocean," he said.

"One day, maybe," she said.

"Sold things to survive?" he said.

"Survive?"

"Yeah," the kid said.

"Isn't that the final destination? The end result, survival?"

"I suppose," he said. "Never really thought much about it. Not like that. Final destination. It's just what people do. People do things to survive. To eat."

"Everyone has to eat," she said.

"What sort of things did you make and sell?"

"Everything. Foods, leather goods," she said, "and jewelry, and potions."

"I know about your potions."

"You do?"

She looked to the kid and he tapped his temple.

"Loco cactus?" he said. "I know about that cactus stuff."

She shook her head.

"No . . . what I make comes from Angel's wings," she said, "and Devil's dues."

He laughed.

"What is funny?" she said.

"I know," he said. "They are healing potions to make people not be . . . what's the word? . . . comfortable."

She nodded.

"In part," she said.

"What is the other part?" he said.

"To take you on a journey."

"Where to?" he said.

"Into your soul."

"I have never tried any of that sort of thing," he said.

"You have," she said.

He shook his head.

"No," he said.

"But you have," she said.

"I ain't."

She pulled her horse to a stop and he came alongside her.

"I gave it to you when we rested back there."

"You did?"

She nodded.

"Your tea."

"Well, I'll be goddamned."

"Are you angry?"

He shook his head.

"I don't feel nothing."

"Not yet," she said.

Then she nudged her horse on.

". . . By the time we get to Appaloosa, you will. You will go on a journey."

"Think I'll come back?"

"That depends," she said.

"On what?" he said.

"On where you go," she said. "And what is revealed."

They rode in silence for a long time, then the kid said, "Hell. I am a traveler. Fact is, uncertainty and journey is all I know."

She nodded.

54

There were a few routes between McCormick's office and James and Bernice Mc-
Cormick's home. Virgil and I walked both.
The first walk provided nothing in the way
of a refreshment stopover. But the second
path crossed Raines Street, and on the
corner of Fifth and Raines there was a café
and card house called the Crow's Nest. It
was a small place that catered to an older
crowd and was named after its yackety old
peg-legged owner, Simon Crow. He ran the
place with his wife, Maureen. She did most
of the work, cooking and serving, and Crow
did most of the talking.

Crow had been a captain in the Army, and
he was not shy about talking to anyone
who'd listen to his war stories. He'd talk
about everything from current events to cur-
rents in the creek. And because he was also
hard of hearing, he talked a lot louder than
needed. Like me, Crow was a West Point

graduate, so every time he saw me he felt inclined to reminisce about things I never really cared to think about.

The only customers that were in the Crow's Nest were two dapper old-timers playing gin and drinking gin. Crow was sitting backward in a chair, watching them. He was talking when we entered. He was filling them full of something about Thomas Edison. He perked up when he saw us.

"Everett Hitch," he said with a salute. "And Marshal Cole. How do?"

He got out of the chair and moved quickly behind the bar. Even though Crow was not young and had a peg leg, he got around just fine.

"What can I get you fellas?"

Virgil pointed to the pot sitting atop the stove.

"Got coffee in that pot?"

"I surely do."

"Worth drinking?"

"It ain't bad."

"Two cups," I said.

"You bet. You bet. Want something to eat?"

"No, thanks," I said.

He got two cups and poured us some coffee.

"Not seen you for a while, Everett. Lots

to catch up on. I was just telling my friends here."

"I'm no friend of yours," one of the old-timers said without looking over.

"Shut up and mind your own goddamn business," Crow said.

"Always do," the old-timer said, "but that never stopped you from minding mine."

"Anyway," Crow said, "the newest electricity generators being made that are in all the headlines recently are going to change life as we know it. I'm sure you have read all about them. Damnedest thing —"

"Let me interrupt you," I said.

"Well . . . well, sure."

Crow set the coffees in front of us.

"Sugar?" he said.

"Please," I said. "Got a question or two for you."

"Okay," Crow said as he set the sugar bowl on the bar.

"You know James McCormick?" I said.

"I did, sort of," Crow said, "but he passed away."

"That is true," I said.

"Yes, I read about it in the paper and was sorry to hear. Paper said he died of natural causes at his home. Hard to figure, him being so young and all."

"He come in here?" Virgil said.

"He did," Crow said.

"Often?" I said.

"You asking me this 'cause you maybe think it wasn't maybe so natural after all?"

"He come in often, Crow," I said.

"No. Not often, but once in a while. He would come in here, his brother sometimes, too. Very smart fellas, knowledgeable, the both of them. James knew interesting facts about a good deal of fascinating things."

"He in here the day he died?" Virgil said.

"Let me think," Crow said. "Let me think . . ."

"He was," the old-timer playing cards said.

He was peering at us over the top of the cards he held in front of him.

"You weren't here, Crow, so you would not know."

"How do you know?" Crow said.

" 'Cause I was sitting in the very chair I'm sitting in on that day, when he came in. Maureen was minding the place and minding her own business while you was off whittling on that wood leg."

"You saw James McCormick in here on Friday?"

The old-timer placed his cards facedown on the table.

"I did," he said.

"What time?" I said.

334

"Oh . . . four o'clock or so, I think."

"He drunk?" Virgil said.

"Don't know for sure," the old-timer said. "Didn't seem so."

"He drinking?" I said.

"Don't know that, either."

"He would drink a little," Crow said. "A beer. Or nurse on a whiskey, but I never saw him inebriated. He was a quiet kind of guy, really. He'd have something to read and was never really interested in conversation."

"I can't imagine why," the old-timer said.

"No, not so, he talked with me. We visited about all kinds of stuff."

"Ha," the old-timer said. "One-sided prattle yack."

"You see him leave?" I said to the old-timer.

"No . . . can't say I did. I was playing cards and didn't really pay him much attention. I just saw him. Just for a periphery really. There was a good amount of fellas in here and things was kinda busy. Maureen was moving about, taking care of everybody."

"He by himself?" Virgil said.

The old-timer squinted at his card partner.

"Don't look at me," his partner said. "I wasn't here."

"I think there was someone with him,"

335

the old-timer said. "Maybe a couple of fel-las, but I'm not sure."

Virgil glanced at me.

"You think?" Virgil said. "Or you're not sure?"

He shook his head.

"Pretty sure there was."

"His brother?" I said.

"No, don't think so."

"One man or two men?"

He gritted his teeth and swallowed like his throat was sore.

"What'd he, them, look like?" I said.

He thought, then shook his head.

"I don't rightly remember. Hell, Maureen would know."

"Where is she?" I said.

"Is there some reason you are asking about him on that day? Was there some kind of foul play, is that it?"

"Where is she?" I said again.

Crow pointed.

"She's not in town. She went with her brother to Dover to help out with his daughter's newborn."

"When will she be back?"

"Oh, a week or so. I got the nigra girls do-ing the cooking and cleaning. If there was a wire in Dover I'd say you could get a telegram to her, but there is not, of course.

Closest town for that is Fletcher, and that is thirty miles. Then their place is up in the hills where the logging is. That's where her brother works. Makes a living up there. Hard goddamn work."

I turned to the old-timer.

"You sure you don't remember?" I said. "Think. Can you remember? Tall men, short, fat, skinny, old, young, one or two, or three?"

"Kind of important," Virgil said.

"Think," Crow said.

The old fella crinkled his nose at Crow like he was something that had soured. Then he put his chin to his chest, trying to remember. After a few seconds, he shook his head.

"Damn sorry about my sieve of a brain. Or what's left of it. Like I said, it was kind of busy in here. And I was winning money. Not to mention I'm afraid I've slept a few nights since then. I just do not recall."

Virgil and I spent the rest of the day trying to find a witness who might have seen James but came up with nothing. No one we spoke with had a clue.

55

The kid was concerned. He'd been concerned for a while. He had the goat cornered. But the curly-haired black doe with wild eyes was getting the best of him. She moved back and forth, staying out of the kid's reach. The kid sure wanted to catch her. He wanted to eat her, too. He wasn't hungry, but his blood lust was up and racing through him. It was pumping hard from just watching the dark and clever doe staying an arm's length out of his grasp.

"You better stay put," he said. "Just stay put."

But the goat had other ideas and kept one eye on the kid at all times. She never took him in square on as she moved. Walking brazenly to one wall, then the other. He tried to quickly reach for her a few times, but she was fast like a cat and managed, ever so easily, to stay a step out of his reach.

But, fuck, he thought, he was moving so

goddamn slow, feeling sluggish. Slower than he was used to moving, and he was beginning to feel uneasy.

"You best stop, you damn goat, 'fore you get my temper up," the kid said. "And you don't want that."

"That is exactly what I want," the goat said.

The kid froze, thinking he'd heard the goat speak.

"Wha . . . what did you say?"

"That's just what I wanted to see," the doe said. "You get your temper up."

Then the goat stood up on her back legs. And when she did, the kid pulled his knife.

"That is what I want," the doe said.

The kid took a step away from her and squinted, trying to focus on the goat.

"Goddamn you," he said.

Then the goat turned slightly, and when she did the kid could see the goat was really the teamster's wife. She was smiling at him with a wicked smile.

"It's you," he said.

"Who did you think it was?"

"A goat," the kid said, and he turned around the room. "A fucking goat."

He turned one way, then the other. Everything seemed unfamiliar. It was a big fancy room with high curtains, flowered wallpaper, and a bathtub in the corner.

"Where are we?"

He'd never seen anything like this before. There was a pair of matching chairs with gold-painted wood and velvet cushions.

"That's the biggest bed I have ever seen," he said. "Need a running jump or a ladder just to get up in it."

He took a step back.

"Whoa," he said.

"What? What is it?"

"It's breathing."

He turned, looking around the room. Everything seemed to be alive.

"Damn."

He stared at her then turned and turned again, looking around the room.

"Why do you figure that everything is alive?" he said. "It shouldn't be, but it damn sure is."

The kid laughed as he reached out and touched the curtains. Then he touched the flowered wallpaper.

"They are growing."

He snapped a look at the big chairs as if they'd said something.

"What?"

He moved toward one of the chairs. He held his knife out at the chair.

"Don't you move," he said. "Not another muscle."

"I'm over here," the teamster's wife said.

He turned to her.

"Where are we?" he said.

"I'm happy you got to see me," she said. "The goat is strongest of all animals in the stars."

"Bullshit?"

"Yes," she said. "That is me, a Capricorn. And you wanted me?"

"I still do."

"What do you want with me?"

"I don't know."

The kid reached out trying to touch things moving about in the turning room.

"Where are we?"

"Your mother's earth," she said.

"How do you know?"

"I can feel her."

"This is Appaloosa?" he said.

"Yes."

He held up his hands. He stared at the knife in his hand and shook his head hard.

"I feel like a . . . a thing?"

"You have been moving about like a mouse."

He pointed the knife at her.

"I could have killed you."

"You still could, I suppose."

"Why would I do that?"

"Because you are a killer."

The kid sat in the huge chair and rested his head in his hands.

"This is good," she said.

She was the goat again. He blinked and shook his head.

"What? What is good?"

"You. As you are."

He leaned forward, resting his head in his hands again.

"When was your first time?" she said.

"What?"

"Killing?"

"I never killed nobody that did not deserve killing."

"Everyone deserves death," she said. "It is part of living."

She crawled up on the bed, then turned to him.

"Make love to me," she said.

"Love?"

"Yes," she said.

He got out of the chair, moved close to the wall, and stared at the wallpaper.

"Come," she said.

He turned and walked slowly to the bed.

She reached out and pulled him up by his hand.

"Lay back," she said.

"No," he said. "You lay back."

She did as he asked. Her face was pulsating. Changing from a goat to her natural self.

"Look, I got no problem killing the marshal

that did what he did to your daddy," he said.

"I know you don't."

"None at all."

"Good."

"But I think you are going to do it," he said. "Take that Sharps and put him to rest."

She shook her head.

"I know what is best," she said. "And I know all of what you can do best, too. So let's take one adventure at a time."

She lifted up and pulled her dress off. She tossed it, then dropped back on the bed, looking up at him.

"Have you ever fucked a goat?" she said.

56

With Simon Crow's wife, Maureen, being away, we had nothing else solid to go on. So Virgil had Book send two of his deputies, Hank, one of the older, more experienced men, and Skeeter, on a ride over to Dover to speak with Maureen to see if we could get an identification of the man or men last seen with James when he was alive. It was a three-and-a-half-day trip to and from Dover.

While we waited, I spent a good bit of time with Martha Kathryn. I saw her show again. And each evening spent with her I was getting more and more comfortable with her. And she was getting more and more comfortable with me, it seemed. The evenings after the show we'd sit on the porch of the hotel and share a bottle of wine and visit about all things, relative and not. Her past was a subject she continued to avoid, but her knowledge and understanding of business and politics allowed for continued lively discussions.

After a dry period, a second round of clouds moved in, and this time the temperature dropped and it rained hard. The soggy days that followed gave Virgil and me no new direction as to what happened to James McCormick. Our thoughts that Baptiste or his partner, Eugene, had a hand in it were still foremost on our minds, but finding proof was another thing altogether.

On Martha Kathryn's next night off, Allie insisted Virgil and I take her and Martha Kathryn to dinner, and thought it would be a good gesture to include Bernice. Allie had not had a chance to get to know Bernice well, but said since she became a member of the social, not to mention had contributed to the Appaloosa Days event, she had truly connected with her. Virgil figured he'd make no more bones about it, and Allie wasted no time extending a dinner invitation to Bernice, and she accepted.

Virgil and I escorted the three of them, Allie, Martha Kathryn, and Bernice, to the newest and supposedly best restaurant in town. It was a small place at the far end of Appaloosa Avenue called Ann Marie's, and it was fixed up to look like one of the lush and stylish places you'd find in Boston or

New York City.

When we entered, it was crowded and dark. A crystal chandelier in the center of the room offered only dim lighting. On our right a bartender behind a long mirrored bar served a few well-dressed customers standing with a foot on the brass foot rail. The walls were wood-paneled and were not spare of paintings. It was too dark to see, but I was pretty certain they were paintings of Englishmen on foxhunts.

The owner's wife, Ann Marie, for whom the place was named, was one of Allie's regular customers. She had her husband secure us a table. His name was Clyde. He met us right away and introduced himself. I guessed Clyde to be about sixty. He was a tall, distinguished man with dark skin and a full salt-and-pepper beard. He wore an evening dress coat with a silk vest and a matching tie and shoes polished as shiny as a West Point cadet's.

"Welcome to Ann Marie's," he said.

"Why, thank you," Allie said.

"Right this way," Clyde said.

He ushered the five of us through the crowd to a round table in the corner next to a bay window framed with velvet draperies.

"Isn't this the most beautiful and romantic

place imaginable?" Allie said.

"It's lovely," Bernice said.

"Thank you," Clyde said. "We here at Ann Marie's are happy to have you. And we will do our very best. We are here to please."

Clyde had some kind of accent, but it was slight and I couldn't place it. German, maybe.

He held out Allie's chair.

"Why, thank you, kind sir," she said.

I held out a chair for Martha Kathryn, and Virgil did the same for Bernice.

"If it is okay with you," Clyde said, "I will start you off with some wonderful newly imported wine we have just received from France."

"Oh, my," Allie said. "France. I love French wine. And why wouldn't I, being Mrs. French and all?"

Bernice smiled.

For some reason Clyde kind of reminded me of a man you might find behind the wheel of a steamship.

Virgil nodded.

"Sounds good," I said.

The corner table was darker than the rest of the room, but there were candles on the table that lit our faces in a warm glow. I admired the ladies in turn. Each one in her individual way was beautiful: Allie, a delicate peach; Bernice, a regal sculpture; and Martha Kathryn, a golden willow.

Clyde placed a menu in front of each of us, then stepped back and smiled.

"I will bring you some fresh butter, bread, and anchovy to start," he said. "Sound good?"

"Sounds perfectly horrible," Martha Kathryn said theatrically with a smile. "Just horrible."

Clyde bowed and smiled.

"Ah, well, I assure you, madam, that it will be perfectly delicious," he said.

"I'm sure it will," she said with a smile.

"By the way," Clyde said, "Ann Marie and I have seen your play. Twice. And it is marvelous and so are you."

"Thank you very much," she said.

"No, thank you," he said. "Just delightful."

"Don't hesitate to come again," she said.

"We just might," he said.

He nodded and moved off.

"Don't think we will at all go hungry here," Martha Kathryn said.

"It's a good thing," Allie said. "Because I'm starving."

Martha Kathryn smiled, looking at Allie, but reached out to hold my hand that was resting on the table. I could tell Virgil was looking at me, but I did not meet his eye.

"You always seem to have an appetite," Martha Kathryn said to Allie. "How do you stay so thin?"

"Virgil chasing me all the time," Allie said with a hearty laugh. "Up and down the halls and through the garden . . ."

Allie stopped talking and stared out the window over my shoulder.

"My word," she said.

"What?" Virgil said, following Allie's look.

"She moved," Allie said.

"Who?" Virgil said.

"Did you see her?"

"No," Virgil said.

"I did," Bernice said.

"Who?"

Allie shook her head.

"There was a woman in the window," Bernice said.

Allie nodded.

"Just staring," Allie said.

"Seemed so," Bernice said.

I turned to the window, then to Allie.

"At what?" I said.

"At us, I suppose," Allie said. "You did not see her, Virgil?"

"Hell, Allie. I was looking at you. When you talk, I listen."

"I'm being serious."

"About a woman looking in the window?" I said.

"Yes," Allie said. "I don't know, there was something about her stare . . ."

"What kind of something?" I said.

"I don't know, the look on her face, it was odd for some reason. Bernice saw."

She nodded.

"Yes," Bernice said. "Rather odd."

"As if she saw something that she needed to look at," Allie said.

"Maybe she was just looking in," Martha Kathryn said. "Admiring the place?"

"Or your beauty, Allie," I said.

"Yes," Martha Kathryn said. "That is it."

Allie blushed and smiled as she shook her head.

"Lord, no," she said. "I know I'm being silly, but it seemed, I don't know, that she was staring at us. Not me, us."

Virgil smiled and scooted his chair back.

"Well, we'll just have to go and see," he said.

"No," Allie said. "I'm just being . . . I don't know."

I offered a smile to Martha Kathryn.

"Most likely staring at you," I said. "Every time we walk down the street together, people look at her. She's famous here in Appaloosa."

Allie nodded.

"That's most likely the case," Allie said.

"Yes," Bernice said.

"I guess I'm just used to that," Martha Kathryn said.

"What'd this mysterious woman look like?" I said.

Allie shook her head.

"I don't know . . . Striking," Allie said.

Bernice nodded.

"Tall, young, strong-looking," Bernice said.

Allie nodded.

"Exotic-like," Allie said.

"Maybe I should go find this mysterious woman and see what in the hell she's up to."

"Go right ahead, Everett Hitch," Martha Kathryn said. "Just don't come back."

57

She had a good view of the door where she stood across Appaloosa Avenue from Ann Marie's. She was down a ways and near the entrance of a billiard parlor, leaning on the wall under an awning. Tacked to the wall next to her was the poster announcing Appaloosa Days. She read all the details, then turned her attention to Ann Marie's across the street.

She was without her normal gypsy attire. Tonight she was wearing a proper gingham dress. It fit her tightly, revealing the muscles and curves of her figure. She carried a small calf-hide purse. It was draped around her neck and hung on one side of her hip. Inside the purse was a nickel-plated Remington .41-caliber double derringer. Normally she wore her calf-laced sandals, but tonight, along with her city clothing, she was wearing her lady shoes. She stood eye to eye with most men in her bare feet, but in her lady shoes with their three-inch heels she was looking down on most passersby.

Her striking appearance got the attention of a man exiting the billiard parlor. He stopped just outside the door and lit a cigarette as he stared at her. Then he turned away, as if he were interested in something else.

"Hello," he said, letting the words drift out into the street.

Then he trained his eyes on her. Waiting for a reply. But she did not even glance in his direction, nor did she say anything.

He turned and started walking toward her. He sauntered more than walked, the cigarette dangling from his lips, the smoke trailing behind him. It was an arrogant saunter, likely fueled by libation.

"Cat got your tongue?"

He kept moving toward her, but she remained focused on the restaurant across the street. Only when he was close enough to spit on did she look to him.

"Howdy," he said.

He smiled and rested his shoulder against the wall, looking at her lasciviously as he smoked.

"What's your name?"

This particular man she did not look down on. He was a big fellow, with a square head and broad shoulders.

She turned away from him, staying focused

on the restaurant. He looked her up and down.

"Ain't you something?"

"Go," she said, without even a glance.

"How much?" he said.

"Get away from me."

"Aw . . . come on."

"Go."

"What the hell are you doing out here if you don't want to make a living?"

"Go."

"Don't you want to have some fun? And make a little money on top of it?"

He flicked his cigarette into the street. Then he reached out to touch her cheek. But before his hand got to her face she had the derringer out and pointed between his eyes. He recoiled with his hands held up in the air.

"Whoa. Easy . . ."

He backed away with his arms raised.

"I didn't mean nothing."

Two men exited the billiard parlor and turned in their direction.

They stopped when they saw the big man with his arms above his head.

"What's going on?" one of them said.

She started walking away. She put the derringer in her purse, turned, and picked up her pace. She walked briskly away down the boardwalk. Her footsteps echoed in the street.

"That whore pulled a fucking gun on me."

He looked to her, moving away.

"You fucking whore!"

She came through the door like a sudden gust of wind and slammed it behind her. The noise stirred the kid where he lay naked, facedown on the bed. He lifted his head. She was twisting her hands and pacing. He watched her, then lifted up a bit and rested on his elbows. He was groggy, confused, and somewhat disoriented.

"What is happening?"

She paced a few times before she said anything.

"I saw him," she said.

He lifted up more and wiped the sleep from his eyes.

"The lawman?"

"Yes."

"What time is it?"

"Nighttime," she said. "Nighttime."

"How did you find him?"

"By chance," she said.

"Where?"

"In a restaurant."

"You talk with him?"

She shook her head.

"No."

"He see you?"

"No," she said. "And it would make no differ-

355

ence. He has not seen me, not really. Only as a much younger person, a child, really."

"Not a good place to ambush someone."

"I was not considering that."

"What are you considering?"

"I don't know for certain."

The kid stayed lifted up, resting on his elbows as he watched her. She was walking circles in the room, agitated like a caged cat. Not meeting his eye.

"Look at me," he said.

She did as he asked but continued to circle.

"Have you changed your mind?" he said.

"I don't know."

"Well, what do you know?" he said.

"Taking happiness away."

"What?"

"Just that," she said.

"How would you do that?"

"My father was no good. He was truly no good. I do not know why I have this feeling. This anger. But he was my father."

He watched her some before he spoke.

"I know about taking away happiness," he said.

She slowed her pace but still twisted her hands together.

"It's what I do," he said.

She crossed to the window and stopped. Her back was to him.

"The tintype," she said.
"What?"
She turned to him.
"Let me see your photograph."

58

By four o'clock the following day, Hank and Skeeter had yet to return to Appaloosa after their trip to Dover to talk with Maureen Crow. We figured they'd have been back by now but that the rain likely slowed them down. There had been nothing more from Victor or any of his hands that rode out of town. And for the moment we were waiting.

I was working with a rank young bay I bought at an auction when Virgil decided to stop by to check on my progress.

"You been busy?"

"The normal," he said.

"Big day tomorrow," I said.

"Appaloosa Days?" he said with a squint.

"Yep, that time."

"Yeah, Allie's not talked nothing else since she convinced the damn city alderman to do the damn thing," he said. "I'll be damn glad when it's over."

"Oh, don't worry, it will never be over

with Allie. She'll figure out some other sort of function after this one's over."

"That ain't even in the least bit amusing, Everett."

After I tired the bay and let him out to pasture, I walked to the barn. Virgil was sitting on the corral fence, watching a red-tail circling in the distance.

"Know what I'm thinking, Everett?"

"I do not."

He turned to me with a serious expression.

"I'm thinking about getting me another one of them Julieta cigars from Wallis."

"Think you might want to get a beer to go with it?"

"I do."

We sat in the Boston House saloon drinking beer as we watched what was left of the humid day begin to cool.

We'd ordered a second beer when I saw Lloyd's little grandson Timothy walk in from the hotel lobby. Timothy was a feisty twelve-year-old towhead who worked helping Allie out at her shop. Timothy was one of the main reasons that Lloyd had moved to Appaloosa. Lloyd figured since he was getting on in years he'd spend as much time as he could with his daughter and her children; both Timothy and his older sister,

Louise, worked part-time at Allie's shop. Timothy rotated his little head around until he spotted Virgil and me. He removed his floppy hat and hurried over.

"Pardon me, Marshal Hitch, Marshal Cole," he said. "Miss Allie asked me to see if I could find you."

"She did, did she?" Virgil said.

"Yes, sir, Marshal, sir, and, well, I done like she said and I found you."

"That you did," Virgil said. "She say what she was needing you to find me for?"

"No, sir. I went by the sheriff's office and Grandpa Lloyd told me there was a chance I might find you at your house or here. So I come here first. 'Cause I figured you'd be here. I'm smart that way. Grandpa said if I did find you here . . . well, he told me you'd let me have a sip or two of beer."

Virgil grinned.

"He told you that?" I said.

Timothy smiled. He nodded hard, then squirmed like he had to pee.

"He did, did he?" I said. "Don't go fibbing, now."

Timothy blushed.

"Okay . . . no," he said. "I made that part up about the beer and you giving me a taste and all."

"That's kind of what I figured," I said.

"You know what happens to fibbers, don't you?"

"They grow up to be liars?" Timothy said.

"They do," I said.

"I was just joshing," he said. "But I'll take a sip."

"No," I said.

"Shucks," he said, and clicked his fingers as if he'd just missed rolling snake eyes.

"What Allie want?" Virgil said.

"She said she needed to see you is all I know. Said it was im*por*tant."

"She's still at the shop?" Virgil said.

"Yes, sir. Marshal, sir, she is."

"Thank you, Timothy."

Timothy remained standing there, looking at Virgil with an expectant look. I fished a nickel from my pocket and flipped it to him. He snatched it out of the air and grinned.

"Gosh," he said. "Thank you."

He turned and scurried out the door.

"Little shit," I said with a smile.

Virgil nodded.

"Duty calls," he said.

The rain had stopped, but a heavy fog rolled in, making the dark night darker. The streetlamps and lanterns in the storefront windows up and down Main Street were fuzzy behind the thick fog. Virgil and I walked along the boardwalk, making our

361

way toward Allie's shop.

When we turned onto Appaloosa Avenue, we could see a crowd down a ways entering the theater for the evening performance.

"Gonna go see that actress tonight again after the show?" Virgil said.

" 'That actress'?"

"Martha Kathryn," he said with a nod.

"I just might," I said. "Never know."

Virgil grinned.

"Well, if you don't know, I do."

"You think so?"

"At supper she was holding your hand like it belong to her."

We crossed the street, close to Baptiste's office. It was dark. The place was closed. Virgil slowed to a stop in front of the office as he puffed on his cigar.

"The sonsabitches."

"They are," I said.

"Just because we ruled out Baptiste and that ass Eugene Pritchard," Virgil said, and then continued walking on toward Allie's shop, "it don't mean that somehow, some way, they didn't have a hand in this."

"No," I said. "They have the motive."

"They do," Virgil said.

As we walked past the theater, Virgil smiled and nodded to the placard near the front door with the figure of Martha Kathryn striking an elegant pose.

"She's a lovely lady," Virgil said.

"She is," I said.

"You two are getting to be mutually exclusive."

"You figure?"

"I do."

"Could be worse."

"Could," Virgil said.

"Better than sleeping alone or with whores all the damn time," I said.

"What happens when the show is over and the curtain closes?"

"Cross that bridge when we get to it," I said.

When we arrived at Allie's shop, Virgil flicked what was left of the cigar into the street and I opened the door.

"There you are," Allie said.

She sat behind her desk toward the rear of the shop. And sitting across from her was Bernice McCormick. She turned, looking at us, then got to her feet. Allie stood up, too.

"Evening," Virgil said as he removed his hat.

"Allie," I said. "Mrs. McCormick."

Bernice's nose and eyes were red, and it was clear that she had been crying.

"Something is . . ." Allie said. "Well . . .

she . . ."

"I'm in fear for my life," Bernice said.

59

She and the kid were in the rear of a large haberdashery on Seventh Street. He was wearing a new black pin-striped suit and a white shirt and a pair of new boots, too. They were tall, black chaparral boots with Mexican heels. She wanted him to be fitted with a pair of shoes, but he insisted on the boots. They made him feel taller and more at ease.

They were standing in front of a mirror and she fitted a crisp-brim black beaver felt hat on his head. Then she stood back, admiring her creation, and nodded.

There were a few other customers moving about as the owner of the place walked the aisles and called out, "I'll be closing up here in a few minutes or so. Don't want to rush you folks, but just letting you know."

She stared at the kid in the mirror.

"Looks good," she said.

"I look like a preacher," he said.

"If you wore shoes you would be more

refined even," she said.

"I ain't wearing no dandy shoes," he said. "Next thing you know you'll want me to carry a goddamn parasol."

"You look handsome," she said.

He studied himself in the mirror.

"Pink paint on a pig," he said with a serious expression.

"I mean it," she said.

She stepped up behind him and smoothed out the shoulders of his jacket.

"It's a very good change," she said. "Makes me see you in a whole different manner."

"Yeah, whole different manner for sure," he said. "Like a preacher about to spread the gospel."

She slid her hand down inside the front of his trousers and whispered, "No," she said. "Not thinking about you spreading the gospel."

She stared at him in the mirror.

"I'm thinking about something much more rewarding. Something that gives back."

She leaned down and bit his neck.

"Ow," he said.

She continued to stroke him under his pants as she stared at him in the mirror.

"You best stop that 'fore I take you down right here," he said with a grin. "Or blow a hole in these new Yankee breeches."

A train whistle called out its wailing cry in

the distance as she continued to stroke him. She removed her hand and took a few steps away, studying him.

"You don't look like a little Mexican any-more."

He put his hands over the bulge in his pants.

"You want to look good, don't you? You don't want your mother to run away when she sees a dark-headed boy with blue eyes and brown skin dressed as a Mexican *chico,* do you?"

"I ain't no boy," the kid said. "No Mexican *chico.*"

"You are close to it," she said.

He turned and faced her with a serious expression.

"No," he said. "I am not."

His eyes were narrow and intense. He stared hard at her. She took a step back, admiring him, and nodded.

"No . . . You are no boy."

She placed her hands on his shoulders, ap-praising him as if he were her creation.

"I would not be here if I thought you were nothing but a simple boy."

She turned him around slowly to face the mirror again.

The whistle of an inbound locomotive blared loudly as he stared at her. It offered a haunt-ing moan that echoed through haberdashery as the rumbling sound of the train neared the station.

"He is grown," she said, staring at him.

He shifted his eyes off her to his own reflection.

"Yes. He is grown up right before us. Here he is, in his gentleman clothes."

He stared at himself for a long time then met her eye.

"You think it's her you seen?" he said. "You really do?"

60

Bernice spent a good amount of time crying before she told us the source of her fear.

Allie shook her head slowly and said, "Can
you believe it?"

Virgil glanced at me and I nodded.

"No reason not to," I said.

"It's just too awful," Allie said. "And you
have to do something about it, Virgil."

"Allie," Virgil said.

"Well," Allie said, "you have to help her."

"We will," Virgil said.

"This is biblical," Allie said.

Bernice nodded slightly.

"Not that it makes it any easier," Bernice
said, "but James and Daniel were half-
brothers."

"Still," Allie said. "My God."

"Do you have proof?" he said.

"Just what I know. It was no secret that
they had different mothers."

"I mean proof of . . ."

"Oh, of course. No, I have no proof. But with me out of the way . . . well . . ."

She stopped talking and stared at the floor.

"What makes you say this? Seeing how you have no proof?"

She met Virgil's eyes.

"It would all be his," she said.

Virgil sat back in his chair.

"There," Allie said. "There is the proof."

"That's motive, Allie, and that is more than understandable, logical," I said. "No doubt. But there has to be some reason for you to say this, to feel you are . . ."

"In danger," Allie interjected.

Bernice shook her head and shrugged.

"I'm sorry . . . it's an overwhelming intuition," she said. "I'm sorry. Simply a hunch."

"Maybe more than a hunch?" Virgil said.

"Nothing firm," she said.

"Did James ever say anything?" I said. "Anything that caused you to worry or be concerned?"

"No, not really," she said. "James was not the type of person to share his emotions. Well . . . at least he did not share them with me."

"But with others?" I said.

"Not really. Not that I know of, anyway."

"What was their relationship like?" I said.

"They were not the best of friends. They argued more than they talked."

"About?" I said.

"Oh, I don't know. Everything and nothing."

"Money?" I said.

She nodded.

"Among other things."

"Like?" Virgil said.

"Oh . . . I can't think of anything too specific, really. I think Daniel resented James."

"Why?" I said.

She shook her head.

"Younger, stronger, smarter, I guess," she said. "I don't know, but there seemed to be a good deal of jealousy on Daniel's part."

"Why did you not say this to us before?" I said. "At dinner. Or before, after we talked with you in the office?"

"I don't know. At first these thoughts were just in the back of my mind, only fleeting. I kept disregarding them, but then the thoughts became more and more constant. Then I became . . . I don't know, just very fearful. But I must say it is instinctual. This . . . This is nothing more than a hunch, I'm afraid. A concern."

"Why now?" Virgil said.

Bernice did not answer. She turned away slightly.

"Has he threatened you in some way?" I said.

She shook her head.

"No."

"But there is something?" Virgil said.

She nodded and tipped her head in the direction of her home.

"I awoke this morning. I heard some dogs barking behind the house. Then I thought I heard something. A noise, sounded like a door closing. I looked out and I . . . I don't know. Perhaps I was seeing things, but I thought I saw someone. I did not go back to sleep. I did not go downstairs. And it was then that my mind began to race. And, I thought it could just be my imagination. Well, then again, it very well might not be my imagination. The following morning, I asked Netta, my housemaid, if she heard anything through the night. She said she heard the dogs for a spell but thought nothing of it."

"Do you think the gunmen that were hired by James and Daniel had a hand in James's death?" I said.

"Well . . . yes. Could be, I suppose. I mean, there is a good chance that Daniel did not personally commit the murder and the gunmen did it. But I don't know."

"When did you first have this notion," I said.

"Suspicion?" she said.

"Yes."

"After the funeral was the first time it truly, completely crossed my mind, but I did not linger on the notion. After the service we all gathered there at Daniel and Irene's house. Irene and some of the ladies from the Appaloosa social made food. Allie, too, thank you, dear . . . and there was a gathering of mourners, company employees, mostly, and their families. Then some of the men he'd hired, not the office workers, the shop people, or the miners but the gunmen, came to the house."

"And did something happen?" Virgil said.

She shook her head.

"Nothing, really, but Daniel stepped out. They talked privately on the porch, then he left with them. Later he came in and said something to me about how sorry he was, and then he took off. He might have said where he was going at the time, but my mind was thinking about . . . well, about everything. About what we are discussing and about James and about how much I was going to miss him."

"Was Edward Hodge one of the men?" I

said. "On the porch?"

"I don't know their names," she said.

"The big fella that came to your house the night James died," Virgil said.

"Oh, yes, him," she said. "He was the main fellow doing the talking on the porch. He seemed angry."

"Any idea what they talked about?" Virgil said. "You catch anything?"

She shook her head.

"No. Sorry."

"And you don't know where they went that day?" Virgil said. "When they left?"

"I do not."

"Any idea of Daniel's current whereabouts?" I said.

She shook her head.

"No." Then she pointed in the direction of his office. "The office, perhaps, home, at the mines or one of the shops . . . I don't know."

"And what about Daniel's wife?" Virgil said. "Irene?"

"What about her?" she said.

"Have you shared this fear with her?" Virgil said.

Bernice shook her head.

"No. And I would not."

"Because?" Virgil said.

"I don't know. I guess I'm just . . . I just

don't want to alarm her. If I'm wrong, something like this could have serious repercussions. And I'm sorry to bring this up now, Allie, to you, too. I know tomorrow is the big event, Appaloosa Days, and, well, I'm . . . well, I'm sorry for this."

"Are you serious?" Allie said. "You just know that you are far more important than any ol' party. Everything is done, Appaloosa Days will take care of itself at this point in time."

"Well, regardless, I don't like to —"

"Stop right there, Bernice," Allie said, then turned to Virgil. "Now what?"

"We will do what we have to do, Allie," Virgil said.

"What does that mean?" she said.

"We need to have a word with him," Virgil said.

"Just a word?" Allie said.

"Allie, we can't just arrest him without having some reason."

"Well, you have a reason."

"Reason, but we have no proof."

"Well, something has to be done," Allie said.

Allie reached out and took Bernice's hand.

"First and foremost, Virgil, taking care of Bernice is of the utmost priority."

"We have had the deputies keeping watch

since James's passing, Allie."

Virgil offered a reassuring and serious smile to Bernice.

"But we will see to it that you will have a guard with you now at all times. Night and day till we get to the bottom of this," he said. "We will keep you safe."

"Yes," Allie said. "Yes."

She squeezed Bernice's hand.

"I would be mortified. Just mortified if something were to happen to beautiful Bernice."

61

Virgil stepped out of Allie's shop with me, and we both turned our attention up Appaloosa Avenue toward McCormick's office. We said nothing for a few seconds. Then Virgil shook his head and turned a little to see Allie and Bernice through the window. Allie was still holding Bernice's hand.

"I did not see that coming," I said.

"No. Me neither."

"I guess it makes as much sense as anything else," I said.

"Does," Virgil said.

"Could be in her head?" I said.

Virgil nodded.

"That, too."

"A noise at night?" I said. "A barking dog. Nothing unusual about that."

"No matter," Virgil said. "Good to have her watched over, just in case."

"Good, in the simple fact Allie would have your hide and mine otherwise."

"That, too," he said.

"Bernice did not come up with anything that seemed too damn firm, though."

"No, I know."

"Makes sense, though," I said.

"Him wanting her gone?" Virgil said.

"Yeah. Like she said, then it's all his."

Virgil nodded.

"But he doesn't seem like the type," I said.

"Capable of murder?"

"Yeah," I said with a nod. "He's not your average."

"No, but everybody is capable. Everybody, Everett, you know that."

"No, I know. We've damn sure been around enough to know all about that."

"Big motive, though," Virgil said.

Virgil gave a brief glance into the shop again.

"Go on," he said. "I'll wait here with them."

I left Virgil on the porch of Allie's shop and walked to the sheriff's office to procure a deputy watchman for Bernice. When I passed McCormick's office I could see that the business was still open. I did not see Daniel, but there were lamps burning and a handful of McCormick's employees were at their desks, busy doing paperwork.

By six-thirty there was still no sign of

378

Deputies Hank and Skeeter when I stopped in the sheriff's office. Lloyd called out the back door to a big, strapping young deputy named Weldon, who was in the rear corral tending to the horses.

"Got a job for you, Weldon," Lloyd said.

I explained in detail to Weldon what needed to be done. He nodded at each of my instructions, as if a puppeteer were lifting his big head up and down by a string.

"Don't let anybody in her house under any circumstances. If she leaves, make sure you are with her at all times."

"Yes, sir," Weldon said.

"She goes out to shop, or eat, or goes out to pee, stay with her at all times."

Weldon glanced to Lloyd.

"She pees outside?" Weldon said. "Thought all them people in them big fancy houses up there had commodes and did all their business indoors."

"Get your shotgun, Weldon," Lloyd said, shooing him outside like a wasp. "And saddle your horse, too. You need to keep yourself at the ready for any and everything, son, understand?"

"Understand," Weldon said.

"All right, then," Lloyd said. "Carry on."

"Yes, sir," Weldon said with a nod, then walked out to saddle his horse.

"Don't worry. He's qualified, Everett. Otherwise he would not be part of this outfit. He's goddamn sure the biggest, most intimidating of the eight deputies we got, but I must confess, he don't often win at checkers. Never, as a matter of fact, but it'd take a goddamn village to bring him to his knees."

Virgil and I left Weldon standing on the porch in front of Allie's shop, holding his shotgun like an Army sentry. Then we headed toward McCormick's office.

"Been thinking," Virgil said.

" 'Bout?"

"Ed Hodge."

"What about him?"

"Could be one of his other gun hands, nothing to do with him. Don't think he had a hand in this."

We walked a ways and I thought back on all of our interactions with him.

"No, it does not seem likely. Does it?"

"No."

I nodded.

"Him coming to the office with James when we locked up his men," I said. "Then coming to the house, raising a fuss with you after James was found dead, then us coming across him on the trail. He's not smart enough to cobble together a front like that."

"No, he's not."

"And then him hanging around, watching us, following us," I said with a shake of my head.

"Not him," Virgil said.

"Then Daniel?" I said.

"Don't know."

"Know something soon enough," I said.

"I suspect we will," Virgil said.

"You thought any about what Allie said?" Virgil glanced to me.

"About what kind of *word* that we'll have with Daniel?"

"Yeah."

"I reckon we will just have to ask him outright," Virgil said.

"And see what he says?" I said.

"Yep."

"What do you think?" I said.

"He won't like it none," Virgil said.

"No," I said. "I don't imagine that he'll take too kindly to the question."

"No," Virgil said. "Don't imagine he will."

62

The kid twirled his old Colt pistol. It was void of blue, and in places it was showing its age with hints of rust. He flipped it first one way, then the other, as he paced anxiously in their hotel room.

"What is the plan?" he said.

"Plan?" she said.

"Yeah, what are we gonna do?"

"About what?"

"Everything."

The teamster's wife was getting dressed behind a screen as she watched the kid. She could tell he felt good in his new clothes. He strutted back and forth, pausing now and again to look in the mirror, stopping periodically to quickly point the gun at his reflection.

"I thought we'd go for a walk," she said.

"Walk? Walk where?"

"Oh . . . Through the nice part of town," she said.

"Walk and do what?"

"Check things out. Find some food. Looks like a nice evening."

"Think that is where she will be? The nice part of town?"

She continued to dress without responding to him. She powdered her neck with a delicate dust that sparkled, then she stepped into her dress.

"Tomorrow we will find her," she said. "Not tonight. Tonight is for us. For the two of us."

"What makes you think we will find her tomorrow?"

"I just know."

"How?"

"Tomorrow is a big occasion here. A party. Appaloosa Days."

"Appaloosa Days," he said. "And you think she will be there?"

"Yes," she said.

"How do you know?"

"I know."

"Damn," the kid said. "Damn. After all this time. After all these years. Son of a bitch."

The kid picked up the tintype off the dresser. He rubbed his thumb lightly across his mother's face in the photo. Then he laid it to rest gently on the dresser and continued to walk back and forth. His mind was racing, she could tell. He was half present and half someplace else with his thoughts as he paced.

"I like parties," he said.

"Everyone will be there tomorrow," she said.

"The lawman, too?" he said.

She did not say anything else to him. She just watched the kid moving to his left, then to his right. Always checking the mirror with each passing. He did not dwell on the idea of the lawman, though. She could tell where his thoughts resided. He stopped in front of the window looking out on the street. He stood for a long time staring out before he said anything.

"Wonder what she does," he said.

She did not reply.

"Wonder where she lives, what kind of home. And with who? I wonder if she is married."

She studied him, then . . .

"I think we will find out soon enough," she said.

"You figure?"

"I do," she said. "Why we are here."

"Among other things," he said.

She stared at him, and he turned his gaze out the window again.

"Wonder what she is like," he said.

"What would you want for her to be like?"

He thought before he answered.

"Hell, I don't know."

"But you wonder."

"Well, hell, yeah. What I said. I guess I have always wondered that. Wouldn't you?"

"Yes. I understand."

" 'Course you do."

He turned and stared at her. Then he grinned and faced the window again. He put a hand on each side of the frame, opening the curtains wider. She could see his boyish reflection in the glass.

"Wonder why she did what she did," he said. "Where she has been all these years . . . If she ever missed me."

He gazed upward, as if he were searching for a star. He shook his head.

"Probably don't give a rat's ass," he said. "Why would she?"

She came out from behind the dressing screen wearing a black dress and walked to him.

"Button me up."

She turned her back to him. He stuck the Colt behind his belt, and did as she asked. The dress was low around her neck and her dark skin glowed in the lamplight.

"I been thinking," he said.

"About?"

"What should I say to her? When I find her?"

"What would you like to say?"

He thought as he worked on the buttons.

"Say what you feel," she said.

"That's just the thing. I don't know how I feel."

"What do you want from her?"

He laughed a little.

"I don't know that, either."

"Are you angry at her?"

He thought and nodded.

"Would you be?"

"I have nothing to do with this."

"The hell you don't. You brought me here. You primed me."

"You say that like I filled you with gunpowder."

"Maybe you did."

"So, you are angry with her?"

"I don't know anger, really."

He finished with the buttons. She turned to him.

"I'm just who I am. And for the most part, I think you could say that I am happy."

"Happy?"

"Yes."

"You are a killer."

He pulled the pistol from his belt and stuck it into her stomach. He stared at her.

"I never knew my mother," she said.

"No?" he said.

"No . . . Only my father."

"Why?"

"She died."

"How?"

"Giving life to me."

63

Lawrence, Daniel's office manager, was removing his dress jacket from the back of his desk chair when Virgil and I entered McCormick's office. There were three other young men in the office, all putting on their hats and buttoning their coats, preparing to leave.

"Good evening," Lawrence said. "Just about to close up here. Can I help you?"

"It's Lawrence," I said. "Right?"

"Yes, sir," he said with a smile and a nod. "What can I do for you?"

"Looking for Daniel McCormick," I said.

"I'm sorry, Mr. McCormick's not in."

"Any idea where he might be?" Virgil said.

Lawrence smiled again and shook his head as he put on his jacket.

Virgil kept looking at him.

Lawrence held up a finger and smiled.

"Excuse me one moment, Marshals," he said, then turned to his coworkers. "That's all, fellas, good day, thank you and see you tomorrow . . . Don't be late."

The three young men nodded, said their goodbyes, then filed out the door.

"Well, I'm not real sure about Mr. McCormick," Lawrence said.

"What are you unsure about?"

"His whereabouts, exactly," Lawrence said.

"You have some idea?" I said.

"Well, yes, I'm sorry, all I know is he went out of town on business."

"You don't know where?" I said.

"No."

"What kind of business?" I said.

"I don't know. Is there something I can perhaps help with?"

"No," Virgil said.

"Sorry. I have no idea what his business was. All I know is he told us he was leaving town for a few days and for us to do our job and do it well."

"When will he be back?" Virgil said.

"I don't actually know. The fact is, he was supposed to return today, this evening's train, but I don't know if he made it." Lawrence turned and looked at the clock on the wall. "It arrived an hour ago, but we've not seen him. Perhaps he went straight to his home . . . I'm not certain. Some of

389

his men were here looking for him as well. Perhaps he's at the house."

"What men?"

"The men he hired for security at the mines. I don't know their names."

Lawrence removed his hat from the hat rack.

"I had everyone stay later than usual, figuring he might have things for us to do. But here we are, and it's been a pretty long day, as we were all here before sunup to get the stuff done that we needed to do. We only have a half-day tomorrow, on account of the street closing for Appaloosa Days."

Virgil nodded, then walked over to a huge map of the McCormick Mining Company on the wall behind a row of desks. He studied it, then turned to Lawrence.

"How long have you worked here?" Virgil said.

"I was the first person hired by the Mc-Cormicks when Daniel and James arrived here to Appaloosa."

Virgil nodded and turned to the map again.

"So you knew James well?" he said.

"Yes, pretty well. He was my boss. Well, both of them, actually. I've worked for them since I first arrived in Appaloosa myself."

"Was James a friend?"

"I guess. I mean, as much as an employee can be a friend . . . This has . . . well, it has been hard. With James's passing, it has been a very difficult time for all of us."

"What can you tell us about James?" I said.

"What would you like to know?"

"Just tell us about him."

"Well, my gosh, we miss him. James was kind. I looked up to him. He treated me, treated all of us, very fair. And like I'm saying, it's been just very sad, difficult."

I nodded.

"What do you do here, Lawrence?" I said.

"Well," he said as he looked about the room. "A lot. A bit of everything — accounting, mostly, I'd say. Accounts payable and accounts receivable, that sort of thing. But I do everything from writing letters to taking out the trash. No job too big or too small."

"What can you tell me about their relationship?" I said. "Daniel and James."

"What do you want to know?"

"Did they like each other?"

Lawrence smiled a bit.

"Yes, they were brothers . . . well, half-brothers."

"Did you ever hear the two men argue?"

He shrugged.

"Some," he said. "As people do managing a business. It's stressful at times."

"Were you here, in the office, on the day James died?"

"Yes."

"Did you see him leave the office that day?"

"No, I was out."

"Thought you said you were here?"

"Oh, well, I was here working that day, but I was out running errands."

"And Daniel was here in the office when you went out?"

"Yes."

"Was Daniel here when you returned?"

"Yes."

"What kind of errands?"

His eyes went back and forth between Virgil and me.

"The usual."

"Which is?" I said.

"Well, I made deposits at the bank. I went to the Western Union office and sent some wires to our vendors, a number of them, actually, which took a while. Then . . . let's see, I went by Hammersmith's hardware and picked up some office supplies. And I stopped at Hal's and had myself a cream soda."

"When was the last time you saw James,

then?" I said.

"Before I left that day. When I returned, he was gone."

"What time did you return?"

"Oh, gosh, around four-thirty, quarter till five. Something like that."

"Did you speak with him prior to leaving the office?"

"Not really, nothing specific."

"Did you talk with Daniel when you returned?"

"No. Not really. I just went about the rest of my day. Mr. McCormick, Daniel, was in his office though."

"Was he alone?"

"Yes."

"When you last saw James, was he acting odd in any manner?"

"Odd?"

"Yes," I said.

"No, I wouldn't say so."

"He didn't appear ill?"

"No. Not that I could tell. No."

"Where, exactly, did you last see him?"

"He was in his office," he said with a point. "Look, I . . . I'm sorry, but . . . is this about his death?"

"What makes you say that?" I said.

"Well. Look, I know it has been speculated

that there was something amiss about his death."

"Speculated by whom?" I said.

"Just what happened, him falling dead on the street. Right in front of his home. All of us here in the office thought it suspect, that is all. One day he is fine and then he collapses and dies. It just seemed suspect." Lawrence frowned and twisted his hands. "Is that right? Did something bad happen to him? Did someone . . . you know?"

"We are just trying to understand some of the business here is all, Lawrence," I said.

"You said you hired on when you first got here to Appaloosa?" Virgil said.

"Yes."

"How was it you came to Appaloosa in the first place?"

"I'm related to the McCormicks. My aunt is Irene, Daniel's, um . . . Mr. McCormick's wife. When I graduated from the university, I came here straightaway and they hired me. Gave me a place to stay."

"You live with Daniel and his wife?"

"Yes, but I'm trying to save money to buy my own home."

Virgil nodded.

"But it is not easy," Lawrence said. "If that is what you are thinking."

Virgil smiled.

"Thinking?" he said.

"I'm just saying there is no favoritism or nepotism at work here. I earn my way like everyone else that works for the firm. Like everyone, in the shops, at the ranch, the mines, I keep my nose to my business and work hard. I take nothing for granted and I avoid taking advantage of the McCormicks in any way. I don't do anything that would rile anyone."

"Does Daniel rile easy?"

"No," Lawrence said a bit quickly.

"No?" I said.

"Well, sometimes," he said, "but if so, it is never unwarranted."

"What is warranted?"

"Oh, you know, typical business things. He likes for things to run smoothly."

Virgil stared at Lawrence, then nodded.

"Much appreciated," Virgil said, then turned to the door.

"Can you tell me what this is all about?" Lawrence said.

Virgil stopped and turned to him.

"We just want to have a word with Mr. McCormick. That is all, son."

We walked out, closing the door behind us.

We crossed the street and started walking

in the direction of Daniel McCormick's residence.

"Don't think there is a person left in town who believes James died of natural causes."

"Keeps everybody guessing, though," Virgil said.

"That it does," I said.

"Except for whoever did it," Virgil said. "They ain't guessing."

"Nope."

We stepped up on the boardwalk and walked a ways, then Virgil gave me a glance.

"Nepotism?" he said.

"An offering . . . a favor to kinfolk," I said. "Like giving a job to a relative."

"Like to a nephew?" Virgil said.

"Yep. That's right. Like to a nephew."

64

We walked straight to Daniel and Irene's place. By the time we approached the house, it was good and dark out. There were two lanterns hanging off the porch posts on either side of the steps, and as we neared we saw someone was sitting near the front door in a rocker. When we got closer, we could see that it was Irene. She was slowly rocking in the chair with a drink in her hand.

"Mrs. McCormick?" Virgil said.

"Hello there," she said.

Virgil removed his hat.

"Pardon the time of evening," he said.

"Not at all," she said. "It is early still. What brings you fellows around?"

"Looking for your husband."

"Well, I am sorry to say he's not in. Might I be able to help you with something?"

"No, just wanted to have a chat with him."

Irene shook her head.

"So sorry, he's gone. But I'm happy to chat. Love to, actually. Can I pour you two a drink?"

She held up her glass.

We could tell this was not her first drink of the evening, and likely wouldn't be her last.

"I thought he would have been home by now," she said. "He might be at the office."

"No," Virgil said. "We were just by the office."

She shook her head.

"I don't know, then. He was supposed to have been on the afternoon train. Returning from a business trip he took to Santa Fe . . . or so he said."

"You mean there is a chance he didn't make the train?"

"I did not say that," she said with a smile. "Regardless, I'm out here on the porch, having myself an aperitif."

She held up her glass again.

"Know what sort of business trip to Santa Fe?" I said.

"Oh, I don't know," she said with a slur. "I don't actually ever really know the ins and outs of my husband's affairs."

She stopped talking, as if she lost her train of thought, and stared off up the street, then turned to us and smiled. Besides her being in her cups, there was a definite detached quality to her manner as she spoke to us. Her eyes had a dead coldness.

"You fellas look as though you need some answers of some sort. Give me a question or two. Let's see what I come up with. Answer-wise."

"That is all right," I said. "We'll catch up with him as some point."

"Oh, what is it, Marshals? Seriously. Perhaps I could be of some assistance?"

Virgil glanced to me and grinned.

"One of his hired hands," Virgil said. "Edward Hodge stopped and paid him a visit here at your house. After the funeral."

"And some of the other men he hired. Yes, indeed, they came by the house."

"Know of a reason?"

"Well, see, I can be of help with that. Since Daniel was to be gone, he was giving them instructions while he's away."

"What sort of instructions?"

"Just to mind the candy store," she said. "Can't be too careful with all that is at stake in my husband's candy-shop world. That's a lot of gold candy."

"Do you know where Edward Hodge and the other men are?" I said.

"Well, there you go, I can be helpful. Mr. Hodge and two of his men came by here earlier. Thought Daniel would be home by now. Likely the rest are at the mine. Watching over the candy . . . Are you sure you don't want to join me for a drink?"

"No, thank you," Virgil said. "And . . . that's all. Good evening to you, Mrs. McCormick."

"Evening, Mrs. McCormick," I said with a nod.

We turned and started to walk away.

"What would you like me to say to him when I do see him?" she said.

"Just that we came by," Virgil said.

"That I can do," she said.

"Let him know we just came for a visit."

"A visit. All right, then," she said.

We turned and walked off. Irene let us get a good ways from the house before she spoke up.

"Is it her?" she said.

We stopped and turned.

"What's that?" Virgil said.

"The bitch wolf?"

65

Virgil shot me a quick glance and we walked
slowly toward the porch.

"Pardon?" he said.

"Is she why you want to talk with Daniel?"

"Ma'am?" I said.

"The bitch wolf said she thinks he's trying to get rid of her, didn't she?"

"Who?" Virgil said.

"Very clever," she said.

She tapped her temple with her finger.

"What are you getting at?"

"Getting at? Oh, come now. No reason to
beat around the bush, Marshals."

"What are you saying, Mrs. McCormick?"
I said.

"Oh, I know a thing or two," she said.

"Like?" I said.

"And to think I was like a mother to her."

We moved closer to the porch.

"It's always the pretty ones, isn't it?" she said.

She chuckled and took a sip of whiskey.

"I never really suspected a thing until a few days ago, though. Not really."

"Suspected what?" Virgil said.

"And then I saw that look in her eye."

"What look?" Virgil said.

"Oh, a look only a woman could understand. But I'm sure you know the look. Handsome men like you get those kinds of looks often. I'm sure."

We edged up even closer.

"I knew of her background . . . She was a prostitute, you know. Before she married James she worked on her back. I did not find that out until later, though. She was well spoken for a whore, I will give you that, not your average streetwalker or barroom trash. She was refined. And I thought, I'll keep quiet. Goodness gracious, everybody has to begin someplace. Me, I was lucky. I was raised to be a princess. My father was quite wealthy, you see. I was brought up with the best of the best. We were very blessed. I had my own servants growing up, three of them, actually, can you believe that? They would fuss over me let me tell you. They would dress me in the finest clothes."

"What are you getting at?" Virgil said.

"Oh, sorry . . . Never know when you reflect you might just remember or find that nugget . . . that, that gold nugget, that seminal point in time, when you made the wrong decision . . . Listen to me, rambling on, talking about fine clothes and gold. Rambling on like a person without etiquette or a point to make . . . James fell for her and she had everyone fooled. Even me."

"What did you mean by her being clever?"

"She turned on him," Irene said. "Right? She rode him right where she wanted him, then she turned on him."

"She turned on James?" I said.

"Daniel," she said.

"She rode your husband?" I said.

"Did she ever."

"Bernice and your husband?" Virgil said.

"All I can tell you is if anybody should be fearful for their life, it's me."

"Why you?" I said.

"With Daniel out of the way, I'm the bull's-eye."

"So Bernice and your husband are . . . ?"

"To put it bluntly," she said. "Fornicating."

"How do you know this?" I said.

"I know. At least they were, there is no telling what's going to happen now. And my nephew, poor thing, he saw this, too, he witnessed them. He knows. Lord knows who else knows. But it's clear that James was murdered, and I do not think he will be the last victim in the saga."

"Who do you think was responsible for James's death?"

"A million-dollar question."

"Do you think your husband killed James?" Virgil said.

"I don't know. I don't think so. But nothing would surprise me at this point in time."

"And her, do you think she killed her husband?" I said.

"No idea. I would like to say yes, but I don't have a clue."

"Before, when we talked with you in the office, you spoke of her fondly," I said.

"That changed," she said. "Didn't it?"

"Now you are accusing her," I said.

"Isn't it funny how something copacetic can quickly become a horse of a different color?"

She leaned forward in the rocker and lifted her rigid body out of the chair. She was not unsteady, but she was not steady, either.

"Now, if you'll excuse me," she said. "I am going inside to refresh my drink."

"Certainly," I said.

She opened the door, then leveled a look to us.

"You boys have a fine evening."

With that, she entered and closed the door behind her.

"Well, hell," I said.

Virgil shook his head some and we started back the way we came.

"Do you believe her?" I said.

"Whiskey talking," Virgil said.

"There is that," I said. "Yes."

We walked a ways, thinking. Then we slowed to a stop and looked back to the house.

"Now what?" I said.

"Need to get Daniel," Virgil said.

"Santa Fe?"

Virgil shook his head.

"We wait," Virgil said.

"What about Bernice?"

"Have to talk with her," he said.

"Confront her, you think?" I said.

"Think we have to."

"Likely deny it."

"Likely."

"Allie will be . . . hell, I don't know what Allie will be."

"None too happy," Virgil said.

"Maybe the two of them, Daniel and Bernice, were in cahoots," I said. "Maybe Daniel's wife hit the bull's-eye thinking she is the bull's-eye. Maybe they planned it out and murdered James. Could be like Doc said. He got poisoned on his way home, then was finished off there at his house with the ice pick."

I pointed. We were close to James and Bernice's place, just across the street and a few doors up from us.

"Maybe," Virgil said.

66

We walked on, and as we neared James and
Bernice's house we did not see any sign of
Weldon. He was nowhere in sight, anyway.
There were no lamps lit on the porch, but
there was some light coming from inside.

"Reckon she's still out?" I said. "Maybe
still with Allie?"

"Might be," Virgil said.

"That notion don't settle real well," I said.
"Not now, anyway, considering what was
just imparted to us."

"No," Virgil said. "Not completely. It
don't."

"Maybe Weldon's inside the house with
her?"

We stopped at the house.

"Want to have a look-see?"

Virgil nodded.

"We're here."

We walked up the steps. I knocked and
after some time, Bernice McCormick's

housemaid, a young, slender woman with a light complexion, answered the door.

Virgil tipped his hat.

"How do?" he said.

She offered a demure smile.

"Hello," she said.

"I'm Deputy Marshal Everett Hitch; this is Marshal Virgil Cole."

"How can I help you?"

"We're here to see Mrs. McCormick," I said. "Is she in?"

"No, sir," she said, shaking her head, "I'm afraid she ain't here right now."

"Know where we might find her?" I said.

She shook head.

"I do not," she said.

Her accent was similar to Effie's. She had that smooth, down-home way of speaking. But her beryl eyes had a knowing and penetrating catlike quality that did not exactly fit her southern speech.

"Much appreciated," I said.

She smiled and nodded.

"Sure enough," she said, and then started to close the door.

"Hold on," Virgil said.

"Yes, sir?" she said.

"What is your name?

"Netta," she said.

"Like to ask you a few questions, Netta."

"Yes, sir? What is it?"

"Know this is hard, with the death of Mr. McCormick and all. But maybe you can help us figure out a few things."

"I'll surely try."

"You were here at the house when James died?"

She nodded.

"I was upstairs," she said.

"Where?"

She pointed.

"Like I say."

Virgil glanced upward.

"Looks like a big home," he said.

"It is."

"What were you doing upstairs? Where were you upstairs?"

"Oh. I was just in Miss Bernice's bedroom."

"Doing?" Virgil said.

"Well . . . um . . . Miss Bernice, she had me pressin' and foldin' her linens in her bedroom. Like I do. She likes her clothes to be clean and pressed."

"Bernice's bedroom?" Virgil said.

"Yes, un-ha, that's right."

"They had separate rooms?"

"What?"

"Bernice and James have separate rooms?"

"Um, I don't know."

Virgil glanced to me.

"Did James have his own bedroom?" he said.

"Um," she said, shifting her eyes, "I don't know nothing 'bout that."

"When was the last time you saw him here?"

"Mr. James?"

"Are there any other men in the house?"

"No, sir. No other mens in the house."

Virgil nodded.

"When did you last see him?"

"When Mr. James leave for work that day."

"Did you hear him come home after work?"

"Um . . . no, sir."

"But you saw him when he died?"

Her eyes shifted between us.

"I did."

"How was it you saw him?"

"What'cha mean?"

"Did you see him when he died, Netta?" Virgil said.

"Oh," she said. "I did. I come down. I heard a crashin' and I come down."

"What kind of crashing did you hear?"

She turned and pointed behind her to the table in the entrance.

"The stuff on this here table. It come off and crashed to the floor and broke all over.

I cleaned it all up like Miss Bernice say."

"Who knocked it off the table?"

"Um. He did."

"How do you know it was him?"

"Well, he knocked it all off and I cleaned it up."

"You did not see him do it?"

"No, sir."

"How did you know it was him for sure that knocked the stuff to the floor?"

"Well, Miss Bernice, she . . ."

"Told you?" Virgil said.

"That's right," she said.

Virgil nodded and smiled.

"There is ice in the kitchen?"

"Sir?"

"Is there an icebox in the kitchen?"

She nodded.

"Why, yes. Yes, sir. There sure is."

Virgil smiled.

"Fair enough," he said. "Much appreciated."

Netta closed the door, and we walked down the steps.

"What do you figure?" I said.

Virgil shook his head as he stared off up the street without answering. He pulled a Julieta cigar from his pocket, bit the tip, then dug out a match and lit it. Once he had it going, he flicked the match to the street.

"Just don't know, Everett."

I glanced to the house door.

"Don't think Bernice had a hand in it," I said.

"No?" he said.

"I don't," I said.

"What makes you say that?"

"Don't know, just don't."

Virgil nodded.

"Don't seem likely," Virgil said. "But . . . at this goddamn point, everything seems somewhat likely."

"Just because they managed two bedrooms," I said, "and Irene McCormick thinks she's fucking her husband and thinks she or they are killers, or the fact that she owns an icebox, or talked her housemaid through the story, doesn't make Bernice the murderer."

"No, it don't," Virgil said.

"One thing for certain that there is no need to lose sight of," I said. "And that is the fact that Bernice was by God sure enough upset and angry when they loaded up her husband's body. If she was acting, I'd say she's a better actress than Martha Kathryn."

67

The following morning the kid woke up hearing the faint sound of music playing somewhere in the far distance. He felt groggy and was blurry-eyed. He turned to the teamster's wife next to him. She was on her belly and sound asleep. He sat up and looked around the room. Her dress and his new suit of clothes were tossed in a rumpled heap on the floor beside the bed. There was an empty bottle of whiskey lying sideways on the nightstand. The music stopped. He checked the time. It was already past noon. He listened for the music but heard nothing.

"Shit. The music," he said. "The party."

He pushed the hair out of his eyes and stumbled to the water basin.

"Wake up," he said.

He splashed his face with handfuls of water, then turned to her. She did not budge.

"Wake up."

She cracked open one eye.

"We don't want to miss the damn party."

She rolled and looked to the clock.

"I heard music," he said.

"Do not worry," she said with a yawn. "The party does not start for another hour."

The kid picked up his coat and trousers from off the floor to shake out the wrinkles. He moved to the window, trying to hear the music again.

"It will be happening all the day long, till nightfall."

"I just want to get there," he said.

She rolled over.

"Do not panic."

"Hell, I ain't panicked."

"I have something for you," she said with a coy expression.

"No. Not now? Get up. Get dressed. Don't you want to get to the party?"

She pointed to one of her bags.

"Bring that to me. The black one."

He walked over to the bag in the corner, picked it up, and gave it to her. She stared at him as she opened the bag. She reached inside and pulled out a fancy wooden box. It had detailed carvings across the top, with a shiny brass latch and hinges.

"What's this?"

"A gift. Here, take it . . . open it."

"For me?"

She nodded. He took the box from her and opened the latch. He stared at what was inside, then met her eye.

"Goddamn."

"That is for you."

"Really?"

"Yes. Really."

He reached in the velvet-lined box and pulled out a brand-new nickel-plated Colt, engraved with a pearl-white handle.

"You like?"

"Like? Like? Hell, yeah I like."

He held it preciously, feeling its weight. He moved it between his hands, left, right, left, right, getting a feel for it. Then he walked to the mirror and looked at the gun in his hand.

"Looks good on you."

He pulled back the hammer, opened the loading gate, and spun the cylinder.

"It looks right for you."

"You think?"

"I know," she said.

He studied the gun, looking closely at the engraving, and whistled through his teeth.

"Never seen nothing like it."

"No more old and rusted firearms for you. You are now a man with a man's proper weapon."

He pointed the Colt, then twirled it forward, then backward.

"And, of course," she said as she reached in the bag and pulled out a box of bullets, "it is worthless without these."

She tossed them on the foot of the bed.

"Don't know how to thank you."

"I do."

She slid what covers were covering her to the side and motioned for him to come to her.

"Come here," she said.

He walked to her. She stared up at him and patted the bed for him to sit.

"Sit."

He sat beside her.

"Let me see it."

He handed the pistol to her.

"See this here?"

She pointed to the engraving.

"The initials?" he said.

"Yes," she said.

"This .44-40 was the prize possession of my father. It is the only thing that I have that belonged to him."

"And you want me to have it?"

"I do."

He leaned in and read the initials: "WLB."

She nodded.

"William Leviathan Brandice."

"I know why you want me to have it," he said.

"I know you know."

68

Virgil and I were standing in front of Allie's shop drinking coffee as we watched Allie putting the final touches on the stage dressings. She was ordering workers where to string up last-minute colorful banners and streamers. Seated on the wide stage was a twelve-piece band warming up for the concert that was set to begin within the hour. All the shop owners had their businesses opened up with their goods on display.

The ladies from the social were helping with the refreshment and food tables that were lined up on the boardwalks on both sides of Appaloosa Avenue. And to Allie's dismay, townspeople were already beginning to show up, streaming in from both ends of the Avenue.

Allie came down from the stage and made her way over to us, shaking her head.

"Can you believe this? Doggone people

are already coming and we are not even ready."

She took Virgil's coffee cup out of his hand and took a sip.

"Just let them do what they are gonna do," Virgil said. "And you do what you need to do."

"Well, that is what I am doing, Virgil," she said.

"I did not say you weren't, Allie."

"Just flustering is all," she said.

"You have done a hell of a job with every-thing, Allie," I said. "A hell of a job. Look-ing great."

"You have," Virgil said. "That is all, there you have it. Now you have to just let things go as they go."

"Oh goodness, Virgil."

"What?"

"Nothing."

Allie saw something else on the stage that did not meet her liking.

"Oh, shoot," she said.

She handed Virgil his coffee cup and hur-ried off to make corrections.

"There she goes," I said.

"Yep," he said.

"Well," I said. "She really has done a hell of a job putting this whole thing together."

" 'Bout killed the both of us."

"Just one more day."

"Yep."

"And it damn sure looks like this is going to be a busy one," I said. "That's a fact."

"We ought to be fishing," Virgil said.

"You don't fish," I said.

"I have."

"But you don't."

Lloyd came walking up past the stage, followed by a huge man wearing a stationmaster's cap. Lloyd spotted us in front of the shop and hurried over. When he was close, he turned about, making sure no one was listening.

"Got a situation," he said.

"What sort of situation?"

"Got us a dead man," he said.

"What?" Virgil said.

Lloyd nodded.

"Who?" I said. "What dead man?"

"Don't know just yet. This fella here is Clifford, the stationmaster from the depot. Tell them what you told me."

"Ten miles up, just past the tower, my section-line men said they found a body in the ditch near the track."

"How'd you find this out?" I said.

"They wired to the depot this morning and let me know."

"And the dead man?" I said.

419

"They picked up the body and loaded him on the handcar. They are headed this way now."

"How long do you figure it will be before they get here?" Virgil said.

Clifford pulled his watch.

"Providing they didn't run into any snags, should be pretty soon, I figure."

We wasted no time making our way over to the depot. When we arrived, there was no sign of the handcar, so we waited. After a short time, we could hear the band start up with a full-throated arrangement, and then, a few minutes later, we saw the handcar headed toward the depot. When it neared, Virgil, Lloyd, and I walked over, followed by Clifford. There was a tarp covering the body. I pulled it back to have a look.

"Holy hell," I said.

Virgil turned to the two men who operated the handcar.

"You the fellas who found him?"

They nodded.

"We are," one of them said.

"You see anybody else there? Near where you found him?"

They shook their heads.

"No," they said.

"Any clear idea how maybe this happened?" I said.

"No idea," the other of the two said. "We just found him like this. Roughed up like he is, we thought maybe he somehow fell off the train."

The other fella nodded.

"Wouldn't be the first time," he said.

Virgil leaned in for a closer look.

"Any bullet wounds?" Virgil said.

They shook their heads.

"None that we could see."

"That's the other McCormick, ain't it?" Lloyd said.

"It is," I said.

I took a closer look. The way his body was roughed up it for sure appeared that he tumbled off the train. But the way his hands and neck were contorted and retracted, the same way James's corpse had looked, let Virgil and I know right away there'd been more to it.

"McCormick?" Clifford said.

The three of us looked to Clifford.

"Another fella came looking for Daniel McCormick here this morning," Clifford said.

"Who?" Virgil said.

"Didn't say his name."

Virgil shook his head.

"Big fella?" I said. "Long red beard?"

Clifford nodded.

"He was. 'Bout my size, I'd say."

"Ed Hodge?" Lloyd said.

Virgil nodded and spoke to Clifford.

"What did he say, what did he have to allow?"

Clifford shook his head.

"That he expected him is all, that he expected Daniel McCormick on the train last night."

"He damn sure don't need to know about this," I said.

"No," Virgil said. "He don't."

Clifford frowned.

"Afraid it might be a little late for that," one of the handcar men said. "Him and two others found us coming in this morning."

Clifford nodded.

"They was here right after I got the wire," Clifford said. "It wasn't like I was needing to tell them, but when they asked about a missing passenger, I just told them what we found is all. Hope that ain't a problem."

Lloyd's eyes moved between Virgil and me.

"This might be the beginning of the end," Lloyd said.

"Might well be," I said. "Might well be."

Virgil looked off up the track, then looked to Clifford.

"Can you get me a list of all the pas-

sengers who bought a ticket on the out-
bound and the inbound train that this here
fella, Daniel McCormick, had a ticket on?"

Clifford nodded.

"Sure thing."

"Much obliged," Virgil said.

69

The kid was spit-polishing his boots with a rag and making a popping sound with each lick.

"Drink your tea," she said.

He looked to her, then at the tea she had just poured. He shook his head.

"No."

"It will make you feel better. Make you feel good."

"I know all about your tea."

"It is not that."

"I don't want to be out of my wits today, not today. I don't need to chase no goats . . . not today."

"This is not that. This is different. It will help you enjoy everything. Help us both enjoy. Look. I have a cup, too."

She took a sip.

"Trust me."

He stopped his polishing and straightened up to look at her.

"This will make today even more special."

"You sure?"

"More than sure," she said, and held out the cup and saucer to him. "Trust me."

He took the cup and saucer. She held up her tea to his and they toasted and drank.

She had one of the hotel workers press the wrinkles out of the kid's new suit of clothes before they left the room. He was a dashing figure, she thought. She felt she, too, was well put together for the celebration. She bathed before leaving and sprayed herself with her best intoxicating gypsy perfume. She applied a dark eye shadow that made her large, dark eyes even more mysterious. She appreciated being different, unique. She was wearing her favorite daytime-to-evening outfit, a sheer, low-cut, white chiffon dress. She had a pair of heeled French shoes and carried a matching parasol. Her dark hair was piled atop her head. She wore large silver hoop earrings and her wrists were full of silver bracelets that made tinkling noises as they walked. As they strolled through the streets toward the party, she got plenty of attention, mostly from men.

"Slow down," she said.

He turned to her and smiled.

"There is no reason to hurry."

He stopped and she stopped.

"We will get there soon enough," she said as she straightened his tie. "We have all day, all night."

Her dark eyes spoke volumes that the kid instantly understood. It was hard for him to compose his enthusiasm, she could tell, but she had an effect on the kid. An effect like he'd never experienced before.

"One step at a time," he said.

She nodded.

"One step at a time."

The kid smiled as they moved onto the crowded Appaloosa Avenue. He did, above all things, like parties, celebrations, the sound of people talking, having fun, and laughing, and the music. The sound of musical instruments was exhilarating to him. He remembered the last party he attended down Mexico way, where he'd sharpened a spoon handle so he could get out of jail and join the festivities. He remembered eating and dancing with the *señoritas,* and the fireworks that night.

Then the kid started to take particular notice of the women as they walked. There were so many of them, all wearing their best clothes, it seemed, and there were all types of females, tall, short, plump, old, and young. Some were beautiful, but some were not. Most of them were under parasols, protecting themselves from the harsh afternoon sun. A sea of parasols, he thought.

"They are like a field of flowers," he said as

he laughed.

"How do you feel?"

He smiled.

"I feel like a bright-and-shiny loaded revolver. Full of powder."

"I told you."

"You did at that."

"You are happy," she said.

"I am."

"Good."

He turned in a circle as they walked.

"So many people," he said.

She smiled as they moved closer into the thickening crowd. In the distance he saw the stage, where the band was playing a lively tune. He took her hand and led her through the crowd and toward the stage. He smiled at her.

"Let's dance," he said.

"I'm not much of a dancer."

"It is easy."

"I dance, but not like this."

"Then dance like you dance."

She held his hand and they moved toward the crowd of dancing people in front of the stage.

"Do you think they will have fireworks later?" he said.

"Oh, I do," she said. "I do think there will be fireworks. I am certain of it."

70

By the time we got Daniel's body to the undertaker and made it back to Appaloosa Avenue, the Appaloosa Days celebration was in full swing, and the sun now cast a looming shadow over half of the street. There were thousands of people filling the street and boardwalks. We stopped on the high rise of the Avenue and watched the crowd.

"By God," Virgil said.

"Last time I remember ever seeing this many people in one place," I said, "it was war."

"Don't look much different now," Virgil said.

"No," I said. "It doesn't."

"Allie's got her hands full," he said.

"She damn sure does."

There were people and parasols going this way and that, from one end of the Avenue to the other. And it was loud. There were makeshift cooking fires with roasting ribs and chicken and lamb. It was a feast.

We had Book, Lloyd, and all the deputies on call, watching and keeping their eyes open for any trouble to break out.

When we found Allie, she was near the stage with Bernice, and Weldon was right there by her side, as we had instructed him to be. Martha Kathryn was with them, too. I didn't see her when we first came up, but she was smiling and planted a kiss on me before I could even say hello. And as loud as it was with all the music and clamoring, it was hard to hear much of anything.

"I was looking for you two," Allie shouted. "Where have you been?"

"We are right here," Virgil said.

"Well, you weren't here before."

"What is it, Allie?"

"Martha Kathryn is going to sing here in a little bit, a sunset serenade, and I don't want you to miss it."

"Wouldn't miss it for anything," I said.

"Plus, we are having the raffle," she said. "And the mayor is gonna make a speech, too, so don't go running off."

"We won't, Allie," Virgil said.

Allie was in full Appaloosa Days mode — ready to strike, giving orders in every direction. She moved off to talk to one of her organizers from the social and dragged Martha Kathryn and Bernice with her like she was corralling sheep, and Weldon tagged along. Martha Kathryn smiled at me and blew me a kiss as she was whisked off. When I turned, Virgil was looking in the direction of McCormick's office. He glanced to me, then started walking and I followed him.

The McCormick office was closed up and there was no sign of Hodge and his gun hands, but Lawrence was present. He was serving punch to a line of thirsty people with his young gentlemen coworkers. A sign let the partiers know that the punch was provided by McCormick Enterprises.

"Look there," I said.

Walking up the boardwalk was Irene. Lawrence greeted her. He grinned broadly, said something that made her smile, and then handed her a cup of punch. She nodded appreciatively, then moved to the edge of the boardwalk, watching the festivities. She did not appear to be drunk, but she did not seem altogether sober, either.

Virgil and I moved on a ways into the crowd and out of her line of sight.

"What do you figure?" I said.

Virgil shook his head.

"Don't think now is the time."

"No," I said.

"Don't think there will be a good time," he said.

We moved on to the other end of the block, away from the loud music, and found Victor and his men gathered around a food table in front of Baptiste's place. For the time being, they seemed subdued. They were lounging, eating, and drinking beer as if they had no care in the world and nothing nefarious or out of the ordinary had happened.

And just about the same time we got our eyes on them, we located Henri Baptiste and Eugene Pritchard. The two of them were sitting on the opposite side of the street on a shaded bench, talking and watching the festivities.

"Don't need your company," Eugene said as we walked up.

Henri nodded.

"We are just enjoying the celebration," he said. "Like everyone else. And it is a good one, no doubt."

"Saw Victor Bartholomew and his hands across the way," Virgil said with a glance through the crowd in the direction of Baptiste's office.

"That so?" Henri said.

Virgil nodded.

"It is a celebration, is it not, Marshal?"

"Not doing anything wrong," Eugene said. "Nothing you can do about that."

Virgil ignored him, as he stayed focused on Henri.

"You expecting trouble, Mr. Baptiste?"

"Just you," Eugene said. "You two are the only damn trouble we got."

"Just protecting our interest," Henri said. "We don't need trouble or threats."

"Have you had trouble or threats?" Virgil said.

"Nothing specific," he said. "Surely, we don't need to go through all that again? Not on this special day of days for Appaloosa."

"McCormick's men threaten you?" Virgil said.

"Why do you ask?"

"Have they?"

"Is there reason to be alarmed?"

"Tell me."

"I do not know what you are referring to, Marshal Cole."

Virgil leveled a stern look at Henri.

"Seen Daniel McCormick?" he said.

Henri looked at him like he was just called a bad name.

"Now, why would I see Daniel McCormick?"

"Have you?"

"I have no business with the likes of Daniel McCormick."

"When was the last time you did see him?"

"I don't make a habit in making contact or associating with crooks and thieves," Henri said.

"Answer the question."

"Not anytime recent," he said. "Why do you ask?"

"How about you, Mr. Pritchard?" Virgil said. "Have you seen Daniel McCormick?"

Pritchard glared at Virgil.

"Why don't the two of you get a piece of pie or go have a dance or something."

"Or lock you up," Virgil said.

Eugene shook his head.

"I have not seen Daniel McCormick," he said.

An exotic woman caught my eye through the crowd. She was an extraordinary-looking lady wearing a shimmering white dress that accentuated her dark skin. She was large and powerful-looking, a robust creature, with strikingly beautiful large, dark eyes. Her wide, full lips were painted bright red. And she seemed to be looking directly at Virgil and me. Then I noticed a small young man next to her. He, too, was dark-skinned, but his eyes were bright blue. He stood beside her, dressed in a black suit with polished boots. He was leaning against a

433

post with his arms folded. Both of them seemed to be looking in our direction. The kid had a smile on his face. And it seemed as if he were staring at Virgil. I glanced to Virgil, but when I looked back, both the kid and the woman were gone.

71

The colors were spectacular, the kid thought, as he walked through the crowd. The sounds were penetrating, but they were also very pleasing. He was feeling more alive than he had ever felt before in his life. He was swaying to the music as he walked. He turned to her and smiled. She was following him, holding his hand. He stopped and then moved off the street and up on the boardwalk. He found a place for them to sit. They smiled at each other, then the kid laughed.

"This is funny?" she said.

"Yes."

"Why?"

"That is him?"

"Yes."

"I just figured someone different."

"How so?"

"I don't know," he said. "Just different."

"He is a formidable man."

"He does not look like much trouble," he said.

"He is deadly."

"So am I."

"I'm glad you feel that way. That he does not seem like too much trouble. But you must beware."

"Just have to find the right place and time."

"I don't want you to get hurt," she said.

"You worried about me?"

"Yes."

"Don't."

"I want nothing to happen to you."

"It won't."

"And I don't want you to get caught."

"I will not get caught, I'll be invisible," he said with a laugh. "Hell, I am invisible."

She studied him some.

"Are you sure?" she said.

"You have not changed your mind, have you?" he said.

She turned her attention out to the people and thought for a moment, then shook her head.

"No."

"Well, there you go. I will just wait for the right place and time. Night will be best."

"Yes," she said. "Nighttime. I like the night."

He pulled the tintype from his pocket and smiled at the photograph, then he looked out into the street full of people.

"There are so many ladies," he said.

"We will find her," she said.

He smiled at the tintype again and shook his head.

"Hard to say."

"You have come this far. Do not be discouraged."

He stared at it. He rubbed his thumb gently across his mother's face in the photograph.

"And you are sure? Sure you saw her?"

"Yes."

"I don't know. She has to be so much younger here, though, in this photograph."

He looked out at all the people.

"It will be difficult to tell."

She shook her head.

"I saw, I know, I have vision."

He nodded, smiled at her, and then returned the tintype to his pocket.

"Come."

He took her hand and they moved on toward the stage, weaving among the people, looking at everything and everyone as they walked. When they got closer, they saw two pretty women step up on the stage. One was shorter, with peach-blond hair, and the other was taller, with dark hair. The smaller woman smiled and waved to the crowd as she picked up a large megaphone. She looked to the bandleader and waited for the song that was being played to end. Then she motioned for another woman, a third woman, to come on-stage. A slender, taller woman walked up and joined the other two. The three women stood side by side.

The teamster's wife squeezed his hand. He looked to her and she nodded to the three women standing up on the stage.

"One of them?" he said.

She nodded.

He reached in his pocket and pulled out the tintype. He looked at it closely, then looked to the three women standing next to each other. Then the woman with the peach-colored hair raised the megaphone and brought it to her lips.

72

"Hello, everyone," Allie said loudly through the megaphone. "I'm Allison French, one of the chairs on the Appaloosa Days committee. And on behalf of the committee, and Mrs. Bernice McCormick here, who donated so generously, we are happy to bring you some special entertainment as the sun sets here on beautiful Appaloosa Avenue."

The crowd whooped and hollered.

"So please help us in welcoming the talented thespian and singer, Martha Kathryn!"

Bernice and Allie walked off, leaving Martha Kathryn standing center stage.

The sun was setting and the last bit of the day's golden light lit Martha Kathryn up like a theater spotlight. She stood tall, with her chin held high, and was stunning in her gown, which shimmered in the waning light. She smiled at the applauding crowd. She spoke out with a confident voice, thanking

Appaloosa, the mayor, the ladies' social, Bernice, and Allie.

Then she sang songs from her show, and instantly everyone in the crowd was enthralled. The whole street remained silent, hanging on every word of her captivating voice. When the song was over, the people went wild with applause. One song after the other she sang, and after each tune the people showered her with adulation, clapping heartily. When she was finished with her last song and took a final bow, the street erupted with a rousing thrilled ovation.

"Isn't she something, Virgil?" Allie said as she clapped her hands hard.

"She is."

"Everett, she is so amazing."

"She damn sure is," I said.

Allie turned to me.

"Don't let this one go, Everett," she said. "Please."

Virgil smiled at me.

"I'll do my best," I said. "She has a mind of her own."

"She has a mind for you," she said. "That is obvious."

When Martha Kathryn stepped down from the stage it was dark out, and the streetlamps and store lights were now providing the lighting up and down Appaloosa Avenue.

I walked over to greet Martha Kathryn.

"Think you got something there," I said. "You might ought to take that up as a profession."

She laughed.

"You think?"

"I do. I also think I might have to find a way to provide my own brand of appreciation."

"Wonder what that will be like?"

"Have to wait and see."

Allie came up and put her arms around Martha Kathryn.

"Oh my God," Allie said. "You were amazing, thank you. My heart is fluttering."

"Thank you," Martha Kathryn said with a laugh, then looked to me. "Think I need a drink before this is all said and done."

"Well, hold on," Allie said. "We are only moments away from the fireworks."

Virgil lingered behind her. His gaze moved off to something behind me, and I followed his look. I turned to see Book with his deputies, Hank and Skeeter. They were coming toward us through the crowd.

"They finally made it," Book said.

"Excuse me," I said to Martha Kathryn.

Hank, the older of the two, removed his hat as he said, "Sorry it took us a while.

Weather and such held us up."

"We figured," I said.

"Rained like hell to heaven it did," Skeeter said.

Hank nodded.

"So what did you find out?" I said.

"The lady," Skeeter said. "She is with us."

"With you?" Virgil said, following Skeeter and Hank's look. Coming up behind them were Maureen and her husband, Simon Crow.

"We brought her from Dover to Appaloosa in her buggy," Hank said.

Maureen stepped up with Simon.

"There you are," Virgil said.

"Yes," Maureen said. "And these nice young men saw to getting me back here to Appaloosa safely."

"And we are grateful," Simon said, chiming in. "Otherwise I would have had to fetch her. Turns out her brother was needed on his job right after his daughter gave birth. Some kind of logging accident happened."

Maureen nodded.

"Nobody was hurt, but it was an emergency and he was needed."

"She would have been there for weeks," he said.

"So what can you tell us?" Virgil said. "This was a long shot having the boys ride over to ask you, but we needed to know. Do you remember who was with James McCormick the day he died?"

"Matter of fact, I do," she said.

Just then the first firework rocketed up. It made a loud boom and lit up the spectators with their expectant faces lifted to the sky, prompting uproarious oohs and ahhs.

73

Another firework lifted skyward with a shrill whistle. Then it exploded in a burst of red, white, and blue sparkles that slowly dropped like a weeping willow tree, then fizzled out and fell to the earth.

Virgil and I found Weldon, who was staring up at the sky.

"Where is Bernice?" Virgil said.

Weldon looked around. He turned one way and then the next. He shook his head.

"She was right here," he said as another rocket exploded. "Just a minute ago. She was right here."

Virgil got Hank, Book, Skeeter, and Weldon's full attention.

"Find her," he said. "Find Bernice McCormick."

Weldon and the others nodded and moved off, looking for Bernice, turning this way and that as they dispersed into the crowd.

Virgil looked to me, shook his head, and

we moved off through the onlookers with their heads lifted to the sky. As we approached McCormick Enterprises, we could see into the office. And we could see Irene. She turned slightly as we neared, and then I could see she was standing with Bernice.

"There she is," I said.

When we stepped up on the boardwalk, we could now also see Lawrence. He was talking with the ladies. When we opened the door, the trio turned to us. Lawrence had a coffeepot in his hand and was pouring them a cup of coffee.

We stepped into the room and Bernice smiled.

"I'm sorry, I did not mean to slip away," she said. "I have never been one for fireworks. I find them unnerving."

"Me neither," Irene said. "I'm afraid we have that in common."

"Coffee?" Lawrence said, holding up the pot. "It's fresh."

Just then Weldon, Book, and Skeeter came up behind us as Lawrence poured coffee for the women.

"Damn," Weldon said. "I'm sorry, Marshal. Won't happen again."

Weldon looked to Bernice.

"Sorry, ma'am. My apologies."

"No, my apologies," she said. "I should

not have run off."

Irene started spooning sugar into her coffee.

"Lawrence," Virgil said.

"Yes," he said with a smile.

"Sit down."

"Pardon."

"Put the coffeepot down and sit."

Lawrence blinked.

"Something wrong?" he said.

A booming firework brightly lit up the office for a few seconds, then faded.

"Do like I tell you."

"What is it, Marshal?" Irene said.

"Sit."

Lawrence nodded, then took a seat behind his desk.

"You two. Both of you," Virgil said to Irene and Bernice. "You, too. Take a seat."

They stared at Virgil, then both women took a seat.

"What has happened?" Irene said. "Something bad, I presume?"

Virgil nodded.

"I regret to inform you. Your husband . . . Daniel McCormick is dead."

"What?" she said.

Bernice gasped.

Virgil nodded.

"What happened?" Lawrence said. "Oh

my God."

Virgil glanced to me.

"He was murdered," I said.

Irene put her hand to her mouth and started shaking.

"My God."

"Where?" Lawrence said. "How?"

"He was poisoned."

"Poisoned?" Lawrence said.

Virgil nodded.

"And dumped off the train."

Irene's chin dropped to her chest, and she began to weep.

Virgil focused on Bernice.

"If something were to happen to you. What would happen with your share of McCormick Enterprises?"

"Well, I . . . I have no beneficiary," Bernice said. "Why?"

She shook her head.

"Well, with no children, there really was no one else."

Bernice looked to Irene.

"No one other than Irene and . . . Daniel."

"So the shares would revert back to the partnership."

She nodded.

"Yes. But we never thought anything like this would happen, especially with James and I being younger . . ."

Virgil looked to Irene as another firework lit up the room.

"Mrs. McCormick?" he said. "Irene?"

Irene lifted her face, meeting Virgil's eye.

"Yes," she said.

"If you were to die, if something were to happen to you, who would be your beneficiary?"

"Why, Lawrence," she said. "He's our only blood relation." Virgil nodded.

"That's kind of what I figured."

Virgil looked to Lawrence.

"You are under arrest for the murder of both James and Daniel McCormick."

"You can't be serious," he said.

"I am," Virgil said. "You were the last person seen with James the day he died at the Crow's Nest."

Virgil pulled out a paper with a list of the passengers who were on the train that he got from Clifford.

"You also boarded the train with Daniel the same day he left for Santa Fe and returned on the night train that evening. It was you."

"No," Lawrence said. "You are mistaken."

In a snap, Lawrence opened the drawer of his desk and reached his hand inside, but I moved quickly on him before he had a chance to pull out the gun he was reaching for. And with my foot I shoved the desk back hard to the wall, pinning Lawrence up against the large map of the McCormick Mining Company.

Virgil stared at Lawrence then turned to deputies Book, Skeeter, and Weldon.

"Take him down to the jail and lock him up," he said.

Then Virgil turned to Bernice and Irene.

"And if I were you, ladies, I don't think I'd take a sip of that fresh coffee."

74

Deputies Weldon and Skeeter escorted Lawrence to jail, and Deputy Book walked a disheveled Irene to her home.

"I don't know how to thank you," Bernice said as we watched them walk away. "I am just so thankful."

"Would you like us to take you home as well?" I said.

"No," she said, as she pulled her shoulders back and looked up to a firework as it whistled, then burst into a bright white light. "I'm going to stay here and enjoy the rest of this party that Allie has done such a marvelous job putting together."

With that, she walked off toward the stage. She stopped and turned to us. She looked off in the direction Irene walked with Book, then said, "I know she thought I was sleeping with her husband. I, too, had heard the rumor. But it was nothing more than a rumor. I loved my husband. Was our marriage perfect? No. But I loved him and he loved me, and I will forever miss him . . . In due time I will make it right with her. After all, we are partners in a gold mine."

She turned and walked off, and just as she disappeared into the crowd, we heard a loud boom.

"That did not sound like any firework," I said.

"Gunshot," Virgil said.

Then we heard another shot, followed by another, then another.

Then we saw a stampede of people running past us, trying to get out of the line of fire.

Virgil and I waited as the mass of scared people passed. Then we could see a handful of horsemen at the end of the Avenue getting fired upon and returning fire. We stayed tight to the buildings and made our way toward the firefight.

A horse took a bullet and dropped its rider. The rider fired as he ran for cover, but went down in a hail of bullets.

We kept on the move and then we could see clearly that it was Hodge and his men having it out with Victor's bunch. It had finally come to blows. A few riders took off, but Hodge was riding his horse back and forth, yelling like a madman, like he was invincible. The gunfire subsided but Hodge rode in circles with his pistol up in the air as he ranted on.

"You sonsabitches," Hodge shouted. "Running off, like a bunch of cowards. Cowards! The all of you! Cowards!"

Then, as if he'd summoned his fate, a single shot rang out. Hodge took a bullet. He stared down at his big body.

"Goddamn it," he said.

Hodge slumped in his saddle. Then he toppled over. His foot stayed hung up in the stirrup, and then his horse took off at a gallop. It passed us, bouncing Hodge on the cobblestone street. Then the horse turned the corner and was gone from sight.

Virgil and I continued walking in the direction of where the bullets were fired. The fight had taken place in front of Baptiste's office. Then we heard a woman's voice call from an alley just behind us.

"Marshal Cole," she said.

We stopped and turned.

"You remember me?"

Then the woman stepped out for us to see her.

"Of course you do not," she said.

"Who are you?" Virgil said.

"I was just a baby when you killed my father."

"Who was your father?"

It was the big striking woman who I had seen looking at us. I could see that she carried a small derringer in her hand.

"Don't do anything stupid," Virgil said.

"Stupid?" she said.

"Just take things easy."

"Nothing is easy."

"Who?" Virgil said.

"He was all I had."

Then we heard another voice, of a young man coming up from behind us.

"Right here," he said.

I glanced quickly and saw it was the young fella in the dark suit that I had seen with the woman. He was holding a shiny revolver.

"This is it," he said.

"Look out, Virgil."

Virgil turned so fast and shot, that the young man did not know what hit him. His pistol fell from his hand and he dropped flat on his back. Then the woman screamed and raised her derringer. Virgil turned quickly on her, but before he fired again I let loose with one shot from my eight-gauge. The blast hit her so hard she slammed back, crashing into a window of the Appaloosa Theater just below a huge poster of Martha Kathryn.

75

When we turned around, the smoke had cleared. But the young man was now — somehow — nowhere in sight.

"Son of a bitch," I said.

"He was hit square," Virgil said.

"Damn sure was," I said. "Had to go through there."

I pointed to a narrow alley opening between the Appaloosa Theater and a mercantile store. The opening was dark and no more than five feet wide. We moved quickly to the side, careful not to expose ourselves in the passageway. We stood with our backs to the theater building.

"Went down hard," I said.

"Did," Virgil said.

I nodded to the street.

"Managed to get his gun, too," I said.

"Goddamn quick," Virgil said.

"Not a good idea to go waltzing in there," I said.

"No," Virgil said. "Not."

"Might be more than these two, too," I said.

Virgil nodded as he opened the loading gate on his Colt, dropped the spent casing on the boardwalk, and put in a new round.

"Recognize him?" I said.

"No, you?"

"No, saw him and the woman, earlier," I said. "They were looking our direction but I didn't think anything of it."

"Never laid eyes on her before," Virgil said. "Or the little fella. And I have no idea who her daddy was that she was talking about."

Another shot rang out down near Baptiste's office. Then a second shot was fired, followed by a horseman riding off the opposite direction. The mounted man fired again toward Baptiste's office as he was galloping away. Virgil took a quick peek into the dark opening where the young fella had to have darted off, then looked toward Baptiste's office. Virgil tipped his head that direction for us to move out and I nodded. We walked away from the opening, to the opposite side of the street, all the time keeping our eye out for trouble. As we moved toward Baptiste's office, we did not see any sign of the young fella Vigil shot or anyone else near the theater.

We stayed tight to the buildings and made our way, moving closer and closer toward Baptiste's office. We stopped when we saw a man sitting on a bench in front of the office. As we neared, we could see who it was.

"Victor," I said quietly.

Virgil nodded.

"Damn sure is," he said.

"Like he don't have a care in the world," I said.

He was sitting on a bench, looking out into the street.

Step by step, we continued toward him. When we were within forty feet of him, we could see he was sitting with his revolver in his hand.

"Put it down, Victor," Virgil said.

Victor did not move.

"Do like I tell you."

We took a few more steps, when Eugene Pritchard stepped out of the office. He turned in our direction, then, without a word, fell face-first on the boardwalk. Victor did not budge.

We took a few more steps, then it became clear that Victor, though sitting stoically upright, was either wounded or dead.

We walked on, guns up, cautious as to what shooters remained active and ready.

The glass was shot out of the office windows and scattered across the boardwalk. There were two men down on the far side of where Victor was sitting. We stayed ready as we approached. One of the downed men was Wayne. He was not moving and there was a puddle of blood near his head. We walked closer, the second body was the big man, Noah, and it was clear by the way he was splayed half off the boardwalk, with his head on the cobblestone street, that he, too, was dead.

We stopped, with our backs to the wall of the building next to the office, and waited for a few minutes to see if there was anyone still fight ready. Then Virgil spoke up.

"Anyone else in there?"

There was no answer.

"Marshals Virgil Cole and Everett Hitch, out here. Come out without your guns and your hands high."

Then we heard a muffled voice from inside the office.

"Marshal Cole!"

"Baptiste," I said.

Virgil nodded

"Thank God," he said. "I'm afraid to move."

"You alone in there?" Virgil said.

"Yes, I . . . I . . . I think so."

"Stay put," Virgil said.

Virgil and I moved closer. There were two more men down. One fellow was crumpled beside the dead horse in the street and another was on the boardwalk across the street from the office. They both appeared to be dead.

We proceeded cautiously.

Then very slowly Victor turned his head toward us. His eyes were open but blood seeped from a bullet hole in his cheek. He stared blankly as we moved closer. By the time we made it to the office door, his head tipped back, staring at nothing, with, now, very dead eyes.

We stood just this side of the office door and waited, listening. Then we heard a horse walking up, its hooves clicking rhythmically on the cobblestone. It was Hodge's horse, coming back to find the other horses he was used to being with. Hodge was still hung up in the stirrup. His clothes were torn and his body was a bloody mess from being dragged around the block. The big bay horse stopped in front of the office, lowered his head, and snorted. We waited for some time before we moved. After it was clear that the firefight was over, we eased to the entrance of the office.

"Baptiste," Virgil said.

We could not see him but we heard him.
"Yes," he said.

"Is there anyone with you?" Virgil said.

"No."

"You can come out now."

"Are you sure?"

"Yes."

A chair on rollers was pushed to the side, then Baptist crawled out from under a desk. He remained on all fours, looking toward us in the doorway. I kneeled next to Eugene and felt for a pulse.

"Is it over?" Baptiste said.

Virgil nodded.

"It is," he said.

Baptiste crawled a bit toward us. He stopped when he saw Pritchard through the open door.

"Is . . . is Eugene . . ."

I stood up and nodded.

"He's dead," I said.

Baptiste shook his head, then leaned to his side and slowly got to his feet. He walked toward Virgil and me. He stopped at the threshold and looked out at the dead.

"My Lord," he said as he surveyed the carnage.

"What happened here?" I said.

Baptiste took a step out.

"They rode up and started shooting, these

McCormick men just ambushed Victor and his men, and us, out of nowhere, they just rode up and started shooting."

He turned to Victor, dead, with a bullet hole in his face, then stared at Eugene, facedown on the boardwalk.

"Eugene and I were just locking up here when it started."

He took a few more steps out and shook his head.

"What made these men so . . . so crazed?" he said.

"Gold," Virgil said without looking at Baptiste.

Baptiste looked to him. Virgil met his eye.

"Makes men do things they otherwise would not do," Virgil said.

76

The kid hid while they searched for him. He found a nice place that was comfortable. He was good at hiding. It was up high and he knew they would not find him, and he could keep an eye on things, too. He could see the marshals and the aftermath of everything. He watched the undertaker's ambulance pick up bodies from the gunfight. A flatbed rolled in and a group of men picked up the dead horse. And he watched as her body was loaded up, too. He did not think things would have gone like this. But then again, he was never really lucky. He thought about her and all that they did together. He thought he would miss her. He never really had anyone who cared a penny for him, not the way she did.

He watched the marshals walk into a shop. He moved so he could clearly see through the window. Three women were inside, the same three women who were on the stage earlier.

He scoffed to himself. Maybe I am lucky.

Maybe this is my lucky day after all. He climbed down from his perch and came out into an alley.

He moved to where he had an even a better view of the shop. Mrs. French's Fine Dresses. He liked the sound of that. He took a step and fell. He looked down where he'd been shot. *Gut shot,* he thought. *That is not good, that is not good at all.* He stayed in the shadows, watching everything and nothing.

After a while the two marshals left Mrs. French's Fine Dresses and walked off up the street. The kid waited until they were out of sight, then he took a step. But he fell again. Blood flowed all the way down his leg and onto his boots, his shiny brand-new boots.

But the kid was determined to make his way across the street. With all the strength he could muster, he walked. When he got to the steps of the shop, though, he had to crawl. One step at a time, he crawled. Through the window he could see the three beautiful ladies sitting at the rear of the shop. It seemed they were just talking, shaking their heads and talking. He wondered what it was they were talking about.

He crawled to the door and pulled himself to his feet by the handle and opened the door.

When he did, the three ladies all turned and looked in his direction. He staggered toward them and they all recoiled at the sight of him.

He smiled.

"Please don't be frightened of me," he said. "It is me, your boy, your son. I have come to you. I have found you. I have finally found you."

The women exchanged looks with each other.

He took a step closer, then fell to his knees.

The three women stood.

He reached into his pocket, pulled out the tintype, and held it up for them to see.

"This is a picture of you."

He looked at the tintype and shook his head. The shot he had received from the lawman had gone through the tintype directly on his mother's face. He shook his head and began to weep. Then he smiled.

"Don't that beat all?" he said. "That is a photograph of you. Or it was."

He sat up like a baby with his hands resting in his lap.

"It is me. You are Helen. And it is me. I am your boy. Don't you remember? Remember what you called me as a boy? 'Cause of my color. Remember what my nickname was. Remember . . . Buckskin. Your little boy. Your boy. Your . . . Buckskin."

He smiled, then slumped forward as his life lifted from his body.

ACKNOWLEDGMENTS

I am forever grateful to Robert B. Parker and the wonderful characters of Virgil Cole, Everett Hitch, and Allison French that he created. And I'm equally grateful to the Parker Estate and their continued support of me throughout the years of carrying on with their Father's legacy and his love for the Western genre. A heritage that allows me to take these colorful characters on adventure after adventure. And a big thanks to Putnam president Ivan Held for his continued wrangling along the way. In the process of the work, I have to first and foremost recognize my wife, Julie. She is the true chanteuse, singing out all the right notes as the curtain opens and the show begins. Like to thank Jamie "Whatknot" Whitcomb for his love of creation, his knowledge of books, and for sharing his words of wisdom. Rob Wood of Rancho Roberto has been over my shoulder and in my head throughout the wordsmithing of these books. Thanks, Pard! Jayne Amelia Larson for shouting enthusiastically, *"Just put him on the horse, Robert!"* Thanks To Trad Willmann for gun handling with me throughout. And, as always, my good friend Ed Harris who brought the iconic Virgil Cole to life. I will always be forever beholden to Ed for including me in this illustrious Parker journey. For without his endorsement, none of this would be possible. And also Viggo Mortensen, and Renée Zellweger. Their voices are and will always be in my head and defining the truths of Allie and Everett. Like to offer acknowledgment to my business team, Allison Binder, Josh Kesselman, and the APA boys — thank you guys for helping me with all the necessary gun work, I know it's tiresome. And a HUGE THANKS to my editor, Sara Minnich! Thank you, Sara, for your guidance and craft! I'm very appreciative of you and all that you do! And lastly, I'd like to thank my mysterious sisters, Karen and Sandra — the Clogging Castanets — who do nothing but laugh, which, as always, is beyond helpful.

ABOUT THE AUTHORS

Robert B. Parker was the author of seventy books, including the legendary Spenser detective series, the novels featuring Police Chief Jesse Stone, and the acclaimed Virgil Cole and Everett Hitch westerns, as well as the Sunny Randall novels. Winner of the Mystery Writers of America Grand Master Award and long considered the undisputed dean of American crime fiction, he died in January 2010.

Robert Knott is an actor, writer, and producer, as well as the author of the *New York Times* bestsellers *Robert B. Parker's The Bridge, Robert B. Parker's Bull River,* and *Robert B. Parker's Ironhorse.* His extensive list of stage, television, and film credits include the feature film *Appaloosa,* based on the Robert B. Parker novel, which he adapted and produced with actor and producer Ed Harris.